AF675096

A Harvest of Ecstasy

by
MATHEW
ATTOKARAN

NIYOGI
BOOKS

Published by
NIYOGI BOOKS
D-78, Okhla Industrial Area, Phase-I
New Delhi-110 020, INDIA
Tel: 91-11-26816301, 49327000
Fax: 91-11-26810483, 26813830
email: niyogibooks@gmail.com
website: www.niyogibooks.com

Editor: Keerti Ramachandra
Cover Design: Vishnu M Nair
Layout: Ganga Rai

ISBN: 978-93-83098-97-2
Year of Publication: 2015

This is a work of fiction. The names, characters and incidents portrayed in it are the work of the author's imagination. Any resemblance to actual persons, living or dead, events or localities, is entirely coincidental.

All rights are reserved. No part of this publication may be reproduced or transmitted in any form or by any means, electronic or mechanical, including photocopying, recording or by any information storage and retrieval system without prior written permission and consent of the Publisher.

Printed at: Niyogi Offset Pvt. Ltd., New Delhi, India

Introduction...

Kerala, a thin strip of land bordered on one side by the Indian Ocean and the other, by the Western Ghats, has a distinct geographic, agricultural and economic character. Being the entry point of the South-Western moisture bearing monsoon winds with a well developed mountain range along the eastern border which helps in precipitation the land is the recipient of copious rainfall. This in addition to the high soil fertility has made the region suitable for growing plantation crops like coconut, arecanut, tea, coffee, rubber and spices. When the story begins in the nineteen thirties, major portions of the region were ruled by somewhat orthodox Maharajas with British administration having minimal influence.

The influence of the British was mainly visible in the few estates that were growing export quality plantation crops. These estates were run mainly by the local Christians and since the products were in the domestic or unorganized sector, it was up to the middle men to garner the produce and then market it.

The spices trade was flourishing long before the Europeans came to Kerala, especially with the Arabs. Almost one third of the State's population is thus Muslim, converted by Arab migrants. Since it was Islam as propagated by the Arabs alone that influenced the Muslims of Kerala, they have a cultural identity distinct from that of the Muslims of the rest of India. A little less than a quarter of the population is Christian, the majority being the Catholics. Christianity was brought in by the Apostle St. Thomas who arrived in Kerala in the first century AD long before the European missionaries and traders who landed on Indian shores at the turn of the fifteenth century. Culturally the Christians of Kerala are also quite different from Christians in other States who are primarily converts after the arrival of the Europeans.

Both these religions, Islam and Chritianity, owe a great deal to the generosity and benevolence of the Hindus and Hindu rulers of the State.Before the twentieth century many Hindu sub-castes practised matrilineal systems, which accorded them a socially superior status. As per historical records, the high position and educational opportunities given to women of the region in the twentieth century had much to do with this tradition.

The Hindu society of the State, in keeping with its love for arts, culture and allied fields, produced many great religious leaders and philosophers like Adi Sankaracharya who built the modern structure of Hindu religion in India, and other progressive leaders such as Sree Narayana Guru who was instrumental in setting up a new religious order and channelling respect and position for the lower castes.

There are also several highly revered temples across the State, which continue to attract a large number of pilgrims from different parts of India. Notable among them are the Sabarimala Ayyappa temple in the south and the Guruvayoor Sri Krishna temple in central Kerala. The Maharajas and their chieftains also nurtured new talent in literature, dance and music. Swathi Thirunnal, a fine composer of classical music and Raja Ravi Varma, the world renowned painter were members of the Travancore royal family.

The rulers were generally magnanimous to visitors from Europe. Even a small group of Jews, who landed on the Kerala coast to escape repression in European countries, were given honourable asylum near Cochin. The fact that St. Thomas received so much freedom to spread the Gospel in the State is proof of the tolerance of the Hindu people and the rulers of the land.

As could be expected, the large Christian population attracted various missionary organisations from across the world, mostly America, and their influence helped Christians to build educational, healthcare and even financial institutions in Kerala.

Communal harmony that existed until about the middle of the twentieth century was very strong. Society was shaped mostly on Hindu philosophy with very little westernisation. Malayalam was the mother tongue, and a deep aspiration to learn English remained in the hearts of Malayalees, both as a status symbol and as a means of obtaining good employment in foreign countries.

The common terms for addressing one's family members, are *Appan* or *Appachan* by Christians and *Achan* by Hindus for father. Mother is called *Amma* and sometimes *Ammachi* generally by Christians. Grandfather and grandmother are called *Appapan* and *Ammama.* Brother and sister are respectively *Chettan* and *Chechi*, and son and daughter are called *Mon* and *Mol. Aliyan* refers to one's brother-in-law. But all these forms are also sometimes used to address familiar people of appropriate age groups.

Eda (masculine) and *Edi* (feminine) meaning 'you there!' are informal modes of address depending on situations and either close familiarity or endearment. Similar is the case for *Poda* (masculine) and *Podi* (feminine) which generally means 'get lost!' said either humorously or in an admonishing tone.

All in all, this region has spun together a special culture with unique customs. Because of the Christian influence, consumption of non-vegetarian food and liquor is more common in the region compared to other parts of India.

The following story represents an era before crass commercialism, garish immorality, religious intolerance and unbridled political ambition reared its head in the State, as is the unfortunate reality at present.

Many were the useful discussions I had with Professor Madhukar Rao about English literature. It is indeed sad that he is not in this world now. Dr. PS Sreekantan Thampi is another with whom I had interaction with regard to various aspects of spices and plantation crops. I would like to thank them as well as Kuruvila Chacko, who did much to improve the manuscript, and Moby Paul for word processing assistance.

MATHEW ATTOKARAN

Chapter 1

Thamarassery is a thriving small town situated on the road connecting the coastal city of Calicut in the South West India to the foothills of Western Ghats. A major trading point, Thamarassery is the centre for the collection of different cash crops grown by small-time farmers in the villages around it. Besides, it is also a supply point for the provisions that are required over and above what is locally grown and for simple implements needed for agricultural operations in the nearby rural outposts.

Five miles east of the town centre, there comes into view the tiny village of Puthupady. The visible prosperity of the village is due to the cash crops, rather than paddy, which are cultivated by the local farmers there. The entrance to the famous estate of Kollegal family lies about half a mile from the centre of Puthupady. A sprawling five hundred acre estate of undulating land offers a spectacular view of the nearby mountains and their rocky projections from the eastern end. During the monsoons the view is more picturesque when streams of water flowing down the hill slopes, glisten in the evening sun like strings of a diamond necklace. One of the larger streams passes through the estate, before emptying itself into the river nearby. With plentiful rain, the generous stream and bounteous ground water, the estate produces a lush growth of crops.

Until the reorganization of the States in 1956 after India became independent, this region was divided into three separate administrative territories. Travancore and Cochin States were ruled by the Maharajas, and the Malabar region which was a district of the Madras Presidency, was under British rule. The Kollegal estate was owned by Mathukutty. He had migrated from the hilly region of central Travancore over forty years ago. An adventurer by heart, he had run away from home to test the relatively unexplored Malabar plains for himself. His early days were a time of struggle. Picking up any odd job that came his way, from running errands, going from door to door selling low priced vegetables and dried fish and even helping a vendor in the local market, he managed to keep body and soul together. He knew he could not go back to his home town since his return would be viewed as nothing short of a shameful retreat.

His natural inclination to work hard saw him employed as a labour hand on a large plantation owned by a maverick Englishman, James Meadows. Meadows had bought this vast tract of undeveloped land a few years earlier and developed the estate on it. Mathukutty found estate work tough to begin with but he was diligent and a quick learner. Meadows, known for his ability to spot talent, saw the potential in Mathukutty and soon the young man was promoted to the position of supervisor. Unlike other small time farmers in and around Puthupady, James Meadows followed a systematic and planned routine. But there was a large tract of land which needed to be developed. The local people referred to Meadows as James *saipu*, a title the Malayalees with which Englishmen were addressed in those days. Very little was known of Meadows, except that he had a wife, an Englishwoman, who had refused to move away from her homeland to a place she described as "god-forsaken and inhabited by uncultured natives."

James on the other hand loved Puthupady and its calm surroundings. Fond of the people of the region, whom he described as 'sincere, honest people untouched by the cunning manipulation veiled under pretentious sophistication,' it was reported that he once derided his own countrymen for not possessing any of the qualities which the villagers naturally displayed.

But Meadows, like any other lonely and single man of his age, was known to have a weakness for women, especially those of the working class. He had promised that if ever a child be born to any woman he copulated with he would honourably marry the mother and set up a home for her. But it was not in his destiny to have progeny. By and large he lived out his existence as a bachelor, in an eccentric yet active manner devoted to the estate and its people.

It was six years before the turn of the century, 1894, to be precise, that Mathukutty swallowed his pride and returned to his ancestral village. By then he was in his early twenties and had earned a fair amount of money. His parents had passed away, but with the help of his relatives he married a young girl, Annama from his village.

When he brought his young bride to Puthupady, James had reached the ripe age of seventy five. Just when senility was creeping in, James was reported to have whispered in a broken tone to Annama, "I may not last long, will be your family's…"

Mathukutty and Annama did not understand the meaning of his mumbling and so attached little significance to the words. But they got a clearer idea, when after a month of age related illness James Meadows passed away, bequeathing the estate to Mathukutty.

Mathukutty was inconsolable at the passing away of his '*saipu*.' He began neglecting his work and drifted into a state of inaction. It was Annama who brought him back to reality, convincing him to carry forward the work left half done by his master and mentor.

"Chetta, however sad it may seem, the *saipu* had dreams and he entrusted them all to your care. You will be failing him and yourself if you waste your time like this," she said to Mathukutty.

In due time, Mathukutty saw the wisdom of her suggestion. His inherent sense of duty and responsibility returned and he set to work. He extended the area of cultivation much beyond the earlier boundary, introducing new crops such as rubber, coconut, arecanut, cassava and some spices.

The dawn of 1930 saw Mathukutty a mature man of fiftynine busy supervising the construction of his home on an elevated portion of his land, about hundred yards from the main gate. The path to the site was deliberately made with a wide curve to reduce the strain for bullocks drawing carts over the slope as well as to present a panoramic view for a visitor approaching the house. For overseeing the construction he engaged a semi-retired master builder from Calicut.

The walls were made of laterite stone blocks quarried from Matukutty's own estate. Plastering was done with a mixture of white lime and river sand. The beams and rafters were made of wood and the dimensions were calculated by the carpenters according to the traditional system. The sloping roof was covered with Mangalore tiles brought from a tile factory in Calicut. All the front rooms had false ceilings made of wood. Only the kitchen and back veranda had bare roofing, so that the tiles were visible from the inside. There was a veranda in the front with a central portico. Both veranda and portico had bulbous pillars made of teak. Overhanging eaves around the house lent it an old world charm. The house was impressive and reminiscent of the traditional houses built by the well-to-do people of the region.

The veranda had cane furniture but Mathukutty's favourite piece was a traditional rosewood easychair with extendable arms and woven rattan seat, now called the planter's easy chair. This was placed on one side of the portico. On the other side was a long rosewood bench with a wooden backrest. Relaxing on this chair Mathukutty discussed the affairs of the estate with the various supervisors who would sit on the bench on the opposite side. Every now and then during the one way conversation Mathukutty would light a new *beedi.*

By the 1940s, the success story of Mathukutty and the fame of the Kollegal estate brought many people from Central Travancore into Malabar, to seek their fortune in plantation crops.

Mathukutty, like his mentor, was a hard working agriculturist. He did not take his prosperity for granted, and having seen many of the complacent plantation owners fall by the wayside, he spent most of his time on the estate or the office. Not trusting anyone to do the job entirely on their own, he ensured that the accounting and sales operations were carried out only in his presence.

When he was deeply engrossed in his work, he would smoke twenty to thirty *beedis* a day. The skin under his finger nails became black, and his hand bore scars from the smoke of *beedi* stubs. But he did not worry about such physical blemishes. The *beedi* was his best friend at work, but once he downed the office shutter and left for home, it was the cosy comfort of his wife Annama that he sought.

Annama, his better half, had radiated a kind of motherliness even as a young girl so it was impossible to think of her as having ever lived through a stage called childhood. But to Mathukutty, despite the grey streaks in her hair and the broadened shoulders in an otherwise diminutive frame, she would always be the sixteen year old blushing bride he had chosen as his life partner.

As for Annama, she was always ready with a mouthwatering meal when Mathukutty came home after a hard day's work. He would drink to his heart's content and relish the traditional fish and meat dishes she prepared for him. But despite his unhealthy company with liquor, smoking and fried food the one thing he stayed away from was chewing betel leaf smeared with slaked lime and stuffed with arecanut.

Though Mathukutty managed to keep off this one vice he never prevented his wife for whom chewing paan was a habit like most women of those days. They believed that the red colour brought to the lips by chewing *paan* enhanced beauty. Though Mathukutty did not approve of this habit he was quite tolerant unlike most men in the village and granted his wife the freedom to pursue this vice.

Mathukutty and Annama had four sons and three daughters. Of the sons two had left the country for good, the oldest one moving to Penang in Malaya and the second to Rangoon in Burma. The third, who was attempting to start a shop in Calicut had passed away after contracting tuberculosis a few years ago. All the three daughters were married off to families elsewhere.

At this stage in their lives all that Mathukutty and Annama asked for was an assurance of continuity of their lineage. The topic was often discussed very emotionally when the couple had had a round of arrack in the evening. They placed their trust in the hands of their youngest son, Thomachan. Annama knew her son. He had been resisting marriage for some time now, despite crossing the appropriate age long ago. She realised that Thomachan had the urge to explore the world and feared that married life would tie him down to the ancestral home. He had seen his brothers make their fortune outside Puthupady, on their own. Further, tales of his father's adventures and success "outside his home" down south were often recounted with a great deal of interest and enthusiasm in the village. It was only natural then, that Thomachan too wanted to be a self-made man, learning the ropes of self sufficiency outside the protective influence of his parents' home.

From hints he gave and some of his actions, Annama could easily gauge the mood of her youngest son. She felt that like his older brothers, Thomachan could also leave home forever. One day she spoke to her husband, "I fear that our Thomachan will leave home soon. You know what happened the last time we allowed the others to do so."

But proud patriarch that he was, Mathukutty brushed aside these worries, "What he needs is a settled life. We should seriously think of taking forward the alliance with Vackachan's youngest daughter Mariam. She's the perfect woman to keep him central to his duties of a family man."

"But she is only sixteen while he's nearing twenty five. Will they agree to the alliance and even if they do, will the marriage work?" What she actually feared was the difference in the status of their families.

Irked by his wife's pessimism, Mathukutty delivered one of his pet sermons, "If a couple complement each other in a marriage there is a good chance their alliance will be a happy one. Call me old fashioned, but it is a fact that being man and woman is enough to complement each other. In addition they need the support of the family, which we will give." After a bout of coughing he added, "And why are you worried about Vackachan's consent? They are a family in decline, hanging onto the last morsel of their former glory. Tell me, who in his position wouldn't want an alliance with the Kollegal family!"

Nodding positively, Annama adjusted the neckline of her white *chatta*, a blouse worn by Christian women of those days, before adding, "I'm all for this alliance . But he has been pooh-poohing the idea of marriage for the last four or five years. How I pray this somehow works out…!" Saying so, she walked away.

Watching her retreating figure, Mathukutty exhaled the smoke from the *beedi* he had just lighted and felt an unnamed fear rise inside him. This marriage had to work or else he knew that the Kollegal Estate too would begin its decline. Throwing the *beedi* away, he followed Annama into the room and said, "He and his grandiose plans to conquer the world. You are right, I'll have to stop it before some foreign woman hooks him and siphons off all his money. He can wear a fashionable suit and sit down to beg in the street if that happens, I suppose."

Those were the good old days. Yes, good indeed, when parents were keen to see their daughters given in marriage to a boy from a well-to-do and respectable family, at least equal in status to their own. Most marriages were arranged by parents because society was conservative and there were few opportunities for boys and girls to meet and mingle. In fact elders ensured that no opportunities to mix arose. As in other parts of the country in Malabar also marriages were not considered a union between a boy and a girl alone, but a strong alliance between two families.

A girl moving to another family was seen in traditional circles as the mother of the next generation, a matter too important to be left to the whims of youngsters. In fact, the first step towards forging an alliance started with the family elders on both sides taking an active interest in finding suitable partners for a successful union, almost like a merger in the corporate sector of today. On the girl's side, charm and possession of an impeccable character were considered valuable pre-requisites, while for the boy his worth rested in financial security either through family wealth or in his holding a lucrative job.

To make the match-making process simpler, strict community norms permitted alliances to be forged only between families of the same religious caste. And Vackachan's family fits the bill perfectly.

Since Vackachan's daughter was educated in a proper school, she was ranked a little higher than other eligible girls. In those days it was common for parents to marry off their daughters as soon as the right proposal came along, regardless of what class the girl was studying in. Women of upper class families did not go out to work, but it was acceptable for women of the lower class to work in the fields or in well-to-do households as servants, but again in some cases only until their family found a suitable groom for them.

The marriage of K.M. Thomachan B.A. of the Kollegal family and Mariam, the pretty daughter of Vackachan was celebrated with the pomp and pageantry expected of a powerful and rich family of Kollegal. Mathukutty, the father of the groom, was particular that the level of celebration was top class. A week before the wedding, he had specifically directed his supervisor, Krishnan Nair to arrange a grand meal for all the workers.

Krishnan Nair had voiced some reservations at first, "Is it necessary, Muthalali?" He belonged to the old world and could not understand what the fuss was all about. "Isn't it enough that we serve your relatives alone?" he asked wondering whether feeding the workers was anything but an avoidable extravagance.

When Mathukutty did not relent, Krishnan Nair remained silent for some time. Then like a pragmatic army general on facing a set-back, retreated only to regroup and came up with, "Certainly we'll hold a great feast for all the relatives and prominent people of the locality." At this the patriarch simply steamrolled his suggestion. "But I want my workers too to take part in the festivities."

Hearing the emphatic tone of his master, Krishnan Nair finally relented. Mathukutty told him firmly, "We can become bankrupt if it comes to that. I want all the workers of this estate to enjoy the great occasion with my family. Do you know how much it means to my dear wife and me to have at least one son to hold aloft the family flame? I don't know how my other boys are, now that they seem to have made their lives in god-forsaken places. But Thomachan, yes Krishnan Nair, he stayed back for me and my wife."

He was serious for a few seconds and then sporting a smile, went about discussing the menu for the feast, "I want a grand feast with buffalo meat and fish curry for the workers also."

To this Krishnan Nair had sounded alarmed, "Will not a vegetarian meal suffice, Muthalali?"

"No. In our family in Kottayam, beef and fish are regular dishes served to guests. I want those same items to be served to all my guests, including the workers," he said, thinking of the tradition of Central Travancore of serving the meat of cow or buffalo at feasts. He was fully aware that perhaps he would be the first one to deviate from the usual vegetarian lunches and usher in an era of heavy dining for workers.

He wanted the typical Travancore style fish curry spiced with *kodampuli* (Malabar tamarind) and left to mature for a day or two to acquire a taste so distinct as to guarantee the ultimate sensory satisfaction for the traditionalists. Keeping in mind their presence, he had also asked for a few of the customary vegetarian dishes such as parboiled rice, cooked vegetables, *papad*, pickles and for the dessert, small ripe bananas to be served with sweetened concentrated *neera*, a sugary syrup obtained by tapping the coconut palm.

As Krishnan Nair made a note of Mathukutty's instructions, little could he imagine the relief which the patriarch felt in finally having someone to carry his legacy forward. As for Mathukutty the patriarch, never in his wildest dreams could he have imagined the twist of fate awaiting his family with the entry of Mariam as his daughter-in-law.

Before the commencement of the Holy Mass in the Church in Thamarassery, Mathukutty scanned the arrangements at home. He felt pleased that everything he had wished for was in place. Krisnan Nair had done a good job. If anything, it only exceeded his expectations. The marriage was of so ostentatious a nature that the Bishop of Calicut himself came to conduct the ceremony along with the two priests assigned to the Church. It was felt that despite all the solemnity of the occasion, the choir played out its music with more raw enthusiasm than subtlety so much so the harmonium was going on full blast disregarding the finer aspects of pitch and musical tone.

After the church ceremony Mathukutty saw Vackachan play the perfect host. Although Vackachan's current financial position was rather modest, there was a time when his family had held powerful posts in the government. Many men from their family were highly educated, with some even serving under the British with distinction in Madras and Calcutta. An alliance with such a family was indeed a matter of pride for the Kollegals.

While Mathukutty was pondering over this, he was suddenly startled out of his thoughts, as in walked the British Collector who had come all the way from the neighbouring town of Calicut, to show his appreciation of the services rendered by Vackachan's family to the Empire. While Vackachan exchanged pleasantries with the Collector, Mathukutty briskly waddled towards the duo and said in his broken English, "Thank you, Collector Saar for coming. I Mathukutty from the Kollegal family, big house and big estate. You come, visit one day."

The Collector murmured a thank you and left soon after, in his car.

When the ceremony drew to a close, the couple were taken in a special, decorated horse drawn carriage which Mathukutty had arranged, to the house of Vackachan, situated close to the church. After a short reception followed by lunch, the wedding party consisting of the couple and the groom's people who had come from Puthupady took rest in a neighbour's house, where after coffee, they left for the groom's house. The same carriage took the couple to Puthupady. When they reached the centre of Puthupady, a band from Calicut escorted the couple and guests in procession to the great house of Kollegal. As they neared the gate, another band of musicians from the nearby Tamil speaking region took over, playing the *Nadhaswaram*, a clarinet-type instrument, while three other musicians played the drums and one sounded the cymbals. With its vibrant tune and stunning drum beats, the effect was truly festive. The crowd thronging the entrance to the house craned their necks to have a glimpse of the couple and the musicians started to play with renewed gusto, in response to all the attention they were getting.

As the couple finally descended from the carriage, the booming sound of fire crackers filled the air, while heaven pointing flower sparklers shot upwards with a whistling sound much to the excitement of the crowd, mostly workers, who had come with their families.

But the function was far from over. As soon as the couple entered the gates, all guests, relatives, close friends, and prominent people of the community took their seats inside the huge makeshift thatched roof *pandal* built with bamboo supports. The *pandal* was illuminated by a few petromax lamps, at the entrance of which the couple were made to stand on *mukali*, a flat slightly raised wooden plank, on which people normally sat down for meals.

"Make sure that the groom is on the right side," Mathukutty whispered to his son-in-law Varghese, a show-off busybody who believed that nothing would work without him at the helm.

After doing as instructed, he called out in a loud voice, "Ammachi come forward to bless the couple before they enter the house."

Accordingly, Mathukutty's wife Annama stopped talking with the guests and came forward to face the couple. With nervous hands, she made the symbol of the cross on the forehead of her son with her right thumb and garlanded him, after which she did the same to her daughter-in-law. She then led the bridal couple inside and seated them on two specially decorated chairs facing the guests. Thomachan's father, as head of the family took charge, and in his booming voice proudly asked the gathering,

"Do I have your permission to offer the sweet to the groom?"

This practice of an elder male of the family, asking the gathering three times whether he can give sweets and water to the groom and bride is peculiar to the Syrian Christian community. When Mathukutty received the consent of the smiling crowd he took a scoop of coconut gratings and sugar from the brass plate kept in front, and put it into his son's mouth. He then repeated the ritual with Mariam, the young bride.

Next was the ceremony of serving water to the groom and bride. Once the formalities were dispensed with, Thomachan's youngest sister Thresiamma led the bride inside while Thomachan followed.

Outside in the great *pandal* the workers were enjoying a feast like they had never had before. People squatted on the reed mats placed in rows, while food was served on plantain leaves laid out before them.

The chief item on the menu was parboiled rice, served from a small narrow cylindrical basket by the volunteers. Other side dishes followed. The beef and fish curry was lapped up in no time. The guests ate to their heart's content, not allowing the food to come in the way of gossip, chatter and jokes. As the day neared its end and the lavish festivities drew to a close, a worried Annama could be heard murmuring to nobody in particular, "I wonder where this extravagance will lead us to, especially with prices of essentials going up by the day!"

Her husband overheard the remark and replied with a chuckle, "*Podi.* Aren't you satisfied with the rise in prices of rubber and coconut? We will gain from that and lose a little on purchase of other goods. So do not worry much about expenses."

Miffed by his response, Annama retorted, "All right, but don't say I didn't warn you. After all, our own marriage was conducted in a humble style. This is unnecessarily lavish."

Mathukutty laughed loudly on hearing this. "Well, you shouldn't be complaining like this, woman. After all, it's your own son's wedding. *Edi*, hard work combined with good breaks has made us prosperous. This is a great occasion for all of us. We will finally have someone to carry forward the family name. I tell you, they will lead us to great happiness and glory."

"That I have no doubt about. He is our son after all," she said, fearing that she would be sidetracked.

"She is ours as well," Mathukutty added.

Annama said, "Just promise me that you won't spoil her. After all she hasn't seen such wealth in many years."

Her husband now understood the crux of the matter troubling her. 'These women!' he thought but then restrained himself from making any comment realising that such tension between a mother and her daughter-in-law was natural. But he also knew that when it came to important issues in the family, mothers knew very well how to show restraint. It would all depend on Mariam now. She, who was new to the house, would have to put in her best to fit into the family ethos if she were to make herself dear to all.

The marriage changed Thomachan for the better. Overnight he became a dutiful husband and a caring family man. It was as if the presence of another to carry the burden of the world lying on his shoulders all these years had lightened his heart. Fortunately for his parents, his urge to explore the world too subsided, as he gladly fell into the routine of estate life. Mathukutty knew that the credit for it lay in the deft handling of his mind by Mariam, who was both a devoted wife and an efficient daughter-in-law.

In traditional rich households, there were servants and cooks who could produce good food. But Mariam outdid them. She presented traditional food with a unique flavour. She also supervised cleaning of the house and made sure that it was neat and tidy all the time. Thus Mariam's entry into the family and into the hearts of its members became easier than anticipated.

For Mathukutty, nothing now preceded in importance his paternal fondness for Mariam. Even Annama despite her initial misgivings, accepted her daughter-in-law as if she was a gift from God himself. And such was the affection Mariam received from Thomachan, that it could easily be said that not even Mumtaz Mahal, the wife of Shah Jahan who built the monument of love, the Taj Mahal in her memory, would have known what unconditional love was.

One Sunday while returning from Church, Mathukutty said to his wife, "We have got ourselves a fine daughter-in-law."

Annama responded promptly, "Daughter, not daughter-in-law! The moment she stepped into our house, I knew a gem had landed amidst us."

Mathukutty raised his eyebrows in surprise at this new found love between the two women, only to lower them, smiling softly to himself. This was an occasion when silence was truly golden and he let it stay that way.

Chapter 2

It was nearly a month now since the wedding. Mariam had become virtually a cornerstone of the household. She was given a free hand to behave like a daughter, and she began to intervene in family issues as well, without rubbing anyone the wrong way. She once even cornered Mathukutty discreetly about his smoking habit. Nobody in Puthupady had ever found this an unusual habit or a threat to health. But Mariam had learnt from experience. An uncle of hers who was a chain smoker had contracted tuberculosis and it was widely believed that excessive smoking had caused it. Naturally, there was a morbid fear of smoking in Vackachan's family, though many of their acquaintances had simply laughed it off as paranoia. Smoking was after all, considered a manly occupation by the simple village folk.

Mariam shared the family's fear and at an opportune moment she confronted Mathukutty, "Appacha, do you really want to smoke so much. It's not good. You will get tuberculosis for which there is no cure."

Mathukutty took the *beedi* out of his mouth and gulped down the smoke, with a feeling of guilt, "Nothing like that, *molae*. I do it because it gives me the energy to work. Nothing will happen to me."

But the concern shown by her made a lasting impression on his mind, and it made him realise how much he missed not having one of his own daughters by his side at this age. However Mariam compensated for that with her loving concern for the family members and soon became their favourite.

It was a time when there began a wave of turmoil in far away Europe. The threat of war loomed and Hitler and Mussolini dominated the news. But here in rural Puthupady they were nothing more than blurry figures with mythological intonations. As far as the villagers were concerned, this was just another time when prices shot through the roof. For the Kollegal family which dealt in different commodities, however, this meant better profits, and enabled them to offset the wedding expenses incurred that year.

"Why don't we buy a car?" Annama popped the question to her husband one day, just before retiring to sleep.

Mathukutty removed his vest and getting into bed, asked softly, "Do you really think we need a car when we have excellent bullock carts?"

Annama then played his own card back at him, "But you only said that the estate produce is getting a good price this year. What is the use of prosperity if it cannot be displayed?" she said with mischievous eyes.

Mathukutty could see in her eyes a dream she had already dreamt in which she was being taken to church in a car with Thomachan and Mariam by her side.

"I'll think about it." Mathukutty said, not entirely shrugging off her request. "It isn't a bad idea for Thomachan and Mariam to go around the village and to Thamarassery as well, sitting in the comfort of a car." The car would be a gift to Mariam, he was thinking. But he was too proud to approve a suggestion made by his wife. He would make his decision known after pretending that he had given it much thought.

Days turned into weeks, weeks into months, and it seemed the idea of buying a car had been swept into a corner of Mathukutty's mind. Christmas was fast approaching. In the meanwhile, Mariam's childhood bronchitis had resurfaced resulting in great discomfort for her with periodical wheezing. Inspite of that she continued to be involved in every aspect of the house, keeping aside her intermittent illness. Annama often told her to stop doing petty chores since it was spoiling the servants. But Mariam enjoyed keeping herself engaged in some work or the other till Thomachan returned from the estate in the evening.

But one day, while seeing her cough incessantly when she was dusting the windows of a front room, Annama scolded her, "Stop dabbling in dirt like this Mariam. It's not good for your health."

"No, no Ammachi! I'm perfectly fine. It's just the dust."

"No. You have to stop and take rest. Next week you have to go to your parents' place for your first Christmas after marriage. What will they say if you keep coughing all the time?" But Mariam simply smiled and continued her work.

That night a concerned Annama told her husband, "Mariam is coughing and I thing she is breathing with some difficulty. We must show her to the doctor."

"What! Let us take her right away! Why wait?"

"Are you mad? Don't get so alarmed about it. We can take her next week when we go to her parents' house. They have a family doctor. For now, she just needs to stop breathing all the dirt and dust of this house."

"Yes, she needs some fresh air. I'll tell Thomachan to take her to the estate tomorrow. The outdoor air will do her good. Actually there is no greater pleasure than watching the crops—the lush green rubber trees and the swaying palms."

The next morning, as the Kollegal house was greeted by a clear sky, Thomachan and Mariam left its premises for the rubber plantations. December mornings in the foothills of the Western Ghats carried a slight chill, and the couple were greeted by it as they rode out the gate. The weather was expected to be better with the bright sun shining down pleasant warmth later.

The bullock cart carrying them had a special spring mounting for comfort. Palani, the cart-man was an old hand, and he had been instructed by Mathukutty to go slowly to avoid any discomfort to Mariam.

The moving bullock cart scattered a congregation of crows which appeared to be holding a local convention with the usual cacophony. In reality they were feasting on a dead rat on the side of the road.

As the cart approached the estate Mariam saw men and women working diligently in the fields. Some were busy preparing beds for sowing the crop using shovels, while others busied themselves in post-harvest operations.

The men wore a short *mundu*–a cotton cloth tied around the waist covering the lower body while the upper body was left bare.

Many of the women too wore a *mundu* with the upper body exposed. This was the traditional attire of the local men and women. But while young women with bouncing bosoms are always a titillating excitement to men, such sights rarely evoked any response among the men working in the field that day. For them, living beside half naked women was not uncommon, being the custom of the land. The straight faced expression of the men in fact was akin to a busy executive in a modern office concentrating on reading the memo in his hand, rather than staring at a well dressed good looking woman walking past him.

As Thomachan and Mariam passed along the narrow path between the rows of rubber trees, Mariam remarked, "How dark it is under the trees!"

"That's because the trees are planted close to each other. This way we can plant the maximum number of trees in the space. If you look, you'll find that every tree leans in the same direction," he explained, happy that Mariam was taking so much interest.

"Why?"

"When one row of trees bends to catch maximum sunshine, the row next to it also follows suit."

"But in what direction do they bend?"

"A good question! I myself have wondered about it often. Perhaps it's the wind direction in the early stages of their growth which decides the direction."

"What are they doing there under the tree?" Mariam asked, pointing to some men carrying some strange looking equipment.

"Oh that? They are spraying a solution of Bordeaux mixture to check the growth of fungus."

"It has a bluish colour," Mariam observed.

"Yes, because the mixture consists of copper sulphate and calcium hydroxide. The intense blue of copper sulphate lends the blue colour to the white of the slaked lime. It's about thirty to forty years since the mix was developed for grape vine cultivation in the Bordeaux region of France. But still it's the best."

Mariam being from a family of government servants did not have much scope to observe the plantation crops at close quarters.

Naturally what she was seeing excited her and she tried to absorb every bit if information. "And what is the young man doing on that tree with a knife?"

"Ah, he is tapping the rubber from it. Let us go near."

They walked to the spot where the young man was slitting the bark and removing a small diagonal strip of thick bark.

"Now can you see the latex flowing from the slit portion? At the end of the cut a small metal strip bent in middle will channel the milk, as latex is popularly called, into the coconut shell fixed over a support, right underneath it. Once everyday the milk is collected this way and a fresh gash is made below the existing one for collection next day. This process is repeated till this part of the tree runs out of its latex generating capacity."

Mariam observed the latex ooze out and then said, "Milk is the right name. It looks exactly like milk. What do you actually do with it then?"

"Let us walk down to the shed," Thomachan said as he guided her down a couple of stone steps and into a processing shed. The shed was dingy, and inside it three or four people could be seen working the latex in different ways. One of them was pouring the rubber milk into a rectangular aluminium tray. Pointing towards him, Thomachan said, "Come Mariam, let me show you. Can you see that man? He is adding this colourless liquid called formic acid to the rubber milk to coagulate it. By evening it will turn into a soft foamy solid sheet."

"But the sheets stacked here are thin and tough."

"That's because the sheets have been passed through the rollers. Look at that man putting one such fluffy sheet through a set of two rollers after adjusting the gap between them. Once the sheets are placed in that gap, he rotates the handle which makes the rollers move in opposite directions to pull the sheet through the gap. The sheet gets thinner as the pressure applied on it squeezes out the water from it. After the sheets are made thinner, they are dried in the adjoining smoke house where hot air and smoke drive out the moisture completely from within the thin yet tough elastic sheet."

"But won't the smoke make the sheet black?" enquired Mariam.

"Yes, to some extent. The preferred colour is golden yellow. If it turns very dark, then it can be used only in the manufacture of tyres, which are black anyway."

"I have read somewhere that to make tyres, you have to vulcanize the rubber."

"Yes," replied Thomas, amazed by Mariam's interest in the subject. "I think you could be of great help in the operations of the estate."

Mariam laughed softly, "I hope your managers won't revolt against a nosy boss, that too a woman."

"Normally they would," remarked Thomachan, "But I have watched you and I believe you have the ability to get them on your side."

"I don't mind. Would it be acceptable for a lady of the house to work in the estate in this part?"

"We will think about it."

Mariam then changed the course of their conversation, "There will be plenty of time to think about it. I have a doubt in my mind that I'm pregnant."

"Really?" Thomachan exclaimed, feeling a sudden rush of joy into his being.

"Mariam you should be careful. Let us return home and tell Ammachi to start preparing everything that is needed to keep you healthy for the coming months. Soups, good food, oil massage and all that!"

"No, please keep it a secret. Let me first tell my mother when we go there in a couple of days' time. She will then inform your parents."

Thomachan saw the logic in that and agreed to her suggestion. "Not a word from me, but promise me that you'll be careful," he said, sounding protective.

"It is fussy husbands like you who spoil their wives unnecessarily," she nudged him with her elbow. "So many women get pregnant every day. And those women, such as those working in our fields, work until a week before the delivery. Yet, no fuss for them and they deliver safely, don't they?"

Thomachan grinned and then replied in a low voice, "But none of them are my wife, are they?" And Mariam blushed and smiled sweetly, as she rested her head on his broad chest.

By the time they reached home Mariam was exhausted. She was gasping heavily while climbing the steps, and then immediately lay down to take some rest, much to Thomachan's relief.

The first Christmas after marriage is celebrated at the bride's place among Christian families in the region. The son-in-law, a new addition to the family is a privileged person and heavy feasting marks his presence on the occasion.The bride too gets an opportunity to reunite with her parents and siblings.

Just before they were to leave for her home, Mariam and Thomachan had their first tiff. Mariam was packing clothes for the trip when Thomachan walked into the room, with little concern for their impending departure. "Chetta, which shirts and *dhothis* you want to take?" she asked.

"Anything you wish. Just pack a couple of sets," he replied indifferently, concentrating more on rubbing his arms with oil.

"What!" Mariam said sharply. "How can you be so casual? All our relatives will be there just to see us. In the church, women will be waiting to have a glimpse of you. You will be the centre of attraction. Don't you want to look your best?"

Thomachan found her concern heartening. He suddenly felt like wrapping his arms around her and hugging her tight, "Okay, Mariam, you decide what I should wear. Take whatever you want me to wear," he said with a smile as he watched her sensual body while she was picking his clothes out of the almirah.

Most men from rich families wore the white *dhothi* for special occasions. To cover the upper body though, young people wore a half sleeved shirt with a front opening that was usually held together with detachable metal buttons. Elderly men like Mathukutty often preferred to wear sleeveless collarless shirts and a *dhothi*. But while at home, no one really bothered about covering the upper body with a shirt. It was also the style of the time to wear a cotton shawl around the neck while going out. This doubled up as a towel if required, to keep the face dry during humid months.

Thomachan and Mariam left for her home with Vackachan. They travelled in a bullock cart drawn by a single animal and fitted with springs to neutralize the jolts caused by the bumpy uneven mud road. Except for a small stretch of road near the town centre which boasted a macadam surface the rest of the road was a network of potholes connected together by raised mud.

On Christmas Eve, the whole family went for the midnight Mass, after which the day of merriment and feasting began. Mathukutty and Annama too had been invited for lunch. Fresh coconut arrack had been brewed and the men drank to their heart's content. Annama eyed the drink longingly. She would have under normal circumstances taken a drink on such occasions but keeping in mind her newly acquired position as mother-in-law, she restrained herself.

Mariam's mother though had never touched liquor before like most Malayalee women of those times.

After finishing their food, as both families retired to rest, Annama approached her husband as he stood in front of the brass-framed mirror in their room, combing his hair

"Are you ready to be a grandfather?"

"Why? What happened?" he asked.

"Mariam is carrying. Her mother told me just now. The expected date of delivery is around the first week of August."

Mathukutty did not know how to express his joy. After a little rest, the couple proceeded to the big living room where most of the guests had gathered. The air was filled with the charm of pleasant conversation mixed with some noisy banter typical of a family get-together on a festive day.

Finally after all the guests dispersed and Vackachan and Mathukutty found themselves in the room, Vackachan went up to

Mathukutty and shook both his hands excitedly, "You heard the good news about Mariam?"

Mathukutty was waiting for someone to mention it so he could burst the bubble growing inside him, "Yes, yes, of course." Then in a tone of affectionate admonishment he said, "Make sure that she doesn't travel in a bullock cart without springs."

Vackachan smiled, "Don't I know what's best for my child?" he replied with slight humour before continuing, "In fact, I would like to request that she stays with us for one month. We will get her checked by the family doctor."

"That is a wonderful idea," agreed Mathukutty, "No trouble or expenses to be spared though," he added.

Towards evening, the family members had an early coffee break, accompanied by a vast spread of sweet preparations and snacks. Mathukutty and his wife prepared to leave as it would take over an hour to get home. With the roads being in bad shape, everyone agreed that they should start early so as to reach before nightfall. In the hilly regions such as Puthupady especially, darkness descended very early in the month of December.

Just before leaving, Mathukutty took Vackachan aside and whispered, "Mariam is gasping and wheezing a lot nowadays. You should ask the doctor to check that as well."

He was acting on the advice of Annama who was becoming worried about Mariam's health. She was afraid that the wheezing if not checked in the early stage would affect her ability to deliver normally. Annama unlike other mothers-in-law, had embraced Mariam as her own daughter despite her initial misgivings. After some small talk Mathukutty and Annama bid goodbye to everyone, got into the cart and proceeded towards Puthupady.

"Thomachan will stay there for a week," Mathukutty said softly to Annama in a voice inaudible to the cartman. "I have instructed Vackachan about her check up," he added.

It was the month of February. Summer had begun to set into Puthupady and its surrounding regions. Thomachan woke up from his sleep sweating profusely and cursing the humidity. He walked out onto the portico to sit down to a nice cup of coffee while looking for the newspaper. He found his father already there, reading the front page. Mariam came in with two glasses of black coffee. She had been feeling sick since the previous night and the exhaustion was reflected on her young face. As soon as she went inside, Mathukutty whispered to his son, "I think we should buy a car."

"But that will cost a lot of money," Thomachan replied, blowing around the rim of the glass to cool the coffee.

Mathukutty ticked him off immediately, "*Eda*, what is money for if not to make our lives more comfortable. The car will be useful to take Mariam to church safely."

"Ah! Appachan thinks only of his pet daughter," Thomachan mocked him, though deep within, he too found the idea attractive.

But not to sound overeager, he continued cautiously, "What will people say? They'll think we have no value for money. Besides you will invite the attention of those taxmen."

"What is there to fear? We have legal accounts for all our assets and we pay what is due to the Government without fail."

Thomachan knew that his father had made up his mind. Thinking of how it would benefit Mariam, he too agreed to the idea, wanting to show extra care and attention to his wife during her pregnancy.

When Annama heard about the car idea she was ecstatic.

"A car! That's exactly what this family needs. Let everyone here know the status and prestige of the Kollegal family."

Mathukutty said almost to himself, "But we need a driver. And that costs extra money."

"Of course we need a driver. How do you expect Mariam and me to go to Thamarassery to buy new clothes otherwise?" she said while adjusting her *mundu* and *chatta.*

Both Annama and Mariam, like all upper class Syrian Christian women, usually wore the pure white fine cotton *mundu* with a fan-like pleated tail in the back and the *chatta.* But when they went outdoors they wore a white half sari over it, both as a mark of modesty and useful to cover the head with when in church.

All the same, the attire was an ironic representation of women from different classes; the upper class indulging in an exaggerated show of modesty, while the lower class walking about in the fields topless!

Once Annama was satisfied with her appearance, she put the final seal on the ongoing conversation. "Now that Mariam is carrying, she can't travel by bullock cart. And then the baby will arrive … Yes, we definitely need a car."

Of course, the main reason behind Annama's excitement was the prestige a car would bring to the Kollegal family. It would raise their status in the village since no one owned a car in Puthupady. Only the PWD Assistant Engineer in Thamarassery owned a car, because the government gave him an allowance to meet his travel expenses. But other than such officers who needed a vehicle to tour different places as part of their job ordinary citizens who possessed a car were given a special status by the local people.

In about a month's time, the car was delivered to the Kollegal Estate. As expected, a sizeable crowd of onlookers thronged around it. Mathukutty allowed them to have a full inspection of the vehicle at first, then losing patience, forced them back to work. He then stood and stared at the vehicle adorning his courtyard. It was a dark blue Ford sedan. A small car, yes, but nonetheless a classic one with a spare wheel attached to its rear while a metal cover shielded the tyre from sun and rain. In front there rested a narrow vertical grill and two head lights mounted on the lower portion of the mud guard close to the bonnet. Two bucket seats had been fitted, one for the driver and another for his companion and a full width seat behind for the other passengers. With Annama, Mariam and Thomachan in the back seat it would be a tight fit, thought Mathukutty. But a car was a car. And Mathukutty was happy to see it occupy the space in front of the portico.

Soon he was joined by Thomachan. Together they inspected every part with great interest, although they did not know the functioning. Annama too appeared with a wide smile, went around it before jumping into the back seat with great satisfaction. Mariam was lying in her room due to exhaustion. Annama ordered

Thomachan to bring Mariam from her room to see the family's latest acquisition.

"The car belongs to Mariam and you," Annama proclaimed. "No, no, it is Ammachi's and Appachan's," he hastily replied, though deep within, he felt glad that they had bought him and his wife such a costly gift.

A young man by the name Govindhan, who had learnt driving in Calicut, was the one who brought the car to the estate driving all the way from Calicut in the company of the supplier's agent. From the time he arrived, Govindhan had started explaining the role of each part of the car, much to the excitement of the family. Since nobody knew how to drive, his word was accepted as final regarding the principle and working of the car. The admiring approval from people around gave Govindhan so much self importance that he started to talk with an exaggerated swagger. Many of his explanations were utter rubbish, but no one was in a position to counter him. Nevertheless it had to be admitted that he was a good driver.

The very next day, Thomachan coaxed Mariam to accompany him to the estate. Mariam obliged. The condition of the road had improved, all the same he ordered Govindhan to drive slowly keeping in mind her delicate condition.

As the car neared the estate, Mariam looked out fascinated by the coconut trees that passed by. The coconut palms were well complemented by the rows of slender arecanut trees swaying majestically to the breeze. Suddenly she remarked, "Look, there's a man climbing the arecanut palm!"

"Yes, they are harvesting the nuts," Thomachan replied, even as he tapped the driver to stop for a moment. He then turned to look out of the window at the man cutting bunches of yellow-orange fruits.

"How beautiful the nuts are!" exclaimed Mariam.

"Yes, they look like miniature coconuts except for the colour," he replied.

Mariam nodded "Does that man have to climb all these trees in order to harvest? Doesn't it take much time? It sounds like a tough job, doesn't it?"

"Watch him carefully, Mariam," Thomachan pointed out.

As soon as the man had harvested all the ripe bunches and plucked some damaged leaf sheaths, he started swinging on the tree. Mariam let out a low gasp, scared that the tree would bend under his weight and break. But suddenly, he latched onto the crown of the nearby tree, transferring himself onto it with great agility. He then went about harvesting the fruit from its crown.

Mariam laughed in wonder, "That was wonderful. So in this way, he can harvest the whole field in just one climb, huh."

"Yes, but only when the adjacent tree is close enough, or, let's say, within catching distance. Come, let us go further," he said, tapping the driver to start the car once again.

They came to an open area, where men were spreading ripe areca fruits to dry. Thomachan, pointing to the adjacent plot explained, "You can see that the fruits are nearly dry in that plot."

"But they don't have the bright colour of the fruits," she remarked.

Thomachan looked impressed with her observation, "That's because when the husk dries it becomes grey-black."

He then picked up a couple of dried fruits and showed her how the husk could be removed with the help of a knife. Mariam saw that the hard nut inside the fruit was round with the top slightly flattened and the bottom slightly conical.

"This is *Kottapaku.* It has a good market in North India where it is called *Chali,*" Thomachan explained

"And that? What are those men doing?" she asked looking into the distance.

"Oh! They are cutting the nuts into half. That variety is called *Parcha.*" It's easier to dry the halved nuts when the sun is not strong. This variety too is much in demand up North."

After walking around a little longer Mariam complained of exhaustion. Immedietly Thomachan led her to the car and they were driven home.

When Mariam was in her seventh month of pregnancy, her parents came to escort her home for the delivery as per custom. Mathukutty and Annama had insisted that they return to Thamarassery in the car, so the bullock cart in which Vackachan and wife had arrived was sent back empty. When the car arrived at Vackachan's house, it caused quite a sensation. The entire neighbourhood came to gape at the car. Had Annama been there, she surely would have enjoyed the attention, but unfortunately there was no place for her in the car.

By the end of July the people in general were alarmed by the events taking place in Europe. The continent seemed to be gripped by war frenzy. While the blame game had begun, the Western nations pointed the finger at Hitler for preparing Germany for war. The news of the impending war had even reached the little known Puthupady. The vernacular papers fuelled hysteria with exaggerated accounts and so called 'first hand' reports.

And in Mariam's house, as the time of delivery drew near, both families were overcome with anxiety due to Mariam's condition. It was as if the war hysteria had put a pause on her plans for motherhood. She was already six days overdue and there were no signs of her going into labour yet. The old doctor checked on her every day, without giving the family any assurance of her condition. Mariam grew weaker with every passing day. Her asthma seemed to be taking control over her mind and body at this critical juncture. Fortunately, the experienced mid-wife who was called in comforted everyone when she finally revealed that the delivery would happen in no more than two days time. The doctor concurred with her observation though deep inside he seemed to be carrying some unnamed worry. Thomachan was by his wife's side, for over a week now. His parents too visited whenever they could.

As the eighth day of waiting finally drew to a close, a heavy shower bathed the entire town in a soaking wet cover. By noon, Mariam went into labour. The mid-wife and standby nurse attended to the delivery while the car was sent to fetch the doctor. It was understood by now that the delivery would take its toll on Mariam's health. But no one had expected what was to follow.

In one of the rooms inside, an old lady from the neighbouring house was leading a prayer group for Mariam's safe delivery. Both Mathukutty and Annama joined in the prayers. But even after the doctor arrived, the delivery had not taken place.

Suddenly the relative calm of the air outside was pierced by a stinging cry. The cry carried in its wake a wave of human anguish and shock. After a second of silence, was heard the eagerly awaited cry of the newborn and then, another unexpected scream from Mariam's mother. Thomachan and Mathukutty looked at each other, before rushing to the room with Vackachan by their side.

But before they could enter, the doctor came out wearing a solemn expression on his face. Taking them aside, he delivered the news in a soft voice, "The baby is a boy and he is okay."

Thomachan could feel something amiss in his words. Impatient, he asked, "And Mariam? How is she?"

Mathukutty came forward as the doctor paused in his reply. "Keep heart, son. The ever powerful God has called her to his abode. She passed away as soon as the baby was pulled out."

Thomachan could feel himself go numb. A sense of emptiness filled his body. Vackachan held his hand and walked him slowly into the room where Mariam's mother and Annama were crying uncontrollably over the blood stained body of their beloved daughter. They moved aside as Thomachan stuttered his way to her side. Not a single drop of tear fell down his cheek. It had not registered yet that his Mariam was dead. Looking at her pale face, he composed himself and kissed the top of her forehead. Then, as if the dam had broken without warning, he looked up at the heavens and let out a singular cry of despair and loss.

Chapter 3

It was the August of 1942. The movement for Indian independence had gained momentum. Mahatma Gandhi, the leader of the freedom movement and his political party, the Indian National Congress had sounded a non-violent war cry to the British. The movement known as Quit India was a protest against the British Viceroy, Lord Linlithgow who had dragged India into the War without consulting any of the Indian leaders. Many of the Indian freedom fighters used it as an emotional plank to arm twist the British into assuring independence for the country as a reward for co-operating in the war effort. Though it was a coercive tactic it was the only means available to them. Some of the more extremist leaders among them were so sore at the British action that they felt India should side with the Germans instead!

But Puthupady remained largely insulated from the miseries of war. Its inhabitants lived their life, protected from any unwarranted happenings elsewhere.

In the Kollegal estate, things were even more removed from the events of the outside world. At least it seemed so. Mathukutty was still grieving over the loss of Mariam. He tried to calm his restless mind by taking care of his grandson Pappachan. And with a two-fold increase in his smoking habit!

Annama on the other hand coped with the situation better. She took over the role of mother of the little boy. Thomachan it seemed had forgotten his duty to the child, either lying almost always in a daze, lost in a world where his Mariam's smile occupied centre stage or keeping himself away from the thoughts of Mariam, by staying away from the house as long as he could. He would immerse himself fully in the operations of the estate and spent long hours reading. He acquired an obsession to learn more about the science and technology of plantation products in general and spices in particular. He would spend long hours in discussion with a retired scientist of the Coconut Research Station, Kasaragod who had settled in his ancestral home near Puthupady.

One day while clearing the table after lunch, Annama broached the rather delicate subject of a second marriage for him, "Shall we go ahead with the proposals?" she said to no one in particular.

"But what is wrong with our present situation," Thomachan replied moodily.

"Now look here," it was Mathukutty speaking firmly. But a bout of coughing halted his words. A little later he said in a calmer voice,

"You are young. You are the head of the estate with lot of responsibilities. You need someone to share the burden. Also Pappachan needs a mother to ensure that he grows up the right way."

"Ammachi is doing that job very well," Thomachan countered in a sullen tone.

"But she will not be there forever. She is getting old. The strain of bringing up a boy will take a toll on her health as well."

Thomachan though would not budge from his stand, "How can a stranger suddenly become a mother to the boy?"

Mathukutty took a deep breath and patiently explained, "There is a reason why elders say that a bad mother is better than no mother at all."

Putting the baby on her lap, Annama added, "Death during delivery is common my son. Look around you. But life has to go on. The men have to remarry for the sake of their child if not their own."

Hearing what he considered callous indifference in their tone Thomachan got up angrily, and in a sharp voice declared, "I refuse to marry again. Nobody can replace Mariam."

Mathukutty lit one more *beedi.* "Of all the people in the world, you are telling me that. I've still not gotten over her death yet," he said gently.

An uncomfortable silence ensued. The elderly couple decided not to push the matter. Life at the Kollegal estate returned to its placid state and Thomachan was left to his own.

As the years passed and the war came to an end, all that remained unchanged were the elements of nature visiting the estate every year like a song on loop. The warm summers sent forth their brightness, while the wet monsoons hid the tears underneath a blanket of rain.

Outside Puthupady, far removed from its boundaries, the world was rejoicing at the end of the Second World War. But Pappachan was nowhere near happy. No, it was not because he harboured a soft corner for the Germans. He was way too young to know anything about them. But what he did know was that he missed home.

Pappachan had been enrolled in a school in Thamarassery, where he stayed with his maternal grandfather, Vackachan. But the child was so homesick that he yearned to return home almost every other day. After several weeks of this, Vackachan had had enough dealing with the boy's daily bouts of weeping, and finally sent Pappachan back home, where he was put in the primary school managed by the Puthupady Church.

Mathukutty had the right connections to get his grandson admission in the middle of the school term. It was not the best of schools; it was not even a satisfactory school by any standards. Only children of estate workers and other labourers studied there. Even the standards of the teachers was depressing. The worst part was that English as a subject was unheard of, seen as an exotic language with no real purpose in one's future pursuits. But then, it was the only school they could find for Pappachan near home.

And then while Pappachan was getting adjusted to his new life, India gained Independence on August 15, 1947. Despite being far away from the freedom struggle, the development brought into the lives of the villagers of Puthupady a kind of special joy as well. And as the rest of India woke up to a new dawn, Puthupady too joined in the celebration of the new found freedom which independence promised.

Leading this new wave of nationalism in Puthupady were the school children. Upon instructions from the school authorities, they took out a procession to celebrate the occasion and then followed it up with an evening of music and dance programmes in the market area.

But it seemed as if the fortunes of the country and the Kollegal family were at variance with each other. For Annama fell sick a day after the celebrations had quietened down.The villagers knew it as nothing more than high fever but it might have been a case of acute typhoid, for within a fortnight she passed away.

This despite the discovery of penicillin by Alexander Fleming in 1920s (and his subsequent Nobel Prize in 1945) considered the magical cure for diseases such as typhoid, in the Western world. But little known Puthupady had not even heard of the drug. It would take a few years more for the region to come in contact with such modern medicines.

Two days after the funeral, Mathukutty, now a shadow of his former self, once again brought up the subject of marriage with Thomachan.

"Now you see son, the situation is different. You must marry again. You are very young and this house needs a woman to look after it."

"We will hire a housekeeper," Thomachan retorted. "I have found a suitable person to run this household, one elderly widow named Thresia. We already have a cook-cum-maid to look after you and Pappachan. So why worry?" he said with an air of finality.

"But they are not family. We need someone to continue the tradition of this family. Your marrying again is the only way out," Mathukutty sounded exasperated.

Thomachan sighed, "I cannot betray my conscience by bringing another woman in Mariam's place. You know how I still feel about her."

Mathukutty tried to reason with him, "I'm also heart-broken. But that should not be an excuse to stop you from leading a normal life. You should think about this matter seriously," he said, giving his son an ultimatum.

But Thomachan remained committed to his earlier stance, "The more I think about it, the less I feel I should replace Mariam in my heart."

"That is indeed noble of you, my son. But Pappachan needs a mother; otherwise the boy will get spoilt."

Thomachan simply waved his hand and walked out.

For Thomachan now, managing the estate had become his entire life. Following in the footsteps of James *saipu*, he decided to experiment. He ventured into coffee cultivation after expanding the area under pepper. Everything was progressing well on that front, so he had little time to worry about his home. He often felt guilty about not showering full attention on his son Pappachan, and in a bid to make amends appointed teachers to personally coach his son in English and Arithmetic. He also made it a point to take him for a drive to the nearby city of Calicut on Sundays.

Almost a year had passed by, when Govindhan drove Thomachan and his son, one bright Sunday morning to the hill station of Ooty, a favourite holiday spot of the erstwhile British rulers, now turned into an elite centre of education in the Madras Presidency. The children of British Officers stationed in South India had studied in one of the many schools dotting the region at some point or the other of their stay. And though the English rule had left the country, the existing British Principals stayed on in the schools and ensured that the high standards of academic excellence were maintained.

That Sunday, Thomachan asked Govindhan to drive the car to one of the better known schools where his old friend Mr. Joseph Francis was a faculty member. After spending the night in a lodge, Thomachan took Pappachan to the school the next day.

"Look Pappachan, how nice the buildings are!" he said, trying to make light conversation as they were led to the staff room, along corridors with rounded pillars. Pappachan just gaped at their size without uttering a word.

"Look at the lawns," Thomachan continued, "How green and beautiful they are! And there, look at that group of boys playing. They are so happy!"

He was obviously trying to condition Pappachan's mind to the news he planned to break to him in the next few days. And when that happened, he did not want his son to feel inferior to the smartly dressed boys running around.

The duo finally located Joseph Francis in the staff room dressed in a suit and tie; Thomachan in his *mundu* and plain shirt looked like a country bumpkin. But inspite of their vastly different styles of dressing, Joseph Francis extended them a warm welcome.They had a long conversation over coffee in the school canteen, after which Joseph Francis introduced Thomachan to the School Principal, Dr. John Miller. A pleasant Englishman in his late 40s, he seemed not to carry any airs about him, warmly shaking hands with Thomachan and Pappachan. It was evident from the greeting Thomachan received that his friend was an influential person in the school.

Later Joseph took them to the dining hall for coffee which was served with hot, crispy vegetable cutlets. Thomachan, used to eating with his hand, struggled with the fork and knife, and watched with a sense of wonder the ease with which his friend handled the cutlery. Pappachan, unmindful of the formalities of the white man, picked up the cutlet with his fingers.

They soon bid Joseph Francis farewell, and got into the car for the long drive back home. Pappachan dozed off as soon as the driver put the car into first gear. Thomachan looked at the sleeping face of his son, ruffled his thick mop of hair with his rough hands and fell into a train of thought.The road back to Puthupady was a winding one concurring with the turmoil inside his mind.

The very next day even before the sun had risen, Thomachan was up and shining, jubilant that he had managed to find a solution to all of the family's problems. He felt like shouting 'Eureka' as Archimedes had done, but he could not out run naked like the genius scientist. All he could do was walk impatiently around the front lawn in a white *mundu*. During breakfast he expressed his views to his father, "Appacha, I have decided to send Pappachan to Ooty for better education."

"Well, I hope that is what he really needs," Mathukutty replied vaguely as if he himself was unsure of his decision.

Thomachan sensing the uncertainty in his father's voice, argued strongly, "But Appacha, don't you see the logic behind it? No doubt it will cost a lot of money, but with our present financial position, we can easily afford it. It will make little Pappachan a better person."

"Are you sure?" asked his father.

Thomachan got up from his chair now, "I can assure you that this step will solve all our problems in one shot."

"All right!" Mathukutty said. He was worried that exposure to the riches and pompousness exhibited by the students of such high-end schools might spoil his grandson even more. Perhaps, even confuse him as to his role in village society; why, for all he knew Pappachan could even turn into a misfit, being of no use to either village or family. Much later admonishing himself for being so conservative he felt that probably his principles need not be necessarily ideal for the next generation.

But the fear returned, after he retired to his room. Some part of him was afraid that like his other sons, his grandson might also migrate to newer parts of the world. He prayed to God that if that were to happen at least may the boy remain happy.

In the summer of 1949 Thomachan took his son Pappachan to Ooty in their faithful old car. Govindhan was at the wheel. A steel trunk carrying the boy's clothes was pushed into the boot. It contained one woollen sweater to combat the low temperatures in Ooty, and many pairs of trousers and shirts. An umbrella had also been packed just in case. Though it rained much less in Ooty than it did in Puthupady, carrying an umbrella wherever one went was a tradition all Malayalees followed. It was a difficult habit to shrug off.

Tucked into the side of the trunk was a small leather box with writing materials, pens, some study books, a few toys, photographs of his parents and grandparents, an atlas and a few other items which the school had listed as necessary. Thomachan had spent a lot of money on purchasing all of them.

By now Pappachan had also grown beyond the homesickness which engulfed him while at Vackachan's place. He was more independent and rarely showed any emotion, a state of the mind which neither his father nor grandfather could fully decipher. Even when he stepped into his dormitory in the boarding school for the first time it was hard to tell if he was happy or felt pain.

Thomachan concluded that he was happy, assuring himself that a good environment in such a top-class school, coupled with plenty of activities and academic pursuits would put his son back on the track.

Thomachan had tried his best to go away without any hurt to his emotional state. He had kept looking at his son playing with his hair and finally when the time came to depart had asked with a slight quiver of his lips, "So son, can Appachan leave now?"

"Yes, Appacha," Pappachan had replied.

"You must eat well. Study and play; that is the hallmark of this school. Not like the primitive school of Puthupady."

"Yes, Appacha."

"You must often write letters to me and Appapan, and also to your grandparents at Thamarassery. Don't forget."

"Yes, Appacha."

Not able to take monosyllabic answers anymore, Thomachan had hugged his son tight for a minute thinking of the day he was born and the aftermath of his birth. His poor Mariam! How she would have loved to hug her son this way and see him off to school. Then setting him free, he had got up and walked out of the building.

During the return journey, Govindhan remarked, "Pappachan must be feeling lonely."

"Yes," Thomachan replied with a stoic expression, wondering though whether the boy's lack of emotion conveyed some other meaning. Maybe everything was for the good, he concluded.

Upon his return, Thomachan found the household in Puthupady resembling a place devoid of its soul. His mother was no more, his wife dead, and now his son was lodged somewhere far off.

As for Mathukutty, the decision to send his grandson and the only real companion in the house away, was nothing short of madness. But such were the ways of the modern generation, he consoled himself. He had left the management of the estate completely in Thomachan's hands and spent his time smoking more and more and wandering listlessly around the house.

But Thomachan could sense the inner loneliness felt by his father. He knew he was to blame for that, and one day in an effort to bring his father back into plantation work, he said after dinner, "Appacha, you are aware that we started growing coffee a few years ago, right? Well, now I have introduced curing. There is a good prospect for its growth."

Mathukutty, looking bored, replied, "I have no doubt about that. But do our workers know how to do the proper curing?"

"Yes. We hired a man who retired from a British company in Mysore."

"Very good! How is his work?"

"He knows his job well, I must concede. We have just begun. You should come tomorrow and see it for yourself."

Mathukutty agreed silently, wondering if the change would enliven his spirits.

The coffee plantations and curing shed were located a little far from the estate, near the stream to be precise, as the curing process required lots of fresh water.

Old man Mathukutty joined his son in the back seat of the car the next morning as planned. Govindan drove rather fast, unmindful of the curves and turns in the estate roads. Mathukutty observed that the condition of the roads had vastly improved since the last time he passed through. "You seem to have transformed the place," he commended his son.

Thomachan replied in a prophetic tone, "There is no future without good roads. Transportation is the key to progress. Before long, trucks and even tractors will have to be brought in to do much of the work here. And without good roads, it will be difficult for them to reach the farthest corners of the plantation."

When the car reached the coffee plantation, the two of them got out. The previous night's rain had made a large puddle in the nearby low lying field. A frog after an impressive acrobatic jump was showing off with a series of croaks. Taking advantage of the situation, a low flying hawk swooped down with the mastery of a Japanese fighter pilot taking part in the *'Tora ToraTora'* operation at Pearl Harbour and picked up an easy meal.

Pointing to a group of women working the crops at a distance, he said, "You can see the women harvesting the coffee berries."

"Is it the good variety, son?" Mathukutty enquired.

"Not yet, Appacha. We have planted *Robusta* variety. Let's wait for a couple more years before introducing the superior *Arabica*."

Mathukutty suddenly felt that he had become out of date in front of his son. Looking at him proudly, he thought to himself, How much more does this younger generation know of the fields and the crops growing in them. And then he realised that with such worldly knowledge at hand, Thomachan must have taken the right decision in sending Pappachan to the school in Ooty.

Both of them continued their walk down the fields and Abdulla, the man hired to introduce curing, joined them shortly. All three of them walked a few yards ahead to the place where coffee berries were spread over mats for sun drying. It was here that the fruits were cured.

"At present we are only making cherry grade. The berries are dried and then the outer skin and rind are removed to get cherry coffee," Abdulla said.

"Please explain to Appachan the other method of processing as well," Thomachan instructed him, upon which Abdulla took on the posture of a learned professor and explained, "The other trade type is plantation coffee where the pulp is removed first, after which the beans are washed free of pulp particles before they are dried. You need plenty more water for this process."

Mathukutty thought for a moment before asking, "Can you tell one type from another just by looking?"

"Yes, a person experienced in processing can determine the difference easily."

"And how is that done?"

"The plantation coffee will have a parchment-like covering. In cherry because the dried skin is removed using great abrasion, the parchment skin does not remain with the bean. That is why plantation coffee is also called parchment coffee."

"Can you convert this coffee into plantation grade?"

"Yes, but I think, it is better to introduce the *Arabica* variety of coffee plants. Plantation *Arabica* coffee will have a good price and good market."

"Will it have a better flavour?"

"The aroma comes only after roasting. It must be heated uniformly, so that there will be controlled charring and that will give rise to fine coffee aroma. Of course, plantation coffee made from *Arabica* beans will give a superior flavour."

Nodding his head in satisfaction, Mathukutty followed his son to the other parts of the plantation.

When they reached home, Mathukutty began smoking nonstop as usual. During the meal he coughed loudly a couple of times. Thomachan looked at him with some concern.

But Mathukutty dismissed his anxiety by saying, "It's the excess of chilli in the curry which is causing this cough. Of course, I'm not saying that the dish isn't superb. After all, only with plenty of masala can fish curry taste good. Mariam used to make very good curry," he recalled. After another bout of coughing he resumed, "Nothing like a true Indian spice such as chilli. What good are foreign spices like your pepper?"

Thomachan smiled to himself, "Appacha, chilli is actually a foreign spice. In northern Malabar, Thalassery for example, chilli is referred to as '*Parangi mulagu*', inticating its Portuguese origin. In Cochin State it is called '*Kappal mulgu*' meaning that it had come through a ship. Of course this name does not reflect the true state but indicate its foreign origin. It was after Vasco da Gama landed near Calicut in 1498 A.D. that chilli was introduced to India. It was available only in the Americas initially from where the Europeans brought it to their continent. But only mildly hot and highly coloured varieties thrived there. Finally the Portuguese brought it to India where a hotter variety was grown."

"Are you sure of that? How come chilli is regarded as an Indian spice then?"

"In the last 450 years, Indians have taken to chilli like a duck to water. Naturally, it has now become a symbol of Indian culinary art."

"I find this news difficult to digest!"

"So it is for many. I have read well and what I am saying is authoritative. And one more thing, pepper is a truly Indian spice. In India there is no craze for it but Westerners love it. So we export all the pepper we produce."

"Well, if you are so sure, I will just have to believe you. But tell me the story of pepper then."

Thomachan was happy to get a chance to display his knowledge of the ancient European's spice expeditions, "Pepper and other spices of the East were sought out by the Europeans. Many sea voyages during the end of the fifteenth century were undertaken mainly to find a sea route to the spice growing parts of the world."

"But were they not getting spices before that?" Mathukutty asked, finding the conversation quite interesting.

His son continued, "Arabs used to import it mainly by land routes. After Alexander the Great of Greece came to India, Egypt became a sort of distribution centre for some of the spices. But even then Europeans could not get hold of sufficient quantities. Besides they wanted to be part of the trade themselves. So Vasco da Gama led a ship from Portugal to India. He took a route around Africa, touching the Cape of Good Hope and landed in Kappad near Calicut in 1498. *Samoothiri* or Zamorin, as the British called the erstwhile rulers of Calicut, received the explorer and his team with traditional hospitality. The Muslim and Arab traders perhaps were not very happy with the competition, but the trade flourished. It is to be noted that the cargo traded was several times the cost of such expeditions."

Mathukutty listened in rapt attention to his son's narration, "Did not the *Samoothiri* fear that the foreigners would produce pepper in Europe and thus end the monopoly of his kingdom?"

"No, he was quite confident that the conditions in Europe would be unsuitable for growing pepper. In fact, he did not act even after hearing that the traders took pepper vine cuttings back home with them. After all, he rightly knew that they could take the cuttings but not the weather!"

Mathukuttu laughed mildly before asking again, "The other day our Malayalam paper was featuring the expedition of one, who is it? Yes, one named Columbus isn't it? It was written that he discovered America. Did that man also begin his expedition in search of pepper and spices?"

"Yes Appacha. He wanted to find a way to East Indies which was then known as the Spice Islands, and also to the South West Coast of India, by going westwards. He believed that the earth being round, he would be aided in his voyage if he travelled around the Atlantic sea from the other side. But before he could reach India he stumbled upon something better! The great continent of the Americas. So even if he did not find black pepper, he found red pepper, popularly called here chilli. Chilli is a gift of this new world, just like other crops such as rubber, vanilla, cocoa and tobacco."

"But Thomacha, what happened to Vasco da Gama?"

"He was the Governor of the Portuguese colony in India. I think he died in Cochin and was buried there but later the Portuguese Government took his remains back to Lisbon, where they built a memorial in his name." Mathukutty drank a glass of water, and satisfied with the knowledge gained got up to wash his hands.

Three months after Pappachan joined the English School in Ooty, Thomachan received a letter from him. This, after he had written nearly six or seven letters to his son, and received none in reply so far. He took Pappachan's letter to his father.

"Pappachan has finally written me a letter."

"Is that so? Has he asked about me?"

"Not specifically. Only that he hoped everybody is fine here."

"Well, did he write in English?"

"Yes Appacha. It was in broken English."

The day he was to pick his son up for the summer vacations, Thomachan left early, so he could visit his friend Joseph Francis first.

"How is Pappachan coping with his studies?"

Joseph Francis took some time before answering, "Frankly speaking, he is just an average student. But he will get through."

"Do you have something more to say? Let me know of it now Joseph."

"Here we give a lot of emphasis to extra-curricular activities especially sports. Your son does not participate in these activities though most students are pretty enthusiastic about them," he replied, upon which Thomachan remained quiet for the rest of the evening.

The next day Pappachan returned with his father to Puthupady to spend the summer vacations. Mathukutty was eagerly awaiting his grandson's arrival. He had asked the cook to make special dishes and sweet preparations for this occasion. Mathukutty found that his grandson had grown in height. He was particularly happy to note that the boy was smartly dressed. Pappachan too seemed happy on seeing his grandfather after so long. But he could not help noticing the signs of age catching up. His face had lost all its vitality and the eyes had sunk deeper into their sockets.

After the initial greetings, Pappachan wished to retire to his room, showing little enthusiasm for a family conversation or for the company of his cousin who had come to spend a few days with them since the school was closed. The boy's name was Mathan who was the second son of Thresiamma. Like his mother, Mathan was a chatterbox.

Thomachan though, was in no mood to let his son get away so fast. Hoping that Mathan's extrovert nature would help his son to open up, he took the boys to the pepper garden. A little breeze had sprung up stirring the leaves of the pepper vines. The rustle of dried leaves drove a squirrel away from them to the tree nearby. As if to applaud its successful retreat, a bird chirped enthusiastically from the branch above.

Thomachan determinedly showed his son all the good work done in the estate during the last one year. He pointed to the vines, "Look there son, all the pepper plants we planted five years ago are now full-grown healthy climbers."

Pappachan and Mathan went near to inspect the plants. Thomachan went on, "They are all trained upon the *Erythrina* tree, which has its own root system but without branches or many leaves. So they provide permanent support for the climbing pepper vines."

"But if it is a growing tree will it not take water and manure from the soil?"

Thomachan could not contain his happiness when he heared the question. But when he looked back to answer Pappachan's query, he realised that it was Mathan, with bright eager eyes waiting for an explanation. To his dismay he found Pappachan busy squashing a little worm with a stick. He quickly recovered and said, "Yes to some extent, but then they are not as expensive as a good wooden pole."

Mathan was now looking with great interest at the fully grown pepper berries. Thomachan said, "You can see the round pepper berries growing as a bunch on a long spike. They look like dark green miniature grape bunches."

"Last year I saw some of the dried pepper brought to the store, but they were black in colour."

Thomachan though slightly disappointed with the disinterest of his own son, explained, "Yes, they turn black on drying."

Like the vicar giving a sermon from the pulpit in the church, Thomachan continued his lecture, "You see the skin of the pepper berry, boys. Outside it, you have green coloured chlorophyll which you also find in leaves. When you leave pepper on the plant for too long, it ripens like any other fruit and then the outside colour changes to yellow first and finally to red."

"But do we allow it to ripen?"

"No Mathan. Before that, we harvest and separate the berries from the spike. Now in the skin there are colourless biochemicals. The tiny cells also have enzymes that can bring about oxidation using atmospheric oxygen."

"What is this en—?"

"Sorry. I recently read about this. I should have put in simple terms." Thomachan closed his eyes for a few seconds and then said, "Enzymes are agents to bring about biochemical changes in a living thing. The food you eat is acted upon by enzymes so that it can be digested. Do you understand? Suffice it to know that they bring about changes."

Thomachan smiled at the boys and proceeded. "Now look, these microscopic cells are a marvel in packaging. Inside it, the biochemicals are all placed separate from one other. When cells are damaged as during drying or upon physical injury, the enzyme comes in contact with the colourless compounds in the skin. Then oxidation occurs and dark coloured compounds are formed. So the dry pepper assumes a black colour."

Thomachan stopped to clear his voice and continued, "That is why it is called black pepper. Because of the ready market abroad and good price it fetches, it is also called 'black gold'!

Thomachan then reminisced about the enthusiasm which Pappachan's late mother had showed when she was taken around the estate. He looked at his son and then at Mathan. Compared to Mathan's bright and eager expression, Pappachan appeared restless. Realising that his son's mind had started to wander, a crestfallen Thomachan stopped explaining and led the boys back home.

Months and years rolled by. Pappachan had fallen into the routine of going to school in Ooty and returning home for the vacations. Elsewhere, major changes were taking place. In 1949, the States of Travancore and Cochin had been integrated. The Malabar District belonging to Madras Presidency was the only Malayalam speaking region which was not a part of the new State. Hectic consultations and public meetings were held by pro-Malayalam leaders, demanding a united Kerala under the banner of '*Aikya Keralam*'.

A few years later Pappachan had completed his schooling in Ooty with just about pass marks.

"He must attend college. It is what we all want," Mathukutty told his son one day. But Thomachan had bigger ideas for his son. He wanted him to take a degree in agriculture. He expressed his desire to his father.

But Mathukutty was not in favour of it. "Seeing the grades he's got, I think placing him in the science stream is a bit over-ambitious! There is no harm in taking a degree in Arts. A degree in economics or commerce will not diminish his status, I suppose."

And so heeding the advice, Pappachan was put in a Catholic college in Calicut. He opted for non-science subjects for the two year intermediate course.

Chapter 4

Karunakaran Muthalali was in an irritable mood today. A construction contractor by profession, he had prospered in Ernakulam. His workers addressed him as Muthalali, which literally meant the 'wealthy one' and this title stuck to his name. But today, the 'wealthy one' did not feel so pleased within. The reason was that he had failed to bag the contract for the construction of a small bridge. He believed that he had given a reasonable bid and expected the contract to land in his hands like all the previous contracts he had bid for recently. But somebody, an unknown name actually, had beaten him to the finish with a lower estimate. Fretting over the loss, he turned to his two older sons who were also partners in his business. The second son, Lakshmanan who had started taking more responsibility made a rational analysis of the loss, "This is not the end of the world, Acha. There are plenty of other opportunities."

"I am not too sure. Besides there are many people entering the construction business. Lots of daring people, especially from the nearby town of Kolencherry are coming up."

The older son Ravindran cut in. "The involvement of the port in the war efforts had opened the eyes of our Diwan and he was keen to develop it further. We have to think in that direction."

"Well, I do see it but…" Karunakaran's voice trailed off, unsure of an alternate plan.

Lakshmanan was the one who was interested in modern technologies. His ambition had been to take up engineering, but his father was not sure if he should invest in his education. Having been brought up in a small town himself, Karunakaran was nervous of sending the boy to a big city like Madras. Moreover his business was thriving at that time, and he needed all the assistance he could get from his sons at the work sites, to ensure that the company overheads remained low. And so Lakshmanan ended up not in an engineering college, but at the construction sites managed by his father.

But the boy had not thrown his interest in engineering away as yet. He collected the requisite study material from an old classmate, a Junior Engineer in the Public Works Department, and started to study on his own.

Karunakaran's third son Ramanathan was doing a degree course in chemistry. Normally chemistry as a subject was not suited to the family's business. But Ramanathan was quite fascinated by the subject and surprisingly his father did the unthinkable by encouraging him to take it up. His fourth son Vasudevan was born after a long gap and was still in primary school. But Karunakaran had noticed that he displayed a great interest in plants.

With four sons, it ws natural that Karunakaran should think of diversifying his business.

"Acha, they are planning to construct bridges to connect the islands of Bolgatty, Vallarpadam and Vypeen to the mainland. We must look into those opportunities," Lakshmanan said.

Karunakaran scratched his chin and replied, "Those are all mega projects. How can ordinary contractors like us handle such work?"

"No, no, not the main work. They are awarding the work to a British Company in Madras. The total estimate is a huge amount, fourteen or fifteen lakhs of rupees!" Lakshmanan added, having done the necessary homework.

"See, that amount is beyond our capacity. Talk about something that we can take up, son."

"My friend in the PWD says that they may give sub-contracts for smaller works. That is what we should aim for," Lakshmanan sounded very optimistic.

Ravindran cut in, "Acha, the PWD Minister Mr. Ayyappan is your friend. Can you not talk to him?"

Karunakan contemplated the idea. In fact he had a firm belief that this type of business, mainly construction of macadam roads, was doomed to end. Concrete would be the king of the future.

With so many bridges required to connect regions crisscrossed by several rivers and streams, only contractors having the know-how of concrete technology would survive. Also, the State had a huge potential for hydroelectric dams.

Capital though, was the most important factor in such projects. And unlike his sons, he was not very familiar with the many financial options provided by modern banking systems.

A few days later, Karunakaran Muthalali called his two sons Ravindran and Lakshmanan and said, "Mr. Ayyappan says that the project for building bridges to the islands may have to be shelved for the time being."

"Why? What is the matter?" Ravindran asked, wearing a worried expression.

"The Union Home Minister sitting in Delhi, Sardar Vallabai Patel is going to stop the independent administration of the Princely States run by the Maharajas. Instead he wants all States to be administered by a democratically elected government and accordingly plans to integrate Travancore State and Cochin State into a new State."

"Have the Maharajas agreed?" Ravindran asked , quite perplexed by the development.

"Of course they will have to agree. What a time to initiate this foolish step though!"

Lakshmanan came to the defence of Sardar Patel, who was popularly known as the 'Iron Man of India.' "I think Mr. Patel is doing the right thing. There are so many princes and Maharajas in our country and not all of them are doing enough for the people. Many of them spend their time and money travelling around Europe, returning to their State only to enjoy the luxury of grand palaces and to ride in their Rolls Royce cars. Maharajas must make way for the people."

"Aye, Lakshmana, you seem to have some Communist ideas ingrained in you."

"Not like that Acha. But unless we are governed by a democratic system, there is no meaning to our Independence."

Karunakaran thought for some time before saying, "Anyway, the bridge project has gone from our hands for the time being. After integration, emphasis will shift to other matters. After that, you may not get another Minister with such foresight for the development of the region."

Ravindran asked, "When is this integration happening?"

Lakshmanan replied, "It is slated for 1949. The new State will be named Travancore-Cochin."

Chapter 5

Resting in the mountains in central Malabar is the town of Kalpetta. From Puthupady, the Ghat road towards this hill town begins after about ten miles eastward. The Ghat road is noted for its hairpin bends and a climb of 2500 feet over just about twenty or twentyfive miles. Kalpetta is home to a few tea plantations.

On one such tea estate, stood a bungalow with front veranda and sloping tiled roof, typically found in South Indian plantations. Its occupant, Peter George had woken up with the rising sun, and sipped tea brought in by his servant. He was in a happy mood today, because by noon his young wife Elizabeth was expected to join him with their three month old baby girl.

Peter once held the position of Field Officer in a tea estate, about twenty miles off Ooty town. While he was working there he got married to Elizabeth who hailed from Calicut. When Elizabeth was in the sixth or seventh month of pregnancy, she moved to her parents' place as was the custom, where she gave birth to a baby girl. It was around this time that Peter got a better job as Assistant Manager in a tea garden in Kalpetta. He had recently moved to the new place and was awaiting mother and child after both had regained their health before joining him. The best thing about his new job was the lovely bungalow allotted to him. All it needed now was the presence of his wife and baby daughter to make it a home.

The baby's christening was done in Calicut with full rituals. Peter who visited his wife every fortnight spent the weekend with his in-laws, Sebastian and Marykutty. Today, as he tidied the house, he thought of the day his daughter was born. It was he who had suggested that the baby be named Molly. He remembered remarking to Elizabeth and her mother Marykutty at that time, "For such a pretty baby, the name Molly is most apt."

Elizabeth had laughed upon hearing the name, knowing well that Peter adored his girl child. "In fact any name would suit her," she added mischievously.

Elizabeth's mother, only too keen to please her son-in-law, readily agreed with his choice.The little baby though was officially christened after Peter's mother, but it was common to give a child a pet name. As Peter took a sip of tea, he smiled to himself thinking of how he and Sebastin, his father-in-law had celebrated the occasion with a round of whisky. Peter also recalled how his father-in-law made any event an occasion for good cheer with drinks. And little Molly found herself with a doting grandfather, who, however was no match for the love showered on her by Peter.

Most tea plantation managers imitated the ways of their erstwhile Western employers and taught their children to address them as Mummy and Daddy.

"I only hope that Daddy doesn't spoil the little thing," Elizabeth had later remarked with a wide grin across her pretty face.

Putting aside the memories, Peter got up to make sure the house was ready for the arrival of its mistress and her young daughter.

In the meanwhile in Calicut, Elizabeth, her parents and the baby got into their Ambassador car which would take them to Kalpetta. Considering the poor condition of the roads the drive was expected to take about three hours. The suitcases were loaded and Elizabeth's mother carried with her a basket containing snacks and sweets popular in Calicut. There were sufficient goodies in it to last the young family at Kalpetta for two weeks. Since good quality fish was available in Calicut, they were carrying a basket of fish packed in ice.

Elizabeth's father, Sebastian, toyed with the idea of taking along a bottle of whisky, but decided against it at the last moment, confident that Peter would have some stocked in his bungalow. Meat also would not be a problem there, he reckoned.

"Has everyone got in?" Sebastian enquired just as the driver came running. After a cursory examination of the boxes and baskets, he closed the boot and got into the front seat.

"Okay let us start," he commanded the driver.

As they were nearing Puthupady on the way to Kalpetta, Sebastian told Marykutty,

"We had promised to visit to Mathukutty Chettan and Thomachan."

Marykutty replied, "We can stop and see them on our way back. Now with the baby it is inconvenient." She was also concerned about the fish in the car. She wanted to reach Kalpetta at the earliest. Once the fish was cooked or fried keeping it for a day or two would not be a problem, considering the cool weather of Kalpetta.

They reached well before lunch time. Marykutty had been worried about getting car sick while driving on the winding roads, but because of the cool weather, no such problem arose. The baby too was fine, managing to sleep through the journey. So it was a thoroughly refreshed group that got out of the car. Peter rushed outside to greet them, ordered his servants to help with the unloading and personally made sure that the baby and the ladies were made comfortable.

"Do you wish to have a bath? There will be plenty of hot water," Peter asked, always wanting to be a good host.

"No Peter. It is quite pleasantly cool here," Marykutty replied massaging her forearms with her hands.

Under normal circumstances Elizabeth would have liked a hot water bath to wash away all the dirt and weariness of the journey. But not today! For she wanted to look around the new house, which she would preside over and be the perfect hostess to the many guests visiting them. It was a beautifully furnished, comfortable house, Elizabeth noted with satisfaction.The drawing-*cum*-dining room had good furniture in place with a large dining table adorning the end adjacent to the kitchen. Two bedrooms too were beautifully furnished and had clean bathrooms attached.

As for Sebastian, Peter knew that taking a bath was not top priority. He poured a peg of whisky and soda for his father-in-law and called out towards the kitchen for some fried pork and banana chips.

He poured himself a small drink as well. Sebastian observed this and remarked, "Why so little? Isn't this cool weather the best time to enjoy a drink?"

But Peter simply laughed. After Sebastian had one more drink, all of them moved to the dining room. Marykutty observed the fine spread laid out by Peter for them. There was pork, chicken and beef.

After tasting some of the vegetable preparations, she exclaimed, "What fresh vegetables! Taste so good!"

'Taste so good! You must also eat them," she said to her husband.

"Yes Marykutty, they are tasty and almost edible," he said, mocking the greens.

"They are always edible," Marykutty scolded him. "You want only meat and fish for every meal. Vegetables and fruits are healthier."

"But then Ammachi, you get only withered vegetables in Calicut," Elizabeth came to her father's rescue. Her mother did not reply, knowing that it was useless to argue when father and daughter joined hands.

When lunch was over they all had a short rest. Soon after, Sebastian and Marykutty took leave. Marykutty's eyes were full of tears when she finally bade farewell to the baby and her daughter.

After a heavy lunch, Karunakaran Muthalali relaxed in his armchair with a big betel leaf in hand. He took a generous scoop of *chunnamb*–watery slaked lime, from a brass pot with his right index finger and smeared it on the leaf. He took two to three pieces of fresh cut arecanut from the *chellum*, the box holding the other *paan* ingredients, and after folding the leaf put it into his red stained mouth and began to chew it. He also stuffed a small piece of chewing tobacco along with it. His wife Janaki Amma was dehusking a big orange coloured arecanut. Once the husk was removed she cut the round nut into pieces to be put into the *chellum* for later use. Janaki Amma was a good looking middle aged woman, who believed that the one feature which contributed to her sexual attractiveness was her full lips, reddened by *paan* chewing. She even considered her lips to add zip to her voluptuous breasts hidden usually by a low cut blouse, the combination which ensured that no man could ignore her presence, just as no woman could look at her without some envy. She was aware that her seductive glances were often helpful in bagging contracts for her husband. She enhanced his chances further by bending low in front of government engineers and local political leaders to display her sexy breasts, while they enjoyed the liquor parties held at her home. Being the only woman in an all male family, she behaved and was accordingly treated like a queen bee.

Once she finished slicing the nuts she also made a *paan* for herself, but unlike her husband she did not add the tobacco.

"How is the work progressing," she asked, while spitting out the *paan* juice. She knew that to maintain her high style, it was imperative that her husband earned well.

"Things are working well Janaki. But there is space for only the older two in our present business. Therefore I am glad that the younger ones are looking towards newer fields," Karunakaran replied, referring to his four sons. The eldest, Ravindran, had moved into his own house after marriage. Karunakaran had already made plans to build a second house for his son Lakshmanan whose marriage had already been fixed.

And even though he was doing well in the construction business, Karunakaran believed that the future lay in manufacturing. He did not have a clear idea though on how to go about it. His wife interrupted his thoughts by enquiring about their third son Ramanathan, who had gone to study Chemistry at Loyola College in Madras.

"Is he going to be a teacher in a college? What will he earn from it? It would be a struggle for him throughout his life," she said with uncertainty. "He is trying to get admission to study in England. He has a fair chance, that's what his friend there said."

"But studying in England will cost a lot of money, won't it?"

"Come what may, let us go for it. We should support him."

"You were not so generous when Lakshmanan wanted to study engineering, which would have been quite helpful for the business now."

"Don't remind me of that. It was a mistake on my part. Luckily Lakshmanan has forgotten about it, but it hurts when I think about it. I must make up for his lost opportunity."

"I hope that Ramanathan will not bring an English wife into this family," she said tartly.

Karunakaran dismissed the idea, "No such thing will happen. He is my son! But you must admit he's taking a different line. I like his bold stand. He has shown courage to take up a new profession. Usually when a family business is thriving, the sons quietly opt to join their father since it's least risky. In fact that is the bane of this country. An agriculturist's son takes to agriculture. A shop-keeper's son takes to shop-keeping," he grumbled.

"And a contractor's son takes to contracting," she finished his sentence.

Karunakaran agreed and said, "Yes, that way Ramanathan has shown enterprise. He is also quite clear about what he wants to do."

"But," he continued after a pause, "Only if he makes a success story out of it."

"He will be all right. Young Vasu for that matter is quite excited about agriculture. He spends long hours with Pillai."

Mr. Pillai was their neighbour who cultivated rice and vegetables. People considered him a walking encyclopaedia on agriculture. Young Vasu was his constant companion.

Karunakaran continued, "Well, that is good. He should specialise in agriculture then."

In 1956, the Malabar District of Madras Presidency was merged with Travancore-Cochin to form the new State of Kerala. *'Aikya Keralam'*—the dream of Malayalees for a united Kerala was thus fulfilled.

Shortly afterwards, in the next General Elections, the Communist Party was elected to power in Kerala State. Comrade EMS Namboodiripad from Malabar was the Chief Minister, and Comrade C. Achutha Menon from erstwhile Cochin State the Deputy Chief Minister. They led the government that was formed in the Travancore city of Trivandrum, now the State capital. Other issues apart, the regional integration of Malayalam speaking areas finally became a reality. The transfer of Government servants, a greater number of marriages between different regions of the present State and expansion of trade—all contributed to make the integration complete.

~

Pappachan meanwhile had begun to show an interest in certain operations of the estate. Thomachan one day took him to the front office where a middle aged man named Mohamedikka served as Head Clerk. He took Pappachan around and explained the various aspects of office management.

"This is the register for all the outbound bullock carts and trucks—and this is where we enter the items taken out—then there is all the incoming material and you see, this is the stock register," he explained one by one.

Pappachan pretended to listen to him as if he was very keen to learn. But Thomachan could sense that his mind was wandering.

"Pratapan bring the stock register," Mohamedikka called out to a youngster who was typing a statement using an old Remington typewriter. The clerk inserted another plain paper, a carbon paper and a sheet for carbon copy and then got up from his chair to search for the register among a stack of files and books kept in an old almirah.

In a bid to impress the young Muthalali, Mohamedikka showed Pappachan the various entries in a patronising manner. Pratapan also stood beside him, aware that by the time the young Muthalali took over he would be presiding over the office as Head Clerk.

Thomachan and Pappachan noticed another young man Majeed, the accountant-cum-cashier also at work. So too one truck driver who approached the accountant, showed some form given from the work spot and collected the money due to him. The three of them were doing a good job and Thomachan made a mental note of it.

"Let Kochu Muthalali work here for a week. We will teach him everything there is to know about running this office," the Head Clerk told Thomachan.

"Would you like to do that?" Thomachan asked his son.

"Yes, Appacha," Pappachan said. It was neither an enthusiastic response nor a totally disinterested one.

Turning towards the Head Clerk, Thomachan said, "All right. Pappachan will come here three or four days a week. Teach him everything. Every week you must spend some time with him. Pappachan, you will then advise Appachan on all matters related to the plantation."

The Head Clerk smiled proudly.

~

Sebastian sipped the morning coffee with more than generous helpings of sugar and milk added to the thick black decoction, sitting at his home in Calicut, while like most denizens of Kerala, scanning the morning Malayalam paper for news of the previous day. The English paper only reached them by afternoon since it was published from Madras city and arrived in Calicut by the mail train. Being an avid cricket follower, he opened the last pages for news of the cricket match between England and Australia. He had heard about Englishman Jim Laker's feat of taking ten wickets in one innings in the Manchester test on radio news the previous evening and was looking forward to reading a detailed account of the same. But cricket was not covered. Laker, the Englishman, had bagged all ten wickets of the visiting Australia team even though the innings was interrupted by rain. By taking nine in the first innings and all ten in the second, England or to be more precise Laker, had stamped Australia out, like an elephant on the rampage. Snapping the paper shut Sebastian threw it on the table beside him.

Just then Marykutty came in and urged him to prepare to leave after an early lunch.

"But why can't we leave leisurely? If we leave by, say 2.30, we will reach Kalpetta by 5.30 at the latest."

"But suppose there is a break down or a flat tyre?"

"I changed the tyres just two months ago and the car is in good condition after the servicing last week."

"If you are so confident, then it is fine. We can leave by 2.30 or even 3."

Marykutty mapped a quick shopping plan as soon as Sebastian gave the suggestion of a late start. She wanted to buy some fresh fish to take to Kalpetta like last time.

When Marykutty mentioned her plan Sebastian welcomed the suggestion. He would be able to get a full description of the cricket test from the English paper which would arrive before they left. This time, he and Marykutty were taking their daughter Elizabeth to her husband's home after her second delivery three months earlier. She had delivered a healthy boy. The older child, Molly, was now over three years old. The new baby became her property ever since his birth. Elizabeth wondered how long this friendly co-existence would last. But she also knew that Molly was a sweet girl and her brother was truly lucky to have her as his elder sister.

This time around, Sebastian and Marykutty planned to stay in Kalpetta for four days. Sebastian was already dreaming of sipping smooth whisky while relaxing in the cold climes of Kalpetta. Elizabeth's sister Celina, and her family, were also driving down from Bangalore to spend a few days at Kalpetta. All the men would have happy drinking sessions, Sebastion was sure of that.

Marykutty was more excited at the prospect of seeing both her daughters together. Besides meeting Celina's two children, it would be a great opportunity to exchange all the gossip that had remained unexchanged. Letters by post were not the best way to convey exciting news!

"Ah! Here we are!" Sebastian said opening the door of the car as it arrived at the bungalow of his son-in-law at Kalpetta. Peter appeared immediately with a man from the estate. He was instructed to take care of the luggage while Marykutty took charge of the precious parcel of fish. Soon they all sat down for tea. Peter took the baby from his wife's arms, as Molly chatted on about the sweet virtues of her baby brother, "Look how he closes his eyes and smiles as I wave my hand over his face. See Daddy, how he does it?" she said excitedly.

"That's because he loves his big sister. Do you also like your baby brother Molly kutty?"

"Of course! He is the best baby in the whole world! You know Daddy, he is called George after your father."

"Yes indeed. It is a nice name," Peter smiled.

Elizabeth meanwhile got busy assuming the role of a hostess. Despite Peter being a stickler for tidiness, she wanted her touch to shine through as well.

The next morning, Celina and her family arrived from Bangalore. Elizabeth was nervous from the minute she walked in. She adored Celina and her husband Rajan. Apart from being a very nice person, Rajan was also a doctor practising near Bangalore, a fashionable city in the neighbouring State. She had kept the house ready for them. They came with their two kids, the elder boy Vijay, eight years old and the second a lively girl, Malini, five years old. Having lived in Bangalore, they spoke English stylishly. She knew that Rajan and Celina had moved to a big and beautiful house which they built recently, all from a letter once sent to her by her sister, mentioning the many details of the house. Peter had asked two of his workers from the tea garden to help during the stay of his guests, upon the special request of his wife.

"What is there for you to be so worried about, Elizabeth?" her mother Marykutty asked presently, "After all, Celina and her husband are nice people, very adjustable."

"The house needs a thorough cleaning up," Elizabeth replied in a low voice.

But her mother did not like anyone fussing too much over familiar people. "Peter has kept the house in tip-top condition. Besides you should not ask him to divert workers for domestic work and cause embarrassment for Peter."

Rajan and Celina got out of the car. Rajan showed little signs of weariness after such a long drive. Their son Vijay though was in a bad mood as he emerged from the rear door. Malini was sprawled across the back seat sleeping. Celina woke her up, as Peter and Sebastian helped Rajan unload the luggage.

"How are Ammama's little ones?" Marykutty came out with a big smile upon seeing her grandchildren.

"Come on Malini, let us get your face washed. Don't you want to see the baby and play with Molly? And how is

Ammama's dear boy? Vijay are you fine?" she continued with her playful banter.

By that time, Elizabeth and little Molly appeared at the doorway, and then on it was a pleasant evening.

After an enjoyable session of whisky drinking by the men followed by a sumptuous dinner, everyone went to bed. Thanks to the cool weather all of them slept well.

The next day being a Sunday, everyone except Elizabeth went to church in the two cars. After breakfast Peter took the visiting couple for a tour of the tea garden.

"Plucking the tea leaves is usually done by women everywhere. At the height of the season we work on Sundays also. Since we do not do any processing here, the harvested leaves are immediately sent to the tea factory for the same," Peter explained.

"Why are they plucking only from the top?" Rajan wanted to know.

"That's because only the two tender leaves and the emerging bud give the best product; so the expression 'two and the bud'. Sometimes to increase the quantity of plucking, a third leaf is also plucked."

Sebastian was fascinated to see that the tops of the plants were flat. He said, "Is the height deliberately kept this much?"

"Yes. It is by cutting and trimming so it is right for the women. If you allow the plant to grow, it will become a tree and then harvesting will be difficult. From above, the top of each plant covers the gap left for it, almost like a jig-saw puzzle."

"Do you know how the tea you drink is processed Vijay?" Rajan asked his son "Perhaps uncle Peter can describe."

Peter gladly explained, "Here in India we make only black tea. In China, Japan and other countries of the Far East, green tea is made. To produce the black compounds and thereafter the special taste, after cutting you have to ferment the leaves at controlled temperature and humidity. It is then heat treated, a step we call 'firing' to complete the oxidation. Then you get the black colour and the aroma that will emerge in the hot cup. After that you dry it in a drier. Then only is the black tea made ready for packaging."

Rajan and Celina looked around the tea garden, soaking in the panoramic view.

Peter let them enjoy the scenery, and then continued, "A few tall trees have been grown around the bushes to lend some amount of shade." Pointing elsewhere, he said, "These leaves are processed into what is called 'orthodox tea'. But more suitable is the CTC type tea."

"I have heard something along those lines. Does it require more machinery?" Celina asked, showing she had some idea of the subject.

Peter nodded in agreement. "CTC stands for cut or crush, tear and curl. It is a continuous process.With more machinery it is a faster method to complete the manufacturing process. We plan to employ the CTC method, once we enter the tea processing sector. It is ideal to process tea of slightly lower quality, such as ours."

"I have also read somewhere that green tea is also made in India," Celina said. Peter looked at her, "Chechi, you have touched upon an interesting topic. There is lot of interest in green tea." Then looking at others he continued, "They do not allow fermentation which is the starting point of blackening. They only do steaming and drying the tea leaves so no fermentation and therefore no blackening occurs."

Being a man of medicine, Rajan who knew about caffeine in such beverages, tried to impress the group, "The main active constituent in tea is caffeine. It keeps the mind awake and drowsiness in check."

Wanting to playfully spar with her husband, Celina said, "That's why tea feels so refreshing when you drink it first thing in the morning. It fully wakes you up, doesn't it?"

"But the taste of tea is due to tannins, I understand," she enquired, to which Peter responded, "Tannin or as the chemists would like to call it, polyphenols. Since there is no tanning process, it's better to call them by their real chemical name. But some aroma is developed during brewing in the cup"

Rajan then added, "Oh, thank you. Anyway polyphenols are good antioxidants and therefore green tea is good for health, isn't it, Peter?"

Peter nodded but disapproving the remark, "But who said that the good polyphenols disappear when we make black tea? Black tea is also good, I tell you." The conversation continued this way, as the group finally made its way back home.

Upon return, they found on the table a fine spread of the choicest dishes prepared under the supervision of Elizabeth.

After lunch, Elizabeth excused herself to feed the baby while Marykutty went to her room to take a nap. Meanwhile, Malini, Rajan and Celina's five year old daughter, was explaining in detail to everyone assembled, the interiors of her new home in Bangalore.

"So how do you like it?" someone asked her.

"Oh it is so big!" she remarked.

But no sooner had Malini started to brag, than there was a knock at the front door. Celina got up immediately to check on the visitor. A salesman from a bottled soda company had come to deliver the soda water bottles. When Celina returned to the room, Elizabeth had joined them and was laughing heartily. Molly and Malini were perplexed at her reaction. So was Vijay. But Elizabeth could not control herself. The baby disturbed by the racket,began to cry. But the laughter continued.

"What is it, Elizabeth?" Celina asked, quite confused. With eyes full of tears, Elizabeth finally managed to stop, interspersing her peals of laughter with broken sentences, "Malini was telling about her new house. She said that it is very big and that Daddy had the best and biggest room in it. She also mentioned about the rooms given to her brother and herself and a special room for guests."

After a pause she continued, "But then you know what Malini said. 'Poor Mummy, she alone does not have a room. So she sleeps in Daddy's room'."

There was some more laughter, this time from Celina also. Marykutty woke up from her siesta in the other room hearing the sound of laughter. The children seeing the adults laugh, shrugged and went out to play, uninterested in what transpired in the mad, mad world around them!

When the world was awakening to the swinging sixties, life at Puthupaday was moving at a pedestrian's pace. Mathukutty was weak and looked older than the octogenarian he was, about to touch ninety. His cough got worse and seemed to erupt from his chest. Often the phlegm was tinged with spots of red. Thomachan was the first to notice it.

"Appacha, there is blood in your spit!"

Mathukutty, who had recently acquired a taste for *paan,* quickly dismissed his worries, "That's because of the *paan* I'm chewing."

After a brief argument between father and son, Thomachan literally forced him into the car and hurried to the hospital in Thamarassery. An X-ray and other medical tests confirmed the doctor's suspicion that the old man was suffering from lung cancer.

The doctor minced no words in conveying the urgency of the situation. "Today you can return home, but tomorrow morning itself, get him admitted to the new Medical College Hospital in Calicut. I will inform the doctor there of your arrival."

Unlike his usual stubborn self, Mathukutty quietly obeyed whatever Thomachan ordered him to do after the diagnosis. Thomachan's sister Thresiamma from Thamarassery came to take charge, and the trio left for Calicut early next morning. Before leaving, Mathukutty kissed the forehead of Pappachan who was crying silently. The other two daughters of Mathukutty came directly to the hospital by evening.

There, the doctor confirmed that it was an advanced stage of lung cancer. Thomachan pressed him for more information, upon which he was told that his father had no more than a few weeks to live. But Thomachan, expecting a miracle, asked the doctor to begin treatment.

A fortnight later, a very weak Mathukutty told his children to take him home. Thomachan suggested continuing the treatment, to which he calmly replied, "I want you to take me to Puthupady so that I can die in my own house. " His children did not protest. They knew it was a dying man's last wish.

Two days after he was brought home Mathukutty passed away. In his final moments he had been holding onto Pappachan's hands, while his eyes presented a picture of sorrow as it darted between each of his children and grandchildren. Thomachan had called the priest from the nearby church to administer the last rites on the previous day itself.

There was a big gathering at Mathukutty's funeral. The family of Vackachan, who himself had passed away a few years earlier, was represented by his widow and some relatives. Sebastian and Marykutty from Calicut, and Peter and Elizabeth from Kalpetta, had arrived as well. As per his wish, Mathukutty was buried in the family tomb of the local church by the side of his wife's mortal remains. The Bishop of Calicut presided over the funeral service.

Thomachan's sister, Thresiamma, had been quite close to Marykutty since childhood. Even though Marykutty moved to Calicut after marriage, they often met at family functions and get-togethers.

After the funeral, Marykutty put her arm around Thresiamma and said in a low voice, "Your Appachan lived his life fully. You should take it as the wish of Christ that he's left us."

"Yes, I understand," she replied softly.

Just then Elizabeth joined them and Thresiamma enquired, "How is Molly?"

"She is doing well and has started going to school."

"Going to school? I thought she was just a baby. And what about the little one, George?"

"Quite mischievous, I must say! And very curious too about things around him. He's very keen to learn new things."

"As good kids should be!" Marykutty added proudly, defending her grandson.

The day after the funeral, Pappachan went early to the estate. As much as he wanted to be involved in the agricultural operations, he was equally desperate to escape the staring faces and enquiring tones of elderly family friends and relatives thronging the house. By lunch, the house had quietened down. When he saw the simple vegetarian meal on the table upon his return he was annoyed. He immediately stomped into the kitchen to ask the cook why there was no fish or meat preparation.

Thomachan overheard him arguing with the cook and remarked, "Pappacha, we are having vegetarian food for forty days. It is a mark of respect for the deceased. It is a family custom and we should follow it without any complaints."

"Yes, Appacha," he replied sombrely. But Thomachan was not to be fooled so easily. He came to know the very next day of his son's trips to Thamarassery and Adivaram, the small town at the start of the Ghat road, where he snacked on mutton *biriyani* and *chapatti* with chicken curry. Pappachan obviously had scant regard for the family custom. He was also seen visiting the *toddy* shops regularly. All this, during the mourning period!

Chapter 6

Sitting atop a concrete coping by the side of the road near her house, Janaki Amma chatted the evening away with a few ladies from the neighbourhood. "Now our Ramanathan is in England and doing very well!" she declared, making it sound as if the whole family was planning a trip to England. "It is in England, that the real world exists," she added smugly.

Just then Janaki saw Karunakaran drive past in his car. She got up hurriedly saying, "I have to go. I will see you all later."

The simple women nodded, mesmerised by Janaki Amma's tales, which unknown to them were partly from her imagination.

As soon as Janaki reached home she asked, "What about Vasu?"

"Vasudevan has received admission to the Agricultural College in Coimbatore, which is one of the best colleges in the country."

"But where is the land for him to work after he graduates? We should have bought some land much earlier."

"Don't worry Janaki. We will see when the time comes. Our children have the brains and can work hard. Isn't that enough to do well in life?"

"I know. Let our neighbours also know now that we are not just old fashioned contractors, but modern in thinking."

It was important for Janaki Amma to show that they had more things than mere money. Contractors commanded little respect in the society. Though many of them were financially strong they used it to advance their prospects in the political or social sphere. Some even held influential positions in religious organisations only because of the money power they commanded. But all the same the whole world believed that for contractors money is not the most important thing but the only thing!

On a cool Sunday morning at around eight o'clock in November, the old Ambassador car dropped Sebastian and Marykutty home after church. Sebastian lit a cigarette and inhaled deeply. Ever since Mathukutty Chettan passed away he had cut down the number of cigarettes he smoked, but compensated by increasing his intake of liquor, justifying it as good for his age.

He held the old fashioned view that the ill effects of alcohol could somewhat be neutralized by eating heavily, especially items like beef and pork.

Upon entering the living room he picked up the day's Malayalam newspaper and relaxed on his favourite easy chair in the veranda, and skimmed through the various news columns. There was nothing exciting in it unlike the English paper delivered in the afternoon which carried news from around the world. Like some of his generation, he too felt that the English had done more for the country than Indians could ever do themselves. While he felt proud of working for English companies, he saw Americans as pleasure seekers unfit for serious matters. The great upsurge of the economy and progress on matters of nation building achieved by the American citizens were unknown to many Indians of that era. Most of all to people like Sebastian who held a die-hard subservient attitude to incumbency!

Marykutty brought him a glass of hot coffee and placed it on the small table by his side. Sebastian took a deep drag, blew smoke rings and said to his wife, "Even after a week they have not found the killer of President Kennedy. It could be the work of blacks or some political group. But what are the FBI and other organisations doing?"

Marykutty said, "What do you mean? They have already found that Oswald or some such person was involved. And he isn't a black or a communist."

"These Cubans are boiling after Kennedy's action in stopping the Soviet missiles. How can you rule out some Soviet involvement?"

"Why, it could be the work of a few Protestants who wish to eliminate a Catholic President," Marykutty, a devout Catholic could think only in one direction.

"Come let us have breakfast. We have to go to Kunnamangalam," Sebastian said going into the house. The breakfast as usual was '*kanji*', a kind of slightly over cooked rice with the gruel water retained. Traditionalists served it with a spoon shaped from coconut shell with a split bamboo handle. Marykutty had prepared dried beans with gravy to go along with the *kanji*. At times, she also made green mango pickle or chick pea curry.

Scooping the *kanji*, Sebastian turned to his wife and said, "Did you know that *kanji* came from China?"

Marykutty replied with a look of annoyance, "What do you mean? It has been here for centuries."

"No, Marykutty, young Balan next door only told me so. He's very well read, you know. It seems the Chinese call it *conji*. Not only this dish, but also many other things are given by the Chinese. He even said our *cheena chatti* is China's … now what was that word he said?" Sebastian paused, racking his brain to recall the correct word.

"Ah yes! It is *wok*; yes *wok*. As for our *Cheena vala,* I'm sure you know that it means Chinese fishing net. In the olden days, according to Balan, one of their natives might have introduced it during his travels to this part of India. A bright boy, that Balan is!"

After finishing breakfast they went into the bedroom to change their attire before leaving for Paulose Chettan's house in Kunnamangalam, a suburb of Calicut.

Paulose, a man of almost seventy years, entered the kitchen to oversee the lunch preparations for his guests of the day - all his friends and relatives. His wife Sophy was giving directions to the maid servant and their daughter-law Mercy was putting finishing touches to the dessert.

"Is everything going well?" Paulose enquired.

"Yes, don't worry, the meal will be grand. You can make sure that all your other stuff is in place, so that the right spirit prevails."

The remark was not lost on Paulose. He smiled knowing that Sophy encouraged him to serve alcohol in the house at get-togethers and functions. Good liquor was essential to lighten up everyone's mood, she believed. Besides, drinking at home had its own controlling influences, especially when women were around. It was the young men who went out for their drinks that she was concerned about.

For that day's get-together though, things had to be grand. Her brother Thomachan was coming from Puthupady. Sebastian and Marykutty were coming from Calicut. They had invited one more couple, their neighbour Narayanan Nair, a retired Colonel from the Army. He had promised to bring good whisky from his military quota. Then there was Paulose's second son, John Paulose and his wife Mercy, who lived with the old couple, as was customary in Kerala.

Paulose had an ancestral house in the middle of a large coconut plantation. John and Mercy had managed the plantation well and were able to generate good income. But of late, John had diversified into copra trading, producing copra on his own by sun-drying the raw material. He had also begun to buy copra from small farmers and sell to expeller operators. Both Paulose and John felt that this diversification in activity was the need of the hour, since there was pressure from the Left Parties on the Government of Kerala to introduce strict land reforms. If implemented the reforms would force them to surrender a large portion of their land to the government for subsequent distribution to landless families.

Around noon the car carrying Thomachan stopped in front of the house just as Col (Retd) Narayanan Nair and his wife Sarada were walking in with a bag in hand. Paulose immediately appeared on the porch and asked, "Where is Pappachan? You did not bring him?"

"He does not take much interest in family get-togethers," Thomachan replied resignedly.

"These young people have their own parties," Narayanan Nair added. Thomachan suddenly looked startled, but then realised that the statement was just a harmless joke.

Before he could say anything, Sebastian and his wife too arrived.

The guests laughed and exchanged greetings after which they settled down on the old fashioned sofas. Whisky and soda flowed and soon the conversation veered to land reforms. Paulose began the discussion.

"I tell you the production of commodities will come down," he said.

Narayanan Nair could not understand what the fuss against land reforms was. Although not someone with a pronounced left leaning, he felt positively about socialistic ideas like land to the tiller. "Why should it be? Actually by giving land to small farmers there will be a better prospect for cash crops," he argued.

Sebastian poured himself another peg of whisky and then joined in, "I'll explain. These beggars do not know the ABC of cultivation. By just projecting Marx you cannot build a society. During British days things were going on so well!"

Soon voices were raised and tempers were getting frayed. Paulose felt it would be better to change the topic.

"Do you know we are also making lot of copra? John is concentrating more on copra trading now," he said loudly.

"But rain and mould growth are the major problem in that," said Thomachan taking the cue.

"Before the monsoon arrives, we will set up a smoke drying facility inside the shed. Of course the smoke lends a brownish colour to the copra and the price of the product comes down," John replied, knowing that only sun-drying gave good quality white copra.

Just then Mercy brought beef *ulathu,* a favourite accompaniment with drinks. The meat, cut into small pieces and generousely spiced was sprinkled with coconut slices.

Resuming the discussion, Paulose pointed to his daughter-in-law and said, "Mercy has introduced a new process to produce white copra with less mould."

"How is it done, Mercy?" Thomachan asked.

Propping herself up on the sofa, Mercy said, "What I do is to smear a thin layer of vinegar on the surface. This considerably controls mould growth. White copra fetches a higher price in the market."

Sophy with some amount of alcohol inside her became resentful of the attention being paid to Mercy.

"You use vinegar? It is too expensive. How can you think of such a stupid move?" she said rudely, much to everyone's surprise.

But Mercy maintained her calm, "Not the expensive coconut vinegar we use in the kitchen, Ammachi. You get white synthetic vinegar which is cheap and best suited for the process."

But Sophy refused to concede defeat, "But then I'm sure it would leave an awful taste in one's mouth."

John realising the danger of this exchange imediately stepped in. He asked Mercy if the food was ready. She replied that it would take another half hour. John was nonplussed for a moment and then he had a brainwave. Knowing that Sebastian and Narayanan Nair were very fond of cricket, he started to talk about the West Indies cricket team that was currently playing brilliantly.

Only Thomachan had no interest in cricket, but John knew that he would be wise enough to understand the change of topic.

"I think Worrell has done a great job in building a West Indian team keeping the future in mind. With such brilliant men like Sobers and Kanhai in their ranks all they really needed was a black man, their own kind to lead them. And now they have one."

Sebastian almost agreed, though the last remark was unwarranted, "What do you mean? Even with a white captain at the helm, they would have done well."

"I think they have beaten England convincingly this time. Even in the last tour of Australia they did very well," Narayanan Nair who was a fan of Caribbean cricket remarked.

John relieved that the tension in the room had been diffused, said, "I personally feel even India is doing a good job under Pataudi."

"That's because he is a Nawab!" Sebastian countered dryly, in an effort not to be outdone.

Narayanan Nair, who was a basketball player in his younger days and had served as the coach of his unit team in the Army, turned the conversation to the National Basketball Association of USA, "Look at this Lew Alcindor. He is a major sensation in basketball. He has adopted the Muslim name, Kareem Abdul-Jabbar."

John was as well informed about the NBA league as the Colonel, "He entered the NBA at the right time, Colonel. By then Bill Russel had left and Wilt Chamberlain was nearing his mid-thirties. But I must admit this Alcindor boy with his 7'2" height will better his contemporaries. He is perhaps even an inch taller than 'Wilt the Stilt' as Chamberlain is nicknamed."

John observed with satisfaction that at last people were taking an active interest in other major sports, that too an American sport, and not just cricket. The conversation thus proceeded, amicably and good humouredly until Paulose finally announced lunch.

The attention shifted to the rich spread of dishes and everyone complimented Sophy and Mercy on the delicious preparations.

After everybody left, Thomachan alone stayed back. He wanted to hold a detailed discussion with his sister and brother-in-law regarding the future of his son, Pappachan. Although his other sister Thresiamma had often talked about ways to make Pappachan a responsible family man and future head of the family estate, Thomachan reserved greater respect for the advice of Paulose.

When all three finally sat down, Sophy asked him, "So what is the matter?"

After the merriment of the afternoon, the mood in the room suddenly turned sombre. John and Mercy discreetly left them and went to their room.

"Actually, Pappachan does take the initiative in some operations. But he loses interest after some time," Thomachan told them.

"Can't you entrust him with full responsibility, at least in some operations?" Paulose asked.

"Well, to be very frank, I don't know! Maybe, maybe not!"

They had a detailed discussion for half an hour after which Mercy called them for tea and snacks. Sophy wondered whether the mismanagement of his birth by the mid-wife could be the reason. Since Mariam had died in childbirth the delivery may not have been totally natural, Paulose felt.

"Anyway let us see how things work with more freedom and responsibility," Paulose said adding, "Perhaps you should move out of some areas and leave them to Pappachan entirely. We will look for a young man with good training in modern agricultural practices, from among our relatives or friends, someone who is reliable and capable of helping Pappachan learn the ropes." Sophy also agreed with her husband.

For the first time Thomachan looked hopeful. Paulose's words had reassured him somewhat.

After tea, Thomachan took leave. "Give my greetings to John and Mercy. I hope we meet soon," he said as he got into the car.

Chapter 7

Towards the end of the Sixties, India's economy was looking up slightly, and was regaining its strength. But immediately the government needed to augument its foreign exchange reserves which had been sorely depleted by the Pakistan war of 1965. The country's import of fuel, fertiliser and cooking oil had increased. To bridge the deficit, special incentives were given to enterprises capable of earning foreign exchange through export.

With this in view, Karunakaran Muthalali and his sons were discussing their plans to set up a spice extraction company like the one his third son, Ramanathan, had worked with after his graduation from Leeds University. "So where do you think this factory should be set up?" asked Karunakaran to his sons, Lakshmanan and Ramanathan.

Now as Karunakaran awaited a response, it was Lakshmanan who spoke first. He was very close to his younger brother and had spent many hours discussing the intricate details of the proposed factory.

"I have located a plot of about fifteen acres on the outskirts of this town, nearly four to five miles from here, Acha," Lakshmanan replied.

Just then Karunakaran's eldest son joined the group. "What were you discussing?" he asked Lakshmanan.

"You tell him," Lakshmanan said to his younger brother. "Explain the project to Chettan."

Only Ravindran, the eldest brother was addressed as Chettan out of respect. All the others were called by their names. Ramanathan began, "In the spice extraction company I worked for in England, they make an essence of pepper, ginger etc, which looks like an oily substance and is used for food flavouring."

"But will this product have all the qualities of the spice?" Ravindran intervened.

"Yes Chetta. Spices like black pepper have aroma which is recognised by the nose and pungency which is felt in the mouth."

"So you use this liquid instead of powder? But before that tell me why is it called black pepper? We all call it just pepper."

"That is because, Chetta, Westerners call chilli as red pepper."

Janaki Amma who had by now entered the room, listened to the conversation curiously, and said, "You mean that I can add this funny oil instead of spice powder to my curries?"

"Not exactly Amma," Ramanathan replied. But just then Ravindran stood up. "Acha, we have to go to the Assistant Engineer now to submit the tender. We can continue this discussion later." Turning to Lakshmanan, he said "You also come with us."

"Yes, I will," Lakshmanan replied. Then he said to his father, "Acha why don't you all come to my house tomorrow? Nirmala and I have finally settled down in the new house and we can have a simple lunch and continue the discussion.

"Okay, a simple lunch, then. We can have the big house-warming later. We will call the engineers, PWD officers and friends."

Janaki Amma interrupted, "Bring Leela also, Ravindran. It sounds interesting. Besides, she can help Nirmala."

Soon, the group dispersed temporarily to attend to their bread and butter business of contracts.

Later that day when her husband returned, Janaki asked, "I forgot to ask you earlier. How was your meeting with Sebastian and Marykutty?"

"It was good. They are fine."

"It's a long time since I've met them. Why are they not coming to Ernakulam?"

"I don't know. They didn't say anything. But I met an Assistant Professor in the Coimbatore Agricultural College."

"Is that so? Did he say anything about our son Vasu?"

"Actually he had taught Vasudevan. He had nothing but good things to say about our son. He said Vasu was not just a good student but he was very respectful to teachers, helpful in nature and what not!"

Janaki Amma could not hide her happiness on hearing this. More things to brag about to the neighbours!

The next morning, after breakfast, Karunakaran and family trooped in to Lakshmanan's house. They were served a cup of tea before being taken around the house after which the men finally settled down for discussion in the drawing room.

Karunakaran started. "Okay Ramanathan, tell us about your proposal for the new industry."

Ramanathan whispered something into Lakshmanan's ears, and then he spoke in a calm voice, "As I have told you earlier, the plan is to make spice oils and oleoresins."

"Explain the improvements in our planned processing method to them," Lakshmanan urged him.

"In the Western world they make a single extraction to obtain oleoresin, thereby getting both the aroma and pungency constituents."

"But what is the improvement in process you were mentioning?" Karunakaran asked Lakshmanan.

"May I explain, Ramanathan?"

"Please go ahead. I think you can explain it better," Ramanathan said with relief.

Undoubtedly both brothers had studied the subject together. Lakshmanan then began, "A new process has been developed by a research group of the Central Food Technological Research Institute at Mysore. Ramanathan has already discussed his ideas with them and he feels that their process is superior to the Western one. In their process, say extraction of pepper. After the pepper is ground and fed into a steam distillation vessel, steam is applied from the bottom. When you cool the distillate, it separates into water and pepper oil."

Karunakaran interjected, "I have seen this process in the hills many times. The people there put lemongrass in a vessel filled with water and then heat it to boiling point. When the vapour of this mixture is cooled, lemongrass oil separates from water."

"That is almost the same thing," Ramanathan took over.

"But what happens to the pungent components?" Ravindran wanted to know.

"Ah! I'm coming to that. Wait. Now after the pepper oil is recovered, the remaining deoiled powder in the vessel is dried carefully and if there are any lumps, they are broken down further. This is then extracted with solvent to produce the resin portion. This portion will have all the pungent principles, colouring matter and some higher boiling oil fractions as well, which escaped the steam distillation."

"This resin portion containing hot principles—the hot sensation is produced by a chemical called piperine—is then blended with the required amount of oil to get pepper oleoresin."

"In what way is this method better?" Ravindran enquired analytically.

"Well, you get more spice oil and only half of it has to be blended for oleoresin. The other half is good quality oil which has a high value and can be used to give aroma to food products."

"Can you not get the oil by simple distillation? Like how the bootleggers distil alcohol," Karunakaran asked, his mind racing once again to the manner in which spurious alcohol was made in remote areas.

"That's a good question," Ramanathan continued with a smile at the reference to spurious liquor. "See, pepper oil is volatile thereby giving off an aroma even when black pepper is ground in a place far away. But upon heating, various chemical compounds present in the oil get charred before they can reach their boiling point. If I may quote a little science here, a substance boils when the vapour pressure breaks the outside pressure, which in this case is the pressure of the atmospheric air. Although vapour pressure continues to increase upon heating, at a stage before it equals the external pressure, the oil constituents get charred; that is why we do not follow the bootleggers' method."

By now Ramanathan was getting carried away in the intricacies of his chemical world. Assuming the pose of a typical scientist he continued, "When you are unable to raise the vapour pressure to equal atmospheric pressure, you do one of the following two things: either reduce the outside pressure by distilling in a vacuum, though such a form of distillation will be very costly, or you can opt for steam distillation. Just think of it this way. If you can't push a car, what do you do? You seek the help of another person. Similarly if pepper oil partially provides vapour pressure and this is supplemented by steam pressure, then it is possible to get the vapours across the atmospheric pressure at around the boiling point of water. The mixed vapours on cooling separate into pepper oil and water."

Ravindran, curious as ever asked, "So you say that the advantage of this process is more quantity of essential oil or volatile oil as you call it."

Ramanathan nodded in agreement. "Not only that, you also get oil unpolluted with solvent fumes. Oddly, in most processing centres in the West, they do not recover the solvent sticking on to the spent residual powder. The newly introduced method has an additional step to recover this by distillation which will increase the economic efficiency.

"You said that piperine is causing the pungency in pepper," his father said. "Is this the one which gives hot taste to chilli also?"

"No. In chilli it is a constituent called capsaicin."

They did not know how the time had passed and were in animated conversation when Nirmala announced that lunch was ready. Lakshmanan joked, "All this while we were talking about food for thought. But right now let us think about food for our stomachs."

All of them moved to the dining room where the ladies had laid out a pure vegetarian lunch.

After the meal and a short rest, they once again assembled in the drawing room. This time the ladies too joined in. Karunakaran could not contain his excitement. "Ladies, Lakshmanan was explaining to us about the proposed project to make spice essence, or what is called oleoresin," he announced.

"What is that?" enquired Janaki Amma. "Can we use it for cooking?" Ramanathan took over the conversation, "Oils and oleoresins are not used in household cooking, Amma. They are industrial intermediates used in processed food like canned soups, spicy snacks, standardised fast foods and so on."

"Oh I see," she replied, then added "But why not in our kitchen?"

"You see, the oleoresin has many advantages, such as being compact which helps it to be transported and stored easily. Further, it is rarely attacked by microorganisms or insects and is highly concentrated. But the most important quality is that it is a precisely standardised flavour ingredient. Such a product if it is not weighed and added correctly nullifies the advantage of standardisation.

In processed food, the flavour strength of the product has to be uniform. This can be achieved only by using well standardised spice oils and oleoresins taken in precise amounts."

Karunakaran was convinced that his sons had considered all aspects of the project.

Looking around the room, the patriarch finally announced, "I think it is a good idea to set up this business because of Ramanathan's technical knowledge and five year's experience in England before coming back home. I will also speak to my friends on other matters. In the meantime I would like Lakshmanan to head the group as he has managerial experience and is very good in finance."

Hearing this Lakshmanan added, "Ravindran is thorough in the technical side. His friend, an industrial engineer, recently returned from Germany. The three of us will shortly visit Mysore and finalise the project."

That was when Janaki interjected, "See, I was telling you we should have bought land in the hilly region of Idukki. Vasu could have looked after it."

She wanted her youngest son also to be a part of the family business. Karunakaran was about to say something when Lakshmanan put forth his plans. "It will not be practical to grow our own raw material, Amma. In the case of pepper we use only a minor grade called light berries that separate during garbling. Also, the chilli will have to come from Andhra Pradesh. And as for ginger, besides our own, we have to import Nigerian ginger as well."

Janaki Amma listened to every word carefully. Then Karunakaran said to appease her, "Don't worry, Vasudevan is a good agricultural expert. Right now he is working temporarily in the government department to gain some experience. I think I will be able to fix him up in a very nice place."

After some more queries and clarifications the group moved towards the dining room, where the ladies had laid out hot tea and snacks for them.

Chapter 8

At the dawn of the seventies, the world was looking forward to a bright future. Sebastian was having his customary discussion with his neibhour who was saying, "But the situation in the Indian sub-continent is far from rosy. East Pakistan has openly begun protesting against what they called the authoritarian rule of West Pakistan."

His friend Sasidharan Pillai added, "The Army which had a major role in the administration and policies of Pakistan is out to suppress the pro-secession movement of Bengali speaking East Pakistan."

"How can our Prime Minister not be concerned about the developments shaping up in the country's Eastern border? Her advisers have warned her about the possible flow of refugees from East Pakistan into the country." For once Sebastian's nationalistic spirit came to the surface, probably because Pakistan was involved. "The last thing I want is to be dragged into a costly war."

"Come let us get going," Peter said, walking towards his car. He was wearing a pair of brown trousers with a light cream full sleeved shirt. The touch of grey in his well trimmed moustache and a complete greying of the sideburns gave him a distinguished look. He was now a Senior Manager in the same Company, with a few additional tea gardens and a factory under his command. But he chose to stay in the same bungalow given to him while he was Assistant Manager. It was a home Elizabeth preferred. With some modifications, including the addition of a bed room and a store room adjoining the kitchen, the house had been made suitable for an extended stay. Its location was also near to the school attended by their children.

Peter had been provided a company car to move around. That day Peter, along with his wife and son George, was on his way to visit Elizabeth's parents in Calicut. A little over a year ago their daughter Molly had moved to Calicut and was living with her grandparents so that she could attend a good college there.

The entry of Molly into the lives of Marykutty and Sebastian acted as the right tonic to enliven their listless existence. Her youthfulness had seeped into their life, making them feel young again.

Molly meanwhile had turned into a lovely young woman and the centre of attraction among young men of the neighbourhood. She wore the traditional sari with such elegance that her grandmother often teased her to take up modelling as a career.

For Sebastian the pampering he showered on his granddaughter was quite unmatched. He loved the famous Calicut *halva* but now his doctor had forbidden him from eating it. But what Sebastian could not enjoy, he insisted Molly should and often compelled her to have his share as well.

"Here, Molly, eat this *halva*. It will make you healthy," he would coax her.

But Molly would reply, "No, I cannot eat this much, Appapa. I will put on weight."

Sebastian would laugh upon hearing this. "Weight! But you are so thin. Here, eat some."

And Molly would reluctantly accept a small piece.

A little before lunch, Peter, Elizabeth and George arrived in Calicut.

As soon as Peter saw his lovely daughter he said, "How are you, Molae?"

"Are you helping your grandmother in the kitchen?" Elizabeth asked after the initial greetings.

"Right now her job is to study well," Peter said with a smile. Sebastian came out and put his arm around young George's shoulder.

"Are you studying well? I want you to become a doctor. We have a good Medical College here."

Sebastian had already begun dreaming of getting George to study next in Calicut. He wanted the company of his grandson as well in his old age.

"He is doing very well in studies. He wants to study chemistry," Peter said with no regret in his voice. Having seen doctors working late hours without even holidays, he did not think it was such a prized profession. True, one could make decent money and gain respect in society, but he wondered if one's personal and family life could be well balanced in such a demanding profession. And finally, Peter said he was happy with whatever the boy chose as long as he did well in the chosen profession.

Elizabeth too harboured dreams of making her son an engineer or a doctor, but had recently resigned herself to their views.

After lunch Sebastian and Marykutty brought up the subject of Molly's marriage. Peter had gone to his room. Only Elizabeth was with them. Marykutty started the conversation. "Molly is already a fine mature woman. No harm in thinking of her marriage. It is not a matter to be delayed"

Elizabeth then poured out her frustration. "Her father thinks she is still his little child."

"Yes, I know. We have to push our view firmly," Marykutty replied. Sebastian then interveined. "If we put it suitably, he will understand."

"Besides, our Syrian Catholic people will demand dowry. Elizabeth, do you have any problem with that?"

"Actually Ammachi, Peter is really worried about that."

"I thought Peter is earning a lot?"

"Not as much. Peter always points out the case of our Malini, you knowAmmachi."

"Yes, you are right," Sebastian added. "Malini is well qualified, also a professional, yet Rajan had to shell out a fat sum."

Marykutty added, "Money is not a problem for Rajan. He comes from a wealthy family."

Just then Peter joined them. Sebastian looking at Peter said, "We were discussing the possibility of Molly's marriage. Because of dowry you should prepare for it."

"I know the problem," Peter replied. "We will think about the matter when it comes to that. First we want her to complete her graduation. There are still two years left for that," Peter replied to his in-laws' query.

"But haven't you earned enough to send her to a good family?" Sebastian asked with a sense of worry.

"Yes, to some extent. But it's not sufficient," Peter replied.

"Jesus will find the solution," Marykutty firmly believed that God will take care of everything.

At the end of their overnight stay, Peter and his family drove back to Kalpetta.

That evening, when Sebastian and Marykutty were relaxing, John, Paulose and Sophy's son and daughter-in-law Mercy paid them a surprise visit. Sebastian was reading the paper and was happy to have someone with whom he could discuss cricket. As soon as the ladies went into the kitchen, John teased Sebastian on an issue he knew Sebastian was touchy about. "Uncle, now a commoner has become the Indian cricket team's captain, and even led the team to victory over both West Indies and England. Howzzat?"

"This Wadekar was selected by a casting vote. The Nawab of Patuadi should have been the captain," retorted Sebastian.

"But all the same Wadekar looks like a sound leader," John argued.

"That is because Patuadi had built a strong team and any fool can lead the team in its present form."

John smiled and was about to say something, when the sound of an auto rickshaw stopping near the front gate deflected their attention.

Sebastian looked up, "Ah, that is Vasu, son of my old friend, Karunakaran."

He went to the gate and escorted Vasudevan to the drawing room, before calling out to his wife Marykutty, "Vasu has arrived. Bring some coffee and snacks. He is coming after a long train trip."

"Come Vasu, let me introduce you to John." Sebstian turned to John and said "He is a post-graduate in Agricultural Science from Coimbatore."

"Have you only just completed your course?" John asked thinking the boy's name was familiar.

"I have been working temporarily in the Agricultural Department in Idukki for the past few months after my graduation," Vasu replied.

Sebastian took over, “But now he is going to be in Puthupady. Your uncle Thomachan you know…”

“Aha, so you are the person? Yes, my parents were saying something in this regard.” John recalled the discussion his parents had had with Thomachan the other day, parts of which he had overheard from inside his room.

He recalled his father having promised to find a suitable person to manage Thomachan’s estate since Pappachan had little interest in it. Subsequently there had been more telephonic conversations.

“But Vasu has a government job, John. If he has to give up that and work for the Kollegal Estate, obviously the pay has to be good.” After pausing to smile at John, Sebastian added, “Also he is the son of my friend Karunakaran, I hope you will all treat him as a member of the family.”

“So are you joining the Estate immediately?” John asked Vasu.

Replying to the query politely, Vasudevan said, “No, uncle Sebastian has asked me to have a look around the place and spend a day or two in Mr. Thomachan’s house first and then decide.”

John nodded, but continued to look at Vasu for long moment.

A few weeks later as Calicut prepared to welcome Christmas, Thomachan paid Sebastian a surprise visit.

“Are you happy with Vasudevan?”

Thomachan smiled, “He is just the man I was looking for. I didn’t know such humble and polite young men still existed in the world!”

“You have to treat him well.”

“You don’t have to tell me that. He may be a few years younger to Pappachan, but he will be made the Estate Manager one day. He is like my second son.”

The two of them sat down to celebrate over a drink. Marykutty brought a plate of fried *karimeen* one of the most preferred delicacies of Kerala. Normally Marykutty cooked the pearl spot fish in a coating of chilli paste in a banana leaf. Sebastian poured half a drink for Marykutty as well. As they were enjoying the drink and fish, the voice of Mrs. Indira Gandhi boomed out from the radio announcing ‘Dacca is now the capital of the free country Bangladesh.’

Karunakaran Muthalali's house was a bee-hive of frantic activity. The new company floated for the manufacture of spice oils and oleoresins was finally registered, with Lakshmanan as the Managing Director and Ramanathan as its Technical Director. Janaki Amma and all the male members of the family–Karunakaran, Ravindran and Vasudevan–were made Directors as well. Ramanathan had returned from a tour of England, France and Germany where he had gone to study the export market and upon his return, Karunakaran wanted to know the potential of the markets outside.

Ramanathan was upbeat. "It is good. My former company will be glad to import from us. All they want is a guarantee for quality."

"But what happened to their production?"

"In the Western world, cost of labour is very high. That makes it more profitable for them to buy these products from a country like India."

"Are you sure?"

"Yes, but they want the best quality. Somehow they have confidence in me, I believe."

"Did you have good response from other places?"

"Some of the clients I visited in Germany have shown interest. We have managed to get good introductions to parties in USA. Lakshmanan will follow them up when he goes there next month."

In another four months the factory was set up in the northern suburb of Cochin City. As could be expected because of the many years of experience running in the family, it was a modern, well designed structure.The various items of machinery were installed without delay and even a well equipped laboratory was set up on the factory premises in a short time. They had conducted the trial production in the presence of the research team from Mysore. Lakshmanan and Ramanathan were also in the process of recruiting personnel for the company.

Once everything was in place, Karunakaran and Ravindran visited the factory and were taken round to see the factory and laboratory. At the end of the tour, the four of them sat in the Managing Director's room. Lakshmanan offered his chair to Karunakaran.

Shaking his head, Karunakaran said, "I cannot accept that chair my boy. Here both of you are the masters. I will sit on the other side of the table," unable to keep the pride out of his voice. "You two have done a great job."

"Nothing would have been possible without your confidence in us," Lakshmanan said sincerely. "Who else would allow us to spend so much money without even checking what we were doing."

"I have full faith in you. And when I trust someone, I go the full way. Continue the good work."

Ravindran, who had been keeping quiet all this while, now spoke, "You have worked well together until now. Continue to support and respect each other." He concluded looking at Ramanathan.

"Chetta I am happy to play the role of 'Bharata' to Lakshmanan's 'Rama'." Ramanathan said solemnly.

When the four men reached home, Janaki Amma was waiting for them impatiently. Before they could relax she started off, "I have found a good girl for Ramu. We have to visit her family this week. Ravindran and Leela will go with us," she said to her husband. "We have everything ready for him, the new house, the fully equipped kitchen, the furnished bedrooms. All he needs is a wife." Ravindran could not hide a mild laughter, noting her haste.

About a week later Karunakaran took Janaki to their new factory. Leela and Nirmala too joined them.The women were highly impressed and proud of the family's achievement when they saw the factory and laboratory.

"This set-up would have cost us a fortune, Lakshmanan. Tell me, how many lakhs were spent on it?" Janaki Amma asked. Lakshmanan laughed and said, "Lakhs? Amma, it's crores."

"Oh, my *Sabarimale Ayyappa*! Crores? How did you manage to arrange for so much money?"

"From banks; we borrow from them and do business."

"So that means you are neck-deep in loans! Is that good? Should you not have remained within your limits?

"This is the way business is carried out now, Amma. In modern manufacturing business, a bank loan is an integral part since repayment takes a longer period. Of course we need to pay the requisite interest and this needs to be shown in the accounting. We even provide for depreciation of machinery and building, and only then arrive at profit etc."

He continued, "It's no good to do a hundred rupee business with your own hundred rupees. With Rs.100, you should do business in thousands by borrowing. Don't worry, we will do well."

On the way back Janaki Amma wanted to stop at the Ernakulam Siva Temple. The ladies offered flowers and coconuts and prayed for the success of the family's new venture.

Chapter 9

In the year 1973, the countries in the Persian Gulf region raised the price of crude leading to an increase in global prices of petroleum products, making them rich beyond their nomadic imagination.

In the years preceding this development, Cochin which boasted of a port of its own, had emerged as a significant commercial centre. The High Court of Kerala was also set up in Cochin as per the agreement signed during the integration of Travancore and Cochin states.

The hinterland of Cochin City was a fertile space bearing a rich wealth of plantation crops which were mainly exported through the port. This provided a great incentive to those seeking to set up processing plants near the city.

In the midst of such developments, the prosperity of the Gulf countries helped further develop Cochin and the rest of Kerala State. Thanks to the long standing relationship the State shared with the Arabs in spice export and other trade dealings, the Arab countries recruited more people from the State for their development related activities. Many Malayalees went as skilled labour. They left behind their families and sent money home regularly. It was thus a period when the economy of Kerala got a fillip thanks to the remittances from the Gulf countries.

It was into such an environment that 'Spice Ingredients Private Limited', the company set up by Karunakaran and his sons, was born. The company with its global outlook presented a great opportunity to the suppliers, job aspirants and bankers. With a progressive set of owners at the helm, the company, fondly called 'Spice Ingredients' or merely as 'Ingredients', seemed well prepared to scale great heights in the export market targeting the West.

Vasudevan hurried through his breakfast of *idlis* and chutney and excused himself saying that he had some urgent matters to attend to. Thomachan had insisted Vasudevan stay with them in the family house, and they usually had all the meals together. Thomachan had watched the boy eat and wondered if he was getting enough food since he still looked lean. But Vasudevan worked hard, exercised a lot and swam in the river whenever the rains were silent. As he left the table to wash his hands, Thomachan thought how nice it would have been if Pappachan too had shown as much enthusiasm for the agricultural operations. Then he could retire from plantation work.

Vasu came back to tell Thomachan, "We are harvesting the coconuts. I am already behind schedule in supplying the promised quantity of copra to John and Paulose Chettan in Calicut." Thomachan nodded and sent Vasudevan on his way.

Vasu walked briskly towards the fields and reached the coconut grove. Chandran who supervised the coconut and arecanut fields was already there. "Have the climbers come?" Vasu asked.

"Yes, saar," Chandran replied, preferring the English 'Sir' to the feudalistic 'Muthalali'.

"It looks like we'll get a good yield this year."

"Yes, saar. I think. Your advice of providing adequate water during the summer season has yielded good results here. It is even better in the arecanut field."

Vasu smiled. "Well I can tell you that next year will be even better. Just wait and see," he said, adding, "After counting, collect them for drying. Let us make good use of the sun."

"Shall we move towards the arecanut field?" Chandran asked him.

The two of them started walking through the damp, well watered earth. Vasu noticed that the climbers were already up on the trees.

He then turned his attention to the other end of the field where the workers had begun dehusking the areca nuts and putting them out for sun drying.

George returning from his college in Kalpetta walked straight into the dining room where Elizabeth had laid out a meal for him. Peter joined them soon after. Peter had been spending much time in Ooty of late, where the headquarters of his tea company was situated. He was tipped to become one of the Senior Managers there. Turning to Peter, Elizabeth said, "Why is Appan saying that George will have to go to Cochin for further studies? Has it anything to do with your transfer? Why can't he study in Calicut like Molly?"

"Appan says that there is a good course in Cochin, which will be suitable for George. Then he can do his post graduation there."

"What is so special about this college, that you are giving it more importance than medical college?"

After helping himself to more food, Peter looked at his son and said, "George is good in his studies, but he dislikes medicine. Since he is not so good in maths, he may not like to do engineering. What do you say George?" On getting a favourable nod from his son he added, "Besides he likes the industrial job which his grandfather has suggested. Appan had got an assurance from his friend Karunakaran that he will offer George a good job if he takes this course."

The next day Peter and Elizabeth drove to Calicut to spend a day there. Molly had completed her B.Sc. in Botany and was scheduled to return home with them. George had stayed back in Kalpetta so that he could continue with his tuition classes. There was a house servant who would look after him while his parents were away.

When Molly saw her parents arrive at the house of Sebastian and Marykutty, she ran out. She was excited to see her parents after a long time. Peter could not help but notice that his little daughter had become as beautiful young woman.

"How is my little child doing? Will you pass your exam?"

"I will get a First Class, Daddy."

"That sounds good."

"If I get a First Class in B.Sc., can I do my M.Sc.?" Molly was quick to ask.

Hearing this, Elizabeth who was busy taking their bags out of the car, came rushing like a tigress, "Now the girl wants to do an M.Sc? There's no time for higher education. It's time to think of your marriage. If you wish, you can take up a job as a teacher in a nursery school, until your marriage is fixed."

Molly looked at her father with a sullen expression. Peter calmed her, "Have patience my child, we'll do something about it."

Peter's reply though angered Elizabeth even more.

"You are spoiling the girl!" she thundered.

Sebastian and Marykutty came outside hearing the argument, and Elizabeth calmed down.

Over coffee, Elizabeth asked her father, "Appa, what course did you advise George to take up?"

"He will be doing his M.Sc. in Applied Chemistry. It is a specialized course in Oils, Fats and Aromatics. My friend Karunakaran, from Cochin, and his three sons recommended the course to me. They have assured us of absorbing him in their company, once he completes the course."

Curious about his father in-law's plans for his son, Peter asked to be told more about the company.

"Karunakaran's third son did his higher studies in Chemistry and worked after that for a few years in England. There he was introduced to a process for making spice extracts. Upon his return to India, he helped set up a family business to produce the same. Since the manufacturing process employed by him will be more cost effective, his former English company has promised to buy his finished products. The English can be relied upon to keep their word. No Indian can excel as Englishmen."

While bragging about his friend's family, Sebastian conveniently put emphasis on the expertise of the English people. This despite Ramanathan having explained to him the role of Indian researchers in improving the existing process.

Hearing her husband's plans, Marykutty sipped her tea quietly, disappointed that her grandson would not be coming to Calicut to continue his education. She had been hoping that with Molly's return, young George would replace her and give the old couple company.

"At least he can do his B.Sc. in Calicut," she said.

"No, Marykutty. It is better that he studies in Maharajas College in Cochin. It will be easier for him then to get admission to their M.Sc. course. Remember, admission to the course is not assured. We have to try hard. Even I would have loved to have him here. But the boy's future is more important."

Peter asked, "But what are his prospects in the company?"

"That is assured. Even with a B.Sc. degree in hand, he will get placed in the company. Karunakaran has promised to take good care of him. But with an M.Sc. in hand, his career can grow faster."

Karunakaran Muthalali's house in Cochin was packed with relatives and friends. The occasion was his third son Ramanathan's wedding, which was to take place in the temple town of Guruvayoor, about 110 km north of Cochin. The marriage party which had assembled at the groom's house was scheduled to leave for the town by bus the next morning, with a stopover for breakfast at Trichur. The wedding was to be held in the Sri Krishna Temple where the ceremony was fixed for 11.25, an auspicious time.

The bride was a girl named Vanya, a graduate in science from a small town called Wadakancherry.

The wedding took place at the appointed time. It was a simple affair with a few select friends of the family since they had planned two different receptions - one by the bride's family in Wadakancherry and another by the groom's side at Cochin. Sebastian and Marykutty had been invited to the temple ceremony.

After the wedding, Marykutty walked towards Janaki Amma and complimented her. "You have a pretty daughter-in-law, just like youself."

She knew that Janaki enjoyed such praise. But she also knew that her favourite grandson would be working for Janaki Amma's son's company one day.

Janaki, as expected, smiled brightly at the compliment and replied, "Did you see her diamonds? Her mother and I specially selected them from Madras."

"I was about to ask about those diamonds. Tell me, how do you manage to have such a fine selection in stones?"

Acting humble, Janaki replied, "Oh, it's nothing. Everything depends on the clarity and cut of the stone; qualities which you are assured of, if you buy from Madras. The stones here are not so pure. Her sari is from Kanchipuram, specially made, you know."

"No wonder it matches so well with her complexion. Well, she is naturally beautiful and any sari would suit her."

Janaki thanked her with a big smile and moved towards the other guests.

The reception at Cochin was a grand affair. Karunakaran had used his influence to get permission to use the reclaimed land for the day and a huge *pandal* had been erected on it. Some of the older citizens said that even for the functions of former Maharajas, such a grand and imposing structure had not been erected. Over a thousand people had been invited.

Sebastian and Marykutty from Calicut, Peter and Elizabeth from Kalpetta and Peter's parents from Trichur were some of the invited guests.

During the reception, Elizabeth asked Marykutty, "Did you buy the gold set for the bride as planned?"

"Here it is. Have a look," Marykutty took out the jewellery box and opened it.

Seeing the jewellery she exclaimed, "What a magnificent necklace. Where did you buy it from?"

"We bought it in Trichur. Your mother-in-law selected it. It is our present. What are you giving, Elizabeth?"

"A stainless steel dinner set." It's quite beautiful. But we have already gift-wrapped it."

Oh it must be quite expensive," Marykutty said. Then looking around, she said, "Where's George?

"He was here a while ago," Elizabeth said and spotted her son in the crowd, "George come here. Have you paid your respects to Ammama?"

George came and greeted his grandmother. Marykutty put her hands on the young boy's shoulders and said, "Aye, George you look smart in your fashionable shirt and pants. If you were a little older someone would have mistaken you for the bridegroom."

"Look Ammama. Daddy also gave me this new Citizen watch."

"It is beautiful, so also your fine shoes."

George smiled, before excusing himself and heading towards a group of youngsters he had just made friends with. Both Elizabeth and Marykutty noted that he showed little interest in the young ladies, some of them sisters of the boys he was talking to.

Marykutty asked Elizabeth, "You have spent a fortune on George's clothes. But why were you so miserly about Molly's? I would have liked to see her in something better. Are you the one spoiling George?"

Just then Peter joined them and said with a cheerful laugh, "He is yet to understand the value of money and that it doesn't grow on a tree, or on a tea plant for that matter. He is an expensive piece to maintain."

"But Peter don't take it lightly. Elizabeth, you must take control and do something."

"No Amma, he insists on wearing such costly outfits. In a way Peter and I are at a loss. But otherwise he is okay. In studies he is good. I am sure he will take control of his life in due course."

In a corner of the *pandal*, a team of musicians from Madras began a session of Carnatic music. The Public Works minister and his retinue had also arrived by then. He was received by Karunakaran and his friend, the Mayor of Cochin. One could also spot many PWD engineers in the crowd. It was as if everyone important in the city had come for the function.

Someone from the guests tapped Peter on his shoulder and pointed to an elderly man sitting in the front row. "That is the

Principal of the Maharajas College," the guest said. Not wanting to lose this golden opportunity, Peter slowly walked towards him. But by the time he reached the front row, he found Sebastian already in conversation with the Principal.

Seeing Peter, Sebastian immediately introduced them to each other, "This is my son-in-law, Peter George. He is a Senior Manager in a Tea Company. He is the father of the boy I was talking about."

Peter shook hands with the Principal and then gestured a namaste in the form of exaggerated respect.

While the trio started a conversation, the bride and groom ascended the small platform and seated themselves for the rituals to commence. The whole place was filled with the fragrance of jasmine, emanating from the flowers around the bridal chairs, and the hairdos of the ladies.

After a brief welcome by Karunakaran, a few more people were invited to introduce the couple to the guests. The Minister presented a boring speech for what seemed like an eternity, but it was compensated by the Mayor, an advocate, who delivered a witty speech to keep the guests in the right spirits.

This was followed by a sumptuous dinner with a wide range of exquisite sweets. While moving towards the food counter, Elizabeth and Marykutty looked around and to their dismay found that they were probably the least impressively dressed women in the crowd. Just then Marykutty caught sight of Vasudevan, who was running around seeing to the guests.

"How are you Vasu? Have you met my daughter, Elizabeth?"

He smiled warmly and greeted them in his usual polite manner. He then led them to another counter which was less crowded.

Chapter 10

Thresiamma, the third of Thomachan's sisters, lived close to Thamarassery where her husband's family owned some land where they grew rubber. They were not as big as the Kollegal family, but they were quite comfortably off. They also owned a grocery store managed by their second son.

It was a tradition that during Easter week, Thresiamma and her other sisters came to the Kollegal Estate for a family get-together. They arrived on Wednesday, took part in the Maundy Thursday, Good Friday, Holy Saturday and Easter Sunday ceremonies and then departed towards evening with their husbands who made it a point to arrive only at the grand finale of the Holy Week: the Easter lunch. A lot of alcohol and plenty of merriment accompanied such get-togethers.

This year too the three sisters arrived as usual, but this time Sophy had a special purpose in mind. She had already discussed the matter with Chinnama and Thresiamma and together the sisters confronted Thomachan after lunch on Holy Saturday.

"We all think that this house needs a woman. Pappachan must get married."

Thomachan suddenly became defensive at their aggressive tone, though he knew he would be happy if somebody could get his son to marry. Only then would the house become a proper home with the voices of children and the comfort of a housewife and would set Pappachan on the right course. Besides, Thomachan knew that age was catching up with him as well, and he wished to retire soon.

Thresiamma took over the conversation upon Sophy's direction, "Presently, this house doesn't feel like a home. It's more like a YMCA. You yourself should have remarried long ago."

"I could not replace my dear Mariam with any other woman. Besides I wanted to give my full attention to Pappachan."

Chinnama, the eldest sister said, "Then you are a fool. What he wanted was a mother."

Sophy cautiously entered the conversation and said, "Let's not think of days gone by. That is neither here nor there. But we can surely think of the future. Pappachan must marry."

Thomachan concurred. "I agree but will he listen?"

"And why not? Every man has to marry and beget children. Is it not what our Church also says? Otherwise he should have become a priest. That would have been wonderful," Chinnama said in a sudden twist of tone.

Chinnama's family based in Palai in South Kerala had traditionally been a supporter of the Church. Her husband's younger brother had become a priest some years ago and the family and parishioners proudly proclaimed his anointment to one and all. It was rumoured that he would soon be ordained as a Bishop. That would be a great occasion for the family.

"I'm all for it. Let's make him agree to the idea. I want all of you to coax him," Thomachan said, knowing well, that despite having raised the subject many times before, all that he had received was a vague response from Pappachan. In fact, he was now afraid to broach the subject in case his son withdrew deeper into his shell.

The three ladies took the first opportunity to pin Pappachan down. Thomachan stood in a corner watching the proceedings, greatly relieved to see that his son was in a relatively jovial mood. That surprised him a great deal. With him, he was always morose and grumpy. But Thresiamma signalled Thomachan to go out so he moved to the living room and sat on an easychair.

It was a happy group of sisters who finally emerged from the room. Shortly Pappachan followed them out and sauntered off towards his room.

"So, that is settled," Thresiamma, the chatterbox among the lot said.

"What is settled?" Thomachan asked impatiently,

"He wants to get married. You have not understood him. So problem solved."

"Really? He agreed?"

"Yes, he needed a little coaxing, that's all. Anyway everything is settled for now. We have even found the right girl." It was Sophy speaking now, ensuring that her agenda remained on track.

"Who is it Chechi? Tell us," the other two led by Thresiamma asked aloud, pretending as if they knew nothing. Even Chinnama joined the act, pretending to be clueless.

"I have an alliance in mind. The girl is the granddaughter of Sebastian and Marykutty of Calicut."

"Yes I know them. Is she good looking?" Chinnama asked.

"She is a beauty. She has recently completed her B.Sc. Her father holds an important position in a tea company in Ooty."

"How old is she?" Thomachan asked.

"About eighteen or nineteen I think."

"But Pappachan is thirty four."

"Age is not an issue. They will agree to the alliance. Who would not want an alliance with the Kollegal family! But how much can they give?" Chinnama directed the query at Sophy, opening up the topic of dowry. An alliance with the rich Kollegal family was a prestige issue and she was sure that rich families would not hesitate to offer any amount of dowry.

"There might be a slight problem as far as that is concerned. But rest assured, they are a good family and every member is greatly respected," Sophy said cautiously.

"But prestige alone is not enough," Chinnama declared, speaking a language of wealth.

Thomachan immediately intervened, "No, no, we need not bother about any dowry. Whatever they want to give to their daughter is fine with us."

Over the years he had thought over the matter long and hard and decided that if a good alliance was found for Pappachan, he would not let money be a hindrance. Even family status and looks of the girl were secondary. All he wanted was for Holy Mother Mary to ensure that the right woman marry his son and lead him into a life of happiness.

Coming out of his thoughts, he asked Sophy, "Is the young lady well behaved?"

"She is a gem of a girl. Don't worry about her. Nobody can get a better bride."

"But are you sure that they will agree for the marriage considering the big age gap?" Thomachan asked again. Besides this, he was also worried that if the bride's family made enquiries about Pappachan and discovered more negatives than positives about him? Even he did not know his son well enough to be sure. Pappachan had always been a loner, but Thomachan had hoped that a woman would bring about a change in him.

Sophy was confident that she could handle any issues related to disparity in age. She had had an informal talk with Marykutty who had expressed a desire for an alliance with the Kollegal family. But the matter of Peter's financial position was causing her some concern. Now that the problem of dowry was settled, she did not anticipate any objection from that side. She said, "Thomacha, you don't know your strength. What is age difference when one has money? You have more money than they can possibly imagine, and you are not asking for any dowry. Don't worry unnecessarily. Just leave the matter to us."

At the Easter Holy Mass the next day Thomachan prayed with sincerity for a good future for his son. His sister's assurances notwithstanding, he hoped that the dream he was presently in, would remain intact and not burst at the prick of a pin. But deep inside, he hoped that Pappachan would not let any form of inferiority complex at marrying a smarter, younger girl come in the way.

The lunch was lavish and the whole family relished the variety of meat preparations and the whisky that flowed freely. Pappachan also seemed to be enjoying himself.

After lunch Sophy took Paulose aside and whispered, "I am sure we can get the consent of Molly's family."

"Yes, from the conversation we had with Sebastian, it does seem possible. They would surely want an alliance with such a prestigious family. What they were worried about was money. Now that is also taken care of."

Meanwhile Chinnama cornered her husband and put across some of her views, "We must get your brother to conduct the marriage and

Holy Mass. By then, I am sure that he will be a Bishop. That would be a prestigious moment for us as well."

"I hope Peter's family doesn't insist on a priest from their family."

"We can convince Peter's father. After all, I doubt if they even have a priest in their family."

In another corner Thresiamma accosted her husband Varghese, who was half drunk, "Once the marriage is fixed, there will definitely be a big feast. We should take a lead in the arrangements. Our grocery store could be of use to Thomachan."

Hearing about his store, Varghese propped himself up and listened attentively. After his wife had finished, he turned into the businessman he was and said, "Yes, yes, we should make all necessary arrangements. We live nearby and should take the lead. We will supply everything including cooks, and even arrange the liquor for the informal get-together."

"Then start planning."

"But is the alliance confirmed?"

"When I am there how can it not be confirmed? Count it as done!"

George was on his way to Cochin to begin his B.Sc. Chemistry course at Maharajas College. He had two suitcases full of clothes bought in Bangalore including pants and shirts of fine quality. He had also bought an expensive pen.

Although Molly was fond of her younger brother, she often worried about his tendency to extravagance. She would tell her mother, "I think you are spoiling him. Why does Daddy pamper him so much?"

"What to do? He insists on having only the best of things. Poor Daddy, he is really struggling to meet his demands."

"But won't it spoil him?"

"Well, may be, but he is a very loving child. He is concerned about all of us. He wanted to buy gold ornaments for you too. He calls Daddy and me misers, saying that the family should begin living in better standards."

"But where is the money for all this going to come from?"

Her mother shrugged, "That is the problem. Let us hope that he changes when he grows up. He is only a young boy, as of now! He studies well."

Molly heard Peter honking and she went out. It was time for George to leave. One by one, they kissed him and bade him a tearful farewell. George hugged his mother and Molly affectionately and then waved a cheerful goodbye as they drove off for Calicut from where he would take the train to Cochin.

In Calicut, the father-son pair lunched with Sebastian and Marykutty. George was very solicitous about his grandparents' well being and they were only too happy with his show of love. After lunch, Peter dropped him at the station and returned to his father-in-law's house. He was to stay there overnight. After dinner Sebastian, Marykutty and Peter sat in the drawing room and talked.

Sebastian felt this was the right time to discuss the marriage proposal for Molly. After explaining the offer from the Kollegal family, he said "So what do you think? We believe Molly is in a way lucky to be married into that illustrious family."

"But isn't he too old for her?" Peter said with some concern.

"Yes in a way. But you should look at the bright side of it. They are a very rich family, he is an only son and they are not insisting on a dowry."

Peter was quite relieved to hear this because it was the one issue he was most worried about. Everything else was irrelevant. He was relieved but also had some reservations. "Is the no dowry business because he is a bit old?"

"I am sick of this talk about age. Why, any young woman would gladly agree to such an alliance. The groom will be more mature because he is older," Marykutty said. "Let us all be happy that good fortune has come Molly's way. Not to mention ours. My own cousin is married to a man much older to her. He married her after the death of his first wife. I haven't seen a happier marriage. She is supremely happy and he adores her. She has already given him four children. Romance is only for a few months. What every wife needs is a mature man to take care of her all her life."

Hearing this, Peter recounted a joke cracked by an American buyer in the Planter's Club, "Marriage is like chewing gum. The flavour lasts for a while but the chewing goes on."

Sebastian laughed upon hearing this, but quickly straightened in his chair and said, "Pappachan is a loner. He needs some company; nothing which a loving wife cannot give. Later on, the presence of children and a happy family will set things straight."

"But have you checked his background?" Peter asked, voicing an unspecified anxiety.

"Yes. Now you can consult your father, and explain the position of the Kollegal family. They will only be happy with this alliance."

Marykutty who was confident about the alliance said, "You do know John and Mercy well don't you? Pay them a visit sometime and talk to John's parents, Paulose and Sophy."

"I will talk to my father when I go to Trichur. But first I must talk to Elizabeth and Molly."

"Yes, do that at the earliest," Sebastian urged.

All said and done, it was a greatly relieved Peter who went to sleep that night.

Chapter 11

Vasudevan had adjusted quickly to his work at the Kollegal Estate. He spent a lot of time learning the various operations of the estate by talking to the people who were carrying out various functions.

Thomachan had given him a room in his own house and despite Vasu's initial objections he was thankful that the old man had persuaded him to accept it. The patriarch seemed to like him very much, especially because of the diligence which he showed in his work.

"Vasu's influence is having its effect on the labour I notice. They look enthusiastic about their work here," Thomachan remarked one day to Pappachan. Pappachan merely mumbled something and walked away. Ignoring his son's indifference, the old man continued to support Vasu in whatever he took up.

One of the projects had been the irrigation of the coconut and arecanut fields in summer. Thomachan approved his plan and accordingly, motors pumps were installed and pipe lines laid. It had yielded good results. Next Vasu came up with the idea of cemented drying yards for the copra. They would help to keep the coconuts from being contaminated with the surrounding dirt and prevent the growth of fungus on the copra. "When I discussed this matter with John he explained to me that the expeller operators would prefer white copra for the manufacture of edible coconut oil. The oil from substandard copra can only be used for soap making. Good quality copra will mean better prices in the market."

Vasu's enthusiasm forced Thomachan out of his self imposed retirement and he found life once again exciting and rewarding. He was more than happy to see his estate being modernised under Vasudevan's supervision. After all the boy had a degree in Agricultural Science and knew what he was doing. However, beneath the surface

Thomachan had perceived a muted conflict brewing between Vasu and his son. Though Pappachan was outwardly cordial Thomachan found his behaviour towards the young man superficial and insincere. He told himself that this problem too would be solved once Pappachan got married. But then the thought that after the marriage Vasudevan would have to find new quarters to live in distressed him. Thomachan would miss his 'adopted' son.

Peter and Elizabeth had dropped Molly off at her grandparents' home in Calicut and were on their way to Trichur to visit Peter's parents. They wanted to discuss the matter of Molly's marriage with them. When Peter's parents heard that it was an alliance from the heir of Kollegal family they were quite pleased. The Kollegal family had agricultural and business interest in Trichur and held a respectable reputation in the town. And they had not asked for a dowry. That was the clincher.

Things moved quickly. According to tradition, a formal seeing-the-bride ceremony at Sebastian's house in Calicut was planned.

Peter's mother who knew the importance of such meetings asked her son, "Who all are coming from Puthupady?"

"Besides Thomachan and Pappachan, Thomachan's sisters from Thamarassery and Calicut with their husbands will come. Probably the Calicut sister's son and daughter-in-law, John and Mercy, will also be there."

Earlier Elizabeth and Peter had spoken to Molly. After explaining everything Peter ended by saying that he hoped his daughter could continue her education in the new family. Immediately Elizabeth said, "What will she achieve by studying more? She needs the support of a husband and family as she grows up. Also, she is going to be the mistress of a big and rich household."

"But is he not a bit old?" Molly asked.

Elizabeth replied, "Yes, he is. But then how can we match the power and wealth of the Kollegal family. Of course we have high status because of your father's position in the Company. Still we are just middle class, my child. But they are lucky too. We are giving them such a beautiful girl."

Molly giggled and went out with dreamy eyes. Any misgivings she might have had about the marriage were dispelled by her grandmother later.

"We have all gone through this phase, molae. What else does a woman want, other than being married into a good family?"

Molly blushed but was still not convinced, "Is he well educated?"

"He has gone to College. But he is not some University Professor to go around flaunting his degree certificates."

"Can I see his photo?"

"You are going to see him in person in a couple of days. I have seen him and he is smart—Look, look how the girl is blushing!" Marykutty laughed.

The formal function went well. Thomachan and his sister, Sophy, her husband Paulose along with their son John and his wife Mercy had come. Marykutty suggested a private conversation between Pappachan and Molly. Accordingly, they were sent into another room. Molly initiated the conversation. She asked him about the Estate, to which Pappachan muttered something in reply.

'So men are also nervous,' she thought, laughing to herself.

Marykutty later cornered Molly and asked whether she approved the boy.

"He is okay," she said blushing.

"So you like the match?"

Molly did not say anything. But there was a smile on her face. Marykutty was relieved. Just then Elizabeth joined them. "What did you think? Did you like him?" she asked Molly anxiously.

"The girl does not want any of us anymore." Marykutty said in a mock disapproving tone.

Before Molly could reply Peter came into the room. Putting his arm around her shoulder he said, "Shall we go ahead with the marriage, darling?"

"Yes Daddy."

It did not matter whether Molly was happy or disappointed with the match. She knew that her parents would be relieved if she gave her consent. Like most parents they too were anxious to get their daughter married in a world where money meant more than any other attribute of the girl.

Molly could hear the general joviality engulfing the group in the drawing room. Now that the basic matter was settled everything else would take its course. Paulose the seniormost member of the groom's family announced, "The '*Sammatham*' or engagement will be held in Puthupady Church on the 3rd of the next month. Then three Sundays will be kept aside for banns."

After a short pause he continued, "The wedding will be held in the Lourdes' Church in Trichur on 27th November just before the twenty five day Nativity fasting starts."

After some whispered discussion among their family, Paulose said, "We have one request to Peter and his father. We would like Father Valathemala of Palai, one of our relatives to conduct the wedding ceremony in Trichur."

Peter and his parents seemed a little surprised, but Poulose continued, "By then Father Valathemala would be a Bishop. And it would be a great honour to have a Bishop to conduct the ceremony."

Peter's father took a minute to recover from the statement, then said, "I don't think there will be a problem. Just to be on the safe side, let me first check with our Vicar. The church comes under the Trichur Bishop. Hopefully, it can be arranged. You will hear from us soon regarding it. There's no reason why our Vicar shouldn't agree."

After a few minutes of good natured banter, with much back-slapping and hand-shaking, the boy's party left.

Elizabeth, Marykutty and Peter's mother were in Calicut in Marykutty's house discussing the shopping to be done for Molly's wedding. Peter too was present listening to the ladies. Hearing of their elaborate plans he said,

"Now that there is no dowry, we can afford to be lavish," as he helped himself to a sponge cake from the plate.

"In that case let's go to Madras to buy a diamond set," Elizabeth said delighted.

But Marykutty did not agree. "Why go all the way to Madras? Peter's mother has already planned to buy the ornaments from her relative's shop in Trichur. After all you get the best gold jewellery there."

Peter intervened, "Amma, we will buy all the gold from our uncle's shop. But perhaps we could get the diamond earring from Madras. Anyway all of you are going to Coimbatore to buy saris. So why not club a visit to Madras with it?"

Just then Molly walked in. Marykutty embraced her granddaughter, and inspected her from head to toe. She then took a couple of steps back and with a satisfied smile observed, "A white silk sari, silver slippers, a pretty net and a diamond ear ring! My sweetie will be the most beautiful bride in the whole world!"

Sebastian came and put his arm around Molly.

"So you are all going to Trichur tomorrow."

"Yes and everyone can stay with us," Peter's mother added. "And when we are in Trichur, we have to order the bouquet and the tiara for the hair. Sister Margareta is the right person for this."

Then Marykutty took over, "And day after, we shall all leave for Coimbatore. Peter has arranged all the money we need."

Sebastian's patience with this talk thinned by now. "Come Peter," he said, "Let the women be happy throwing away good money on gold and silk. We will spend it on better stuff"

Peter smiled and reached for the bottle of whisky he had just brought for his father-in-law.

It was the night before the wedding. Peter's family home was full of guests. The house was decorated with coloured lights and tables laid out for dinner. In a room upstairs some close friends and relatives of the family had a round of drinks after which dinner was announced. It was an elaborate menu with chicken, pork, fried *karimeen* and *varaal* fish curry in coconut milk prepared in the typical Trichur style. The *varaal* fish, also called snake fish due to the shape of its head, was a favourite among the Christians of the Trichur area.

After dinner, all close relatives gathered in the hall for the purification ceremony. A collective gasp was heard when Molly walked into the room, resplendent in a peacock blue Kanchipuram sari and a beautiful gold and blue stone studded necklace with earrings to match. She had also put a blue *bindi* on her forehead, unusual for a Christian woman. She slowly approached each of the elder relatives present in the room with hands joined and stood before them seeking their blessings.

"What a beautiful young woman!" an older cousin remarked. Everyone seemed in agreement. Elizabeth who had overheard the remark, felt very proud and happy.

As per tradition, Peter's eldest sister smeared a drop of coconut oil on Molly's forehead and washed her toes with water. This was a symbolic oil bath given to purify the body.

"What is to be done now?" Molly's nervous aunty asked of no one in particular, much to the amusement of the crowd.

"You have to offer sweet and water," someone from the crowd said. As she went to get the plate with the sweetened coconut, an elderly person said, "You have to first seek permission from all of us." The crowd laughed good humouredly.

After that Elizabeth introduced Molly to a group of women who wanted to see more of the bride-to-be and her dress. One of them remarked, "What a fine silk sari! Where did you buy it?"

"In Coimbatore. Here you get only the traditional kind."

Another lady remarked on the beautiful necklace of fine cut blue stones set in gold. Molly had worn matching blue and gold glass bangles.

"What perfect matching! What taste! Is it your selection?" another woman enquired of Molly with genuine admiration.

Elizabeth felt a surge of pride. Molly replied, "This is my brother George's gift to me."

"You mean, our George?"

Elizabeth added, "Yes. He wanted to get the finest possible present for his dear sister. He does have good taste."

"But where did he get the money for all this? Isn't he still studying?"

"Of course, we sent the money to him," Elizabeth bragged, making it look as if sending a large amount of money to their son was just a minor matter for them. But she remembered Peter's concern when he received George's unusual request for such a large amount. He was convinced that their son had expensive tastes and was stubborn about getting his wishes fulfilled.

Elizabeth put that incident out of her mind and enjoyed the appreciation his gift was drawing. While the men had been bowled over by the beautifully dressed bride-to-be, the women were giving points for the dress and ornaments she had worn.

Elizabeth suddenly remembered a line she had recently read in a magazine, 'While a man sees a beautifully dressed woman, a woman merely sees a woman in a beautiful dress!'

She was happy with the tremendous impression her daughter made. One woman even went on to say, "No wonder she got a marriage offer from such a prosperous family." Elizabeth felt puffed up by that remark.

When night fell, a number of mats and mattresses were spread wherever there was space and guests lay down to sleep waiting for the big day to dawn.

The next morning Elizabeth had to go around urging her relatives to have breakfast of *kanji* and bread with pork curry, some vegetable preparations and green mango pickle as side dishes.

"Nothing like pork with *kanji,*" remarked a veteran of innumerable weddings.

"Ho, *kanji,* stupid thing," a youngster sneered and went for the bread.

"I say there is no food like *kanji.* It nourishes the body and the mind," the old man advised the boys.

"I can see that in you!" the youngster retorted while a few of his friends sniggered.

Overhearing the exchange a smart middle aged man stepped in, "Uncle Sebastian was once telling us that *kanji* came from China."

Another man chipped in, "That is true. I say it with authority. Just last month I had some *kanji* or *conji* as the Chinese say, for breakfast in a five star hotel in Hong Kong. I saw most of the Chinese were heading for it so I also took it out of curiosity."

"How was it?" one of the youngsters enquired.

"It tasted all right. Actually it felt overcooked and had too much salt. There were pieces of meat in it also."

The old man was happy to hear this and said, "The Chinese are very smart people."

In the meantime Molly had a light breakfast. "You better go to your room. The beautician has come," Elizabeth said and shooed her daughter inside.

At nine in the morning, the bride came to the drawing room which was cleared of all furniture. She was made to sit on the lone chair in the middle of the room for the traditional ritual of offering the sweet by the eldest member of the family. As soon as Molly sat on the chair, the photographer took over. He clicked pictures of her from different angles, and then made her relatives stand alongside her for multiple shots.

The wedding was fixed for ten. A little before the fixed time, the bridegroom's decorated car arrived at Molly's house, to take her to the church. According to tradition the bride was not to be kept waiting in the church. So the bridegroom would arrive early and send his car to fetch the bride. She would be escorted by a close relative, in this case John and Mercy. Peter and Elizabeth received them. Since Molly's entire family wanted to accompany the bride, the groom's car was used only as an escort vehicle. Molly sat in the decorated bride's car, sandwiched between her paternal grandparents. The seating arrangement was not very comfortable, but then considering the importance of the occasion, her grandparents adjusted themselves allowing her to take up more space. Peter took the wheel, with Elizabeth sitting by his side. Sebastian, Marykutty and George travelled with John and Mercy in the groom's car. All others got into whichever car was available, including the taxis arranged by the family.

Molly in a white silk sari, her face covered by a white veil, wearing a white and silver coloured bridal tiara over her neatly tied hair, with a bouquet in her hand was truly grace personified. As she stood in front of the church façade she looked like an angel of God.

Pappachan was sweating profusely in his three piece suit even though it was the end of November. George looked smart in a light two piece with a flowing tie nattily knotted unlike the bridegroom's clumsily knotted one. Most of the male guests wore a *mundu* and shirt.

The marriage ceremony was conducted by the Bishop of Palai with two priests assisting in the ceremony. During the Holy Mass many men stepped outside. For them there were better things to do than attending a boring Mass. The women mostly spent the time watching other women's saris and jewellery.

As soon as the ceremony was over Peter called Elizabeth to one side and said, "You know that the couple will stay here and leave early morning for Puthupady to get there in time for lunch?"

"Of course I know."

"I hope you have arranged for the couple's bedroom to be nicely decorated?"

"Yes. Your sisters have taken that responsibility. I have asked Celina to keep an eye on the arrangements and help where necessary."

When the wedding party finally reached Puthupady the next day, it was nearly one o'clock. Inside a huge *pandal* erected for the occasion, lunch was served for all the workers and local people. Despite the seating for four hundred people at a time, there were three sittings starting from 11.00am. It was a regular custom in some villages for guests to begin eating well before the arrival of the bridal couple. So often the bride's party, prominent guests and close relatives were seated together, while the newly wed couple were seated on an elevated podium in a specially decorated area of the *pandal.* The sumptuous meal began after the ritual of giving sweet and water.

In the evening a cocktail dinner was hosted by the groom's family. Vasudevan was in charge. Thomachan had cautioned him, "The party should be top class, Vasu. There are executives coming from Ooty and Bangalore."

"Everything is taken care of."

"There will be four or five top officers of the tea company from Ooty. It was I who had suggested to Peter that they come here and not to Trichur since it's easier for them to travel to Puthupady. The executives will be coming with their wives. Didn't you say that your teacher, Professor Vishwanathan from Coimbatore was also invited? If he and his wife come, it will be great."

"Yes he has promised to come. I told him that you are keen on meeting him. I may be not be able to attend to them because—"

"I will look after them myself. They are personal guests of mine."

The venue looked splendid. Vasudevan had arranged for a caterer from Calicut to provide the food and a popular orchestra from Calicut played popular Hindi film songs by Lata Mangeshkar and Mohammed Rafi.

At the insistence of his aunties, Pappachan wore his wedding suit. Only this time Vasudevan helped him tie a proper knot. The only other person from the family wearing a suit was George. Being situated at the foothills of the Western Ghats and the fact that night was fast descending, the weather was cool. Peter was in a regular pant and shirt , but the three officials from Ooty and the professor from Coimbatore were wearing suits.

The real colour of the party though was provided by the ladies. With the worry of arranging the marriage function behind them finally, all of them took this occasion to display their beautiful saris and glittering ornaments.

Thomachan took Professor Vishwanathan of the Coimbatore Agricultural College around and introduced him to a few people and eventually came to Sebastian and John when the host was called away to meet some newly arrived guests. The three of them talked about the start of the One Day Cricket World Championship planned for the following year in England.

"But I tell you, that One Day cricket is just pyjama cricket. They are degrading cricket into a commercial enterprise," the Professor put forth his view and then continued, "My real interest lies in tennis."

"Oh, the newcomer, what is his name John, aah yes, Jimmy Connors. He may be the future champion. By the way this is John. He is a producer and dealer in *copra*."

"Nice to meet you, Mr. John. Coming back to tennis, I am so thrilled to see a black man, Arther Ashe in tennis. If he wins, he will be the first black man to win Wimbledon."

John an amateur player himself, chipped in "A friend of mine who visited Europe recently talked of a young Swede by the name Bjon Borg. He said that Borg was a steady player with good temperament. He seems like a match winner, they say." It was John's ambition to watch Wimbledon live one day.

The others nodded, and the Professor suddenly changed the topic, "Sports aside, what I really wanted to know is why so many of you Malayalees are Christians. Both of you are Christians so perhaps you could educate me."

"Let me start if John doesn't mind."

Sebastian, who had read a bit about the origin of Christianity in Kerala was confident of explaining the matter properly. John smiled and asked him to carry on.

"After the death of Christ, while St. Peter and other Apostles travelled to Rome, St. Thomas came to Kerala. He spread Christianity here and later died in Madras. During his stay he spread the new religion. So when Vasco da Gama landed, Christianity in India was already about 1500 years old."

"In that case I suppose in other parts of India, almost all the Christians are converts by the Portuguese or the English, Mr Sebastian?"

"Yes Professor, that is why they are a little westernized in dress and behaviour. But here the Christians are not culturally westernized. We eat meat and drink a little as these are not taboo in Christianity."

"I have also generally noticed that speaking in English is not very common here. But I can deduce the reason from your explanation."

Just then Thomachan brought Pappachan and his lovely bride towards the group and introduced the men to the couple.

After most of the guests had gone, Thomachan called Vasudevan aside and said, "You have done splendid job. You worked hard and made everything move smoothly. Thank you, thank you very much."

"Oh it is nothing. Everyone helped."

"I appreciate your modesty. Some day God will reward you. You are my true son."

Pappachan and Molly were to stay in Puthupady for two days and then travel to Kalpetta to visit Molly's parents.

Elizabeth had been pleading with George to spend time in Kalpetta when his sister and brother-in-law were there but George insisted on leaving the next day. "I can't miss my classes," he said.

"It's just a matter of one week. I'm sure it will not be a problem."

Peter also tried futilely to persuade George to change his mind.

But George was adamant, "No Daddy, please explain to Mummy. I am leaving with Appapan for Calicut just now so that I can take the morning train to Cochin."

Molly was crestfallen, but quickly composed herself and hugged her brother. George bade his family farewell and got into Sebastian's car. As the car drove away Molly thought that whatever her brother's shortcomings were, neglecting studies was definitely not one of them. She felt proud of him.

Vasudevan was busy in the estate when he was joined by Thomachan. "How is your cottage? Is it comfortable?"

"It is fine Appacha."

"Why don't you come to our home for lunch?"

"No. The man you have assigned cleans the house, cooks for me and frankly I am quite happy with the arrangement."

"I am glad to hear that. How is everything here? I have been so busy with this wedding I have not been in touch for some time."

"That is all right Appacha. We are continuing with the rubber tapping. The production has gone up, but the price has dropped."

"Can the fall in the sales of cars be responsible for the lower demand for tyres and therefore the price of rubber?"

"It could be one of the reasons. I wonder if the tyre manufacturers are experimenting with use of synthetic rubber for making tyres. But this price volatility could also be the usual trade fluctuations."

"What about *copra* production?"

"Oh, that is doing perfectly fine. We now supply *copra* to John who is doing pretty well in business. The price of coconut oil is good since quite a lot of it goes towards hair oil production. Have you seen the bottled variety of plain coconut oil available in the city? It has an intense nutty flavour. They heat the *copra* to a high temperature and then expel it. The North Indian market loves the oil, both for hair and massaging purposes. Oddly North Indians don't like the coconut flavour while cooking. They use it only for cosmetic purposes."

"You want to give the processing segment a try?"

"No Appacha. But do you think it is a good idea?"

"Vasu, if you feel it's worth a try, I will definitely support you."

"Maybe we should discuss with John and think of doing something together."

"Good. You think about it and let me know. But what about growing pepper? Your brothers may need it for their factory."

"Not much. They only want immature light berries. Our pepper is too good for their requirement. We must produce the Malabar Garbled type for the grinding industry abroad."

"Well Vasu, you just carry on with your plan. I have full confidence in you and your ideas."

Thomachan turned towards home. Vasu walked with him.

"One of these days you must dine with us. Let Molly settle down first. She will really cheer up our home, like my dear Mariam did."

Chapter 12

"There are two types of oils–Essential oils and Fixed oils," the professor said, to his M.Sc. students in Maharajas College. "Essential oils are used for making essences and hence the name. They are volatile and usually have a fine aroma."

George was one of the eight students listening to him with rapt attention.

The professor's voice reverberated in the classroom, "Fixed oil on the other hand is viscous, non-volatile and without strong aroma. Can anyone give an example of fixed oil?"

A girl replied, "Coconut oil."

"Yes. There are others as well like sesame oil and mustard oil. These are vegetable oils used for cooking. But do you know that there are fixed oils of animal origin? Like ghee, lard and tallow. Such oils are used for cooking. Perhaps tallow was more used in soap making and in the olden days for candle making. Some of the more recently developed oils in India are soyabean oil, palm oil, sun flower seed oil and so on. Have you heard about canola oil?"

None of the students could recall having heard of it. So the teacher continued, "In Canada they modified the rape plant by genetic manipulation to produce oil with low saturated, low molecular fatty acid as the component. So in the name 'canola', 'can' comes from Canada, 'o' stands for oil and 'la' for low acid. Like rape seed oil, you can produce canola oil in large quantities easily. In fact, it is fast on its way to becoming one of the more popular oils."

He paused to ensure that his students had absorbed the information then continued, "Now coming back to essential oil or volatile oil, can someone give an example of the same?"

George raised his hand and said, "Lemon grass oil."

"Yes, you have orange oil, sandalwood oil, eucalyptus oil etc. But unlike fixed oil which is also called fatty oil, essential oil is made only from plants.

"Actually there is one more class of oils, mineral oil which you get from crude oil like petrol, kerosene, paraffin oil etc. But they are not edible and therefore let us not worry about that for now."

The lecture continued for a whole hour. Everyone liked the professor's method of teaching. George was convinced that he had chosen the right subject to study. He wrote a detailed letter to Molly explaining the fine things he was learning. He did not forget to write her name as Mrs. Molly Pappachan. Adding the family name as a surname was not common.

But while the classes were definitely interesting George did not find the hostel suitable so he got himself a comfortable lodge, for which he had asked his father for more money.

Lakshmanan and Ramanathan of Spice Ingredients were busy in discussion with the Senior Manager of a national bank about getting a long range loan for the working capital. After Ramanathan explained the manufacturing process to the manager, Lakshmanan took over the discussion, "You have seen the specialized machinery and the laboratory in our possession. This is because we have faith in the industry."

The Manager spoke, "Yes, all that is okay. But I am going by the financial position of your company."

"Look your bank has reached this height by supporting emerging industries. I can give hundreds of cases where what looked like a venture of uncertain future really took off to make a mark."

"Well, Mr. Lakshmanan, I have no doubt that you will do well, but..."

Lakshmanan then explained how his brother had worked in an English company which now found that it was cheaper to source the products from his company because of lower labour cost here. He then described the performance of the English company for the last five years with balance sheets as proof. Lakshmanan knew the importance of relevant documents and had asked Ramanathan to acquire the copies of the balance sheets from his former company. "But the critical point to be considered is quality of the products produced," Lakshmanan said smiling at the bank manager

"Yes indeed, Mr. Lakshmanan, please explain what you are doing to ensure quality."

"All our processing vessels and equipment are food grade stainless steel. We also have an improved process in place and set up a modern lab. Last week the Technical Manager of the English company was here. He met our team and left satisfied. Here is the letter of approval he mailed us upon returning to England. So there is nothing to fear."

"Who said anything about fear? But I have to make an independent assessment of the situation, don't you think?"

Lakshmanan sighed, before saying, "There's one last thing, Sir, and that is the reliability of the party which runs the industry. You have been funding my father's business for many years now. I myself have had several discussions with you several times."

"Well Mr. Lakshmanan, let me assure you that on that count, the bank has no fear." It looked like the manager was satisfied.

Just then a young woman, the receptionist, carried in a tray holding three cups of coffee and a plate of roasted cashew nuts. The Bank Manager was attracted to the cashews. He relaxed and started eating them between sips of coffee. After refreshing himself, he announced suddenly, "I say, if you can serve such fine cashew nuts and coffee, I am sure that you can produce quality products for export."

There was loud laughter from all. The girl was beaming with pride and said, "Shall I pour some more coffee, Sir?"

"Why not? We have to work together in future. Let us start on a fine note. Mr. Lakshmanan, give me a copy of your customer's balance sheets, letter and other documents. I will present all this to the Board. I can't sanction this large sum on my own, you see."

"But any sensible bank will take your recommendation as you have a reputation for honest assessment."

'Yes rightly so, and no sensible bank can afford to miss an opportunity to lend to a worthy emerging industry,' mused the Bank Manager. With a few more pleasantries exchanged, the Manager left. Lakshmanan and Ramanathan came back and called for more coffee.

"The fish is nibbling!" observed Ramanathan.

"The fish is biting!" Lakshmanan said confidently.

Life on the Kollegal Estate rolled on as usual. The Estate was doing very well under Vasudevan. Pappachan was less and less involved in its running, especially after his marriage.

Although Thomachan tried to be with Vasudevan in the field operations, poor health kept him indoors most of the time. Molly used to accompany him on these outings but after he preferred to stay indoors she continued to spend some time in the field. Vasudevan was always courteous to her and explained the working of each section to her. Molly found such sessions interesting. In her otherwise mundane life, these visits to the Estate's operation centres were exhilarating. But being the mistress of the estate she had to restrict her interactions with outsiders.

A lot of Molly's time was spent preparing food for her father-in-law and taking care of him when he was unwell.

"Why don't you look around the factory first and then we shall talk," Lakshmanan said to the young job aspirant, Mr. George Peter, sitting in front of him. George had completed his M.Sc. with a First Class and as suggested to him, had applied for a job at Spice Ingredients. Lakshmanan had asked George about the course and why he was interested in taking up this job. George had replied, "What I have learned in the course will be useful to this industry"

Ramanathan joined them. "Yes, I know the syllabus is pretty comprehensive," he said.

Lakshmanan then asked him, "So, how do we proceed from here, Ramanathan?"

The decision to employ George had been taken long ago. The interview was a mere formality.

"I think we should take George around the factory till his appointment letter is prepared," Ramanathan said.

"Very good," Lakshmanan replied. "Why don't you take him around the factory and laboratory? I may not be the right person to explain the operations to him."

"Come George, let us go. I will explain everything to you. I want you to understand the practical side of manufacturing. By the end of the tour, you'll have added to your knowledge."

"Thank you, Mr. Ramanathan. I want to learn as much as possible."

George was quite excited to see all the equipment and machinery and was impressed by the clean factory floor and the neat way in which everything was arranged.

"So did you like our factory?" Lakshmanan asked him upon their return.

"I think I will enjoy working here. And I hope to learn much from Ramanathan Sir," George said modestly.

"Where will you stay? We may be able to fix up some accommodation nearby. What do you say Ramanathan?"

His brother agreed.

George immediately replied, "Please don't worry. I have found a good lodging for myself in the city. I will shift there in a few days" time. No problem."

After shaking hands with Lakshmanan and Ramanathan he walked towards the gate, with his head held high. On the way, he failed to respond to the graceful and friendly smile of the girl at the reception.

Around this time most of India was connected by the Subscriber Trunk Dialling service offered by the telephone department. George managed to get the STD code number of Puthupady in

Calicut circle and after a couple of failed attempts got connected to the Kollegal House. The phone rang for a long time before it was picked up.

"Is Molly there?" George asked.

"No, sorry she is outside. Shall I call her?" the voice on the other side replied.

"Sorry to trouble you, this is George Peter, Molly's brother from Cochin. I will call after ten minutes. Can you ask her to wait near the phone?"

Not quite used to long distance calls, the person could not enquire further. As he himself could not go out, he called Kamalam, the middle aged cook to fetch Molly.

Kamalam sent another servant to find Molly. As soon as Molly received the message, she ran back to the house.

Kamalam was outside when Molly walked in.

"It is Mon, Kochamma."

"What Mon, Kamalam?"

"Your brother from Cochin."

"Oh! George?" she said panting, when the telephone started ringing again.

"How are you Molly?" she heard her brother say.

"Wonderful, darling George. How is everything with you, Monae?"

"I am an Assistant Manager in an exporting company."

"Oh I am proud of you. Also you are a post-graduate in a technical subject and an assistant manager. How happy I am! How do you like the job?"

"Great. I get a chance to practise what my Professor preached," he said, laughing at his own expression.

"How is the work? Is it too much of a strain? You must take care of your health," she said.

"I enjoy the work."

After talking to her brother, Molly had a smile on her face.

She felt good inside and went into the kitchen to thank Kamalam.

Molly thought that this was the first time Kamalam had actually answered the phone. Previously she had merely shouted at it saying "There is nobody here," without lifting the hand-set!

"It was your Appachan who took it. He struggled to come to the phone, then talked to your brother and gave me instructions to fetch you."

Molly immediately went into Thomachan's room to thank him, but when she saw his face she was worried.

"What is the matter Appacha?"

"Nothing. I'm not feeling well. My mind is not at peace."

When Pappachan arrived that evening, she told him that Appachan needed to see a doctor.

"We will do something about it," he replied casually.

These days there was very little conversation between Molly and Pappachan. It seemed as if Pappachan was suffering from an extreme level of inferiority complex and a sense of inadequacy. It was even rumoured that he often visited a place near Adivaram, where he drank heavily.

Molly waited for a day and then in an act of defiance asked Vasudevan to take Thomachan to the doctor in Thamarassery.

Vasudevan felt that the small set-up at Thamarassery was inadequate and so he used his contacts in Calicut and arranged for a detailed check up at the Medical College Hospital.

"We may have to admit him for a day. Let us do all the necessary tests, Madam."

"Yes, Mr. Vasudevan."

"What about Mr. Pappachan? Will he not be accompanying us?"

Molly said in a firm voice, "Forget Pappachan."

Vasudevan was surprised for a moment but recovered instantly. However awkward it might be to leave Pappachan out of the plan, there seemed no other option.

"His blood sugar is high and the kidneys are in very poor shape," the doctor told Molly and Vasudevan after the detailed examination.

"Do you have a nurse available there?"

"Yes, it can be arranged," Molly said and looked at Vasu. The doctor continued, "He needs insulin injection as well as some tablets. Let us monitor his condition for a month. If there is no improvement, we may have to start dialysis. You can arrange for the same at the hospital in Thamarassery. I will talk to the doctor."

After that visit Thomachan was completely bed ridden. Pappachan made fleeting appearances during which he listened impatiently to his father's whispers. Pappachan had no time for his family. He remained out a lot. Where he went nobody quite knew.

Soon Molly was by her father-in-law's bedside most of the time. She watched the old nurse closely to see how the injections were given. Around this time Pappachan moved out of their bedroom to the guest room. In a way Molly felt relieved that she was sleeping alone.

Chapter 13

Within a month of joining Spice Ingredients, George came up with some useful recommendations for improving the working of the factory. Ramanathan liked his suggestion to increase the capacity of the cooling system for recycled water that was used in the condensers. Overall the company was doing well as most of their customers from the West were quite impressed by the quality of products coming out of the factory.

Noting the aggressive way Lakshmanan was taking orders and insisting on promptness of dispatch, the Factory Manager was a bit worried.

"Sir, you are taking the orders even before the raw material is procured," he complained one day.

"That is what is necessary. After all, you do know that the raw material will be available once the harvest season begins. So, we should plan accordingly."

"Backward integration even in production. Unless we do things which are ordinarily considered difficult, we cannot stand out from the ordinary," cut in Ramanathan who had entered the room just then.

"Well said Ramanathan," his brother complimented him.

But the Factory Manager seemed unconvinced. "But Sir how can you trust the raw material suppliers so completely? What if they, especially the good ones, desert us for some other buyer who will pay them more?"

"Don't worry about that. Ramanathan and I have a back-up plan, if needed. In any case we will neither take sub-standard produce nor will we pay any extra money."

"But then Sir, how can you get quality raw material in time?"

"Do you know what a business man who has already invested substantial money into his venture fears the most?"

Lakshmanan paused to clear his throat. Then in a firmer tone said, "He wants prompt payment. He will take his margin all right, but more than that he will wish for prompt payment. I have learnt this while working with my father in our contract business. Once the raw material arrives, there will be no delay for payment from our side."

The Factory Manager seemed somewhat relieved. But Lakshmanan did not stop talking, "These operations are like a relay race. Each man has a role to play. The man who runs the last lap should have faith in his colleagues."

In Puthupady Thomachan's condition was not showing any signs of improvement. His kidney function was deteriorating, but the doctors were managing to hold off dialysis with effective medicine. His sugar level was maintained thanks to regular insulin injections. Molly watched and learnt how to give an injection from the nurse whose physical condition, Molly thought to herself, was as bad as Thomachan's kidney.

After feeding Thomachan a little bit of *kanji*, Molly stroked his hair and asked, "How do you feel Appacha?"

"I don't worry about me…"

"Don't worry Appacha, we will all look after Pappachan."

"I am not too much bothered about him either. It is you who I'm worried about."

"Why Appacha, I am fine."

"It's graceful of you to say that. You are a wonderful girl. I cannot ask for anything more."

"Why do you worry about everything? You will be all right."

"No, I know that my kidney will not last long."

"Appacha, I have made a decision. I will donate one of my kidneys if the doctor approves it."

"Don't Molae. Don't even think of it. You are too young and have a long way ahead of you. I think my kidney will hold on."

"You should not think so negatively. We are here to help you."

"All I want is your happiness," Thomachan replied weakly.

When Pappachan returned home that night, Molly told him about his father's worsening condition. "It would be nice if you spend some time with him," she suggested.

As usual, he murmured something and went into his father's room. Seeing him, his father said, "Look Pappacha, I may not last long. All my hope had been in you."

"Yes I know, but what can I do for you now?" There was a note of impatience in Pappachan's voice.

"I am not happy about the way you look after my Molly."

"I give her whatever she asks for. Nobody prevents her from doing anything she likes either. What more do you want?"

"Look my son, it is love she needs. Think well, are you really a good husband to her? You live your own way. Money and material wealth are not enough. What a wife needs is love and companionship."

"Yes Appacha," he made his standard response, and left the room grumpily.

Meanwhile in Ooty, Peter had become the Senior Manager of the tea company. Elizabeth found the cold engulfing the place too uncomfortable for her liking. But she soon discovered that warmth came from many sources, not just from her husband Peter, but also by sipping the tea brewed from the tea leaves made by his Company. She started drinking plenty of hot tea to keep herself warm and had even learnt how to make a good 'cuppa'.

Watching her enjoying her tea one day, Peter asked, "Ever thought about the various qualities of tea?"

"What do you mean Peter?"

"Tea has aroma and body."

"Aroma I get. By body do you mean the strength and bitterness?"

"It is not bitterness. It is astringency."

"What is this astringency?"

"Let me try to explain. When you eat an unripe banana, you get a choking feeling in the throat and a mild feeling of dryness, almost like dehydration in the mouth. This is the real feeling of astringency. When you chew arecanut you get a similar feeling."

She tasted another sip and said, "Yes, now I understand. I do think that keeping the cup open for some time makes the tea lose some of its aroma."

"Yes, aroma is developed immediately after brewing."

"You said the other day that tea is also taken cold with drops of lemon juice?"

"True. Then you get to enjoy the astringency along with the fine flavour of lemon, like a touch of sourness and sweetness mixed together. Aroma is not important in cold tea. In fact Chinese take green tea, warm of course, but there also aroma is not very important."

"Then why do they drink it at all?"

"Many astringent substances are liked by people. In a way it neutralizes any feeling of nausea. Some even prefer it without sugar and milk. But remember, tea has caffeine which is a stimulant and is addictive."

"But Peter, coffee can also offer all these qualities."

"How can you compare tea and coffee?" Peter sighed, thumping his forehead with his hand, and they both had a hearty laugh over it.

Elizabeth added, "Every man for his own child!"

"Not only that. I don't know much about coffee except that I can spell it without using any of the original letters in it, 'kauphy'," Peter said.

A couple of weeks later, he took Elizabeth to the factory. The Production Manager explained to her the importance of each step in tea processing. Finally they entered the tea tasting room. A man was sitting there with a row of funny looking cups in front of him. He was the official tea taster.

Observing the curious look on Elizabeth's face, the Manager started to explain.

"These are special cups, Madam. Observe that porcelain cup without a handle, where you put tea leaf and pour hot water. The quantities and even time of brewing are standardized. The cup has serrations on top. Then the lid is placed on the cup and the tea is poured out into the flatter cup."

"But it has two handles. Is it to compensate the lack of handle for the taller cup?" The tea taster and the manager laughed at her query.

"It is convenient to hold the cup with both hands. See now he is taking the freshly brewed tea into his mouth."

"He is making a lot of noise."

"That is to feel the brew in all parts of the mouth. He is taking it in with a slurp. Now as you can see he is taking it to the sides of his mouth, so that he can make the correct judgement."

"But he is spitting it out."

"He tests over twenty samples a day. He cannot drink all of them. Besides, he has to judge only the organoleptic qualities in tea, and for that it is better that he does not consume the beverage."

"Can I try too?"

The Manager spoke to the man who was doing the tasting. Elizabeth tried many samples with instructions from the expert. He pointed out the salient features of each.

"If you are interested and want to be trained, we can use you as a taster. In fact we need more tasters to evaluate the tea. When the season is at its peak, the load on the present tasters is indeed high. Not only does it delay our work, but sometimes their judgment may get awry."

For some time Elizabeth mulled over the suggestion. "Why not? I would love to do it, but first I must ask Mr. Peter," she replied.

She did not want to cause any inconvenience to her husband. Often junior executives tried to encourage wives of Senior Managers only to gain favour with their bosses. But she felt this particular request was genuine.

Molly took the syringe apart, washed it in boiled water, allowed it to cool and then placed it in a small stainless steel vessel filled with water. She kept the vessel over the stove. She was sterilizing the syringe in Thomachan's room when Vasudevan entered unexpectedly.

"Madam is now a professional nurse," he smiled.

Molly frowned at the way he had addressed her. Thomachan immediately knew that she did not like to be called Madam. "You can call her Molly, Vasu. After all you are my second son," Thomachan said, feeling a strange glow of happiness to be in the company of two of his favourite people.

"Then should I address you as Chechi?"

Molly looked at him and said, "No Chechi either. I have a name."

Thomachan smiled. Instantly Molly also looked at Vasudevan and smiled.

When he saw Molly preparing the insulin injection Thomachan pushed his sleeve up and turned to lie on his side. With expert care Molly inserted the needle into his left upper arm, and emptied the insulin into his body.

"There you are!" she said, gently withdrawing the needle.

Vasudevan watched as Molly removed the needle and washed the set with water. He said, "I understand that disposable syringes are available in the West. They are made of plastic."

"Is it? How do you sterilize them then?" Molly asked, curious.

"They are sterilized in the manufacturing plant by irradiation, after packing in a hermetically sealed pouch. You can open the pouch and straight away use the syringe. No boiling is required."

"How convenient it would be if they were available here!" Thomachan observed, "Actually I am feeling very well now."

"Yes, the insulin and tablets are having their effect on you."

"No Molly. It is due to your care and love. No medicine can replace that!"

Vasudevan joined in with sincere appreciation. "Yes the care Mada,–er, Molly gives is indeed praiseworthy. Kamalam was telling me how well Appachan has been looked after."

"Now Appachan can walk around the house. Maybe he should take a walk outside," Molly suggested, brushing aside the compliments coming her way.

"Yes, Molly, that's a good idea. Vasu, take me to the estate. Being cooped up here is no good. I must get into my garden."

Molly went to the kitchen, to bring a cup of coffee for Vasudevan.

When she came back with coffee and snacks Vasudevan said, "So tomorrow both of you should come to the estate. I want to show you the tender arecanut processing we have begun."

"Oh you have started doing that? It is called '*kali*' something, isn't it?" Molly exclaimed.

"Yes it is *kalipak* or *kali* areca nut."

Just when Vasudevan was about to leave Molly said, "Perhaps you could bring the car, Mr. Vasudevan? We wouldn't want Appachan to walk too much and strain himself on the very first day."

"If you want me to drop 'Madam' why can't you drop 'Mister'?" Vasudevan asked half indignantly

Molly blushed and Thomachan let out a low chuckle.

The next day Vasudevan came with the car. "Good morning Appacha, good morning, mad.. Molly," Vasu said with a smile. Molly laughed and replied, Good morning Mist.. er, Vasu." Thomachan felt happy to see Molly laugh openly. He could feel the carefree happiness inside the young woman. Vasudevan helped both of them sit in the rear seat, after which he got into the passenger seat beside their old driver Govindhan.

"How are you, Govindhan?"

"How are you Muthalali? Are you feeling better? I am sure that our workers will be happy to see you back in the fields."

"I'm good now. What about your health, Govindhan?"

"I am okay, except that I am getting older, Muthalali."

"Aren't we all, Govindhan, aren't we all!" Thomachan said wryly.

After a short drive they reached the arecanut garden. A few workers were as usual dehusking immature arecanuts.

Vasudevan had thoughtfully arranged for a chair for Thomachan to sit on. Then he asked one of the workers to bring a knife. He cut a green nut and said, "These are green or tender areca nuts. They are harvested at six to seven months after fruit-set. For fully ripe nuts you have to leave these on the tree for a further two to three months. At this stage, the outer husk turns dark green. You see, the inside is so soft that a finger nail can easily be driven into it."

He then cut a small piece of the fruit and gave it to Molly. She chewed it for an few seconds and exclaimed.

"Oh my God! This is strong stuff! It's making me feel strange."

"Yes, Molly. The polyphenols are at the highest concentration during this stage of harvest. Besides there is a very low level of an alkaloid called arecolin. It acts on the central nervous system."

He then took a small piece of processed arecanut and said, "Now chew this."

Molly chewed it, "Yes this is mild. I can see the difference."

"Now what happened here is that processing the fruit helped tone down its strength."

Both Thomachan and Molly were listening with full attention as Vasu proceeded,

"The first step is dehusking. The whole tender inner kernel which is like a ball is first extracted and then cut into various shapes, depending on the market preference. Both longitudinal and transverse cuts are employed to get the right variety. Today we are making a popular variety called *choor*. This is made by longitudinal cuts alone. Depending upon the thickness of the longitudinal cuts, there are further sub-divisions. The next step is boiling the cut pieces. There you can see water being boiled in a copper vessel. Now they are putting the pieces into the water. They continue the boiling until some polyphenols in the nuts get extracted into the water. Then the boiled pieces are ladled out, as you can see there. The pieces are kept for about half-an-hour to cool. The same water is used for boiling three to four batches of sliced nuts."

"Why can't they use fresh water each time?" asked Molly.

"That is to get the extract sufficiently enriched as you will understand in the next step which is the *kali*-making. The enriched but still thin extract is concentrated by boiling it for a long duration in a flat metal vessel kept over open fire."

"How much more?"

"The extract is"—Vasudevan had to stop as a worker came and caught his attention. There was a brief conversation between them.

Molly's thoughts went back to her childhood days. Her little brother, George had in his mischievous ways, tasted a liquid in a bottle which had looked like the extract of arecanut that was now being made. It happened to be some Ayurvedic medicine which was very bitter. George had spat it out and was jumping about screamimg and crying. The scene was quite comical. Molly had laughed heartily then and even now the memory brought a smile to her lips.

"What was I saying?" asked Vasu looking at Molly.

"Umm? What?" she asked, still thinking of George.

"Yes. The extract is concentrated nearly ten-fold. It first assumes the colour and thickness of honey and on further heating becomes thick, almost a pasty liquid which turns progressively darker; a sort of glossy dark brown colour."

Molly went near the concentrated extract and took a few drops on her finger. She showed this to Thomachan, who asked Vasu,

"What is the advantage of doing this?"

"You will understand in the next step, Appacha."

Saying so, he instructed a worker to start the *kali*-coating. They put a basket of boiled and nearly cooled cut arecanut slices into a wooden vessel shaped like a small boat. Then a worker took some thick *kali* with a ladle made of coconut shell and poured it over the cut pieces, after which he spread the *kali* thoroughly in a sideways sweeping action, until the nuts were coated with them.

Resuming his explanation, Vasudevan said, "Now you can see a dark coating over the pieces. The next step is drying after which the surface will get a glossy dark coating. This is *kalipak*. There is a huge market for this in South India."

Thomachan had a last question, "When you chew the *paan* then, why does it stain your mouth red?"

"There's no sure answer for that one. But I reckon it has to do with the oxidation of polyphenols of arecanut in the alkaline condition brought about by slaked lime. There is also the formation of compounds called quinones and further secondary products which are red."

"Betel leaf has no role?"

"No, betel leaf only gives the fine flavour, mainly from the essential oil in the fresh leaf."

Molly looked at her father-in-law and said, "I think we are good for the day. Let's return home."

Chapter 14

"Next week I am leaving for Bangalore for some Company work. Are you interested in joining me?" Peter who had just finished his tea, called out to his wife. Elizabeth came in from the kitchen but did not say anything.

Peter said, "I will be going in the Company car with the driver. If you join me we can stay with your sister Celina and Rajan for a day."

As soon as she heard this, she immediately showed interest.

"Yes, I will come. How many days will the trip be?"

"I have a meeting scheduled for next Monday. I can take an additional day off and we could go sightseeing."

"In that case, why don't we leave early morning on Sunday, immediately after Mass. We can spend a day at Mysore. You will enjoy seeing the Mysore Palace and Brindavan Gardens. We could then halt there and start early for Bangalore on Monday."

"Okay, then let us skip the Mass and start at 6 am on Sunday," Peter suggested. He was not a deeply religious man. In fact Peter had little real faith. He followed the holy obligations like going to Church and community prayer, only to be accepted by society. His suggestion found favour with Elizabeth, although she was reluctant to skip the Mass.

"Now we have installed a brand new sprinkler cooler system for condenser water," Ramanathan said, during an official discussion with George.

He replied, "Yes I noticed that. In fact in a day or two we should be able to connect this cool water to our condensers."

"But what is it that you are doing to the receiver set?"

"Ah, that? Mr. Ramanathan, right now we are having only two compartments for siphoning off condensed water. I would like to put an additional compartment."

"Why, do you suspect any leakage of oil?"

"I don't know. There is a possibility of droplets getting mechanically entrained. Anyway let us put this modification everywhere."

"Very good, George. I appreciate your enthusiasm to try out something new."

George was happy that his efforts were being appreciated, but more than that he was pleased that the Company gave him adequate freedom to pursue his ideas.

Mohamedikka had been the Head Clerk at the Kollegal estate for a long time and was close to Thomachan. Very often Thomachan used to take his advice on matters relating to the functioning of the property.

Keeping this familiarity in mind, Mohamedikka arrived at Kollegal House one day to meet Thomachan. "How are you Mohamedikka? Is life good?"

"Good Muthalali. We all wish that you could come to the office and spend some time with us."

"Is Pappachan not coming there?"

"Yes, yes, he does. He comes and spends some time with Majeed. He does not give us any guidance."

"But you are all very experienced. You do not need any guidance. I cannot move about like before." After a pause Thomachan added, "Is there something on your mind that you wish to tell me about?"

"Nothing Muthalali, except that Majeed has too much work. Handling both the accounts and cash section is tiring for him. Could you not hire a new person to handle cash?"

Thomachan sensed something fishy about that request.

"Okay, I will do something about it, Mohamedikka."

Thomachan called Vasudevan and recounted the conversation he had with the Head Clerk.

"See if anything can be done about it," he told Vasudevan.

At six on Sunday morning, Elizabeth and Peter began their journey to Bangalore via Mysore. It was very cold at that time in Ooty. By noon they reached Mysore city. They took a room in a vegetarian hotel situated in the centre of the city, enjoying the vegetarian lunch on offer. They relished the sweet, *Jilebi.*

"It is indeed nice to have a sweet at the end of the meal. But it is unusual for an ordinary vegetarian meal!"

"People here enjoy sweets, not like us who want only meat and more meat. Come let us go see the Mysore Palace."

When they reached the Palace, Peter invited the driver to join them. But he declined the offer, having seen the Palace many times before. He preferred to rest before resuming their journey.

"Mysore is a city of palaces, but this one is the real Palace. It is a good tourist attraction," their guide explained earnestly, as Elizabeth listened with childlike interest.

"The construction was started in 1897 and completed in 1912. A British architect, Henry Irwin was assigned the job. It is a three storied grey granite structure with a pink marble dome and five storeyed tower."

He continued to give various details. When they entered one of the rooms, he said, "See, these doors have been recovered from the old palace which was partly destroyed by fire. This door is made of pure silver and other one of ivory.

Turning away from the doors, he said, "Every year, the festival of Dasara is celebrated in either September or October. On the tenth day of the festival, known as *Vijaya Dashami*, a parade of caparisoned elephants and decorated floats starts from the Palace grounds."

He continued, "Today being Sunday, the entire Palace will be illuminated at night. It is indeed a spectacular sight with 96,000 lights enveloping the Palace compound. Don't miss it."

"Can we see the trophy room?" Peter asked. He wanted to show the stuffed animals that erstwhile rulers had hunted. The guide took them to the trophy room where antlers and heads of many animals,—nilgais, bisons, deers,—were mounted on the walls. There was a magnificent tiger occupying the prime spot.

Elizabeth and Peter were very impressed by the taxidermist and the Palace management who had done an excellent job in preserving these trophies.

“Let us go back to the hotel and rest for a while before we proceed with our trip,” Peter said.

"Are we going to see the Brindavan Gardens also?" Elizabeth asked.

“Of course! I have seen it once, but I don’t mind going once again, especially in the company of my most beautiful wife.”

“Oh! You con man!”

The drive to Brindavan Gardens took about forty five minutes. Being Sunday there was a big crowd. There was still some time left for darkness to fall, after which the garden lights would be switched on. But even without lights, the garden was captivating, dotted with fountains, terraced gardens and manicured hedges.

“This is a garden built in the Mughal style. Its design is similar to that of Shalimar Gardens near Srinagar in Kashmir,” Peter explained. Elizabeth interrupted him, “Is it not based on a French Garden?”

“No it was based on the Mughal gardens. During those times there was no electricity for lighting. Perhaps you are talking about the introduction of the lighting, when you say French.”

A little later the lights were switched on, transforming the place into a dreamland. The lights added colour to the water flowing out of the fountains and the play of colours in the water was creating a magical world of its own.

“Now you see why I made that comment earlier? This is a place for romance. Many movies were shot here.”

“An ideal place for honeymooners,” Elizabeth replied dreamily.

“But come, let us rush back to see the Palace illumination.”

As they neared the city, heavy traffic slowed them down. They finally managed to reach the Palace.

“It is indeed a wonderful sight,” Elizabeth remarked as she stood amidst the large crowd gathered there.

"See how uniformly the lighting is done. Even the glow is harmonised. And the lights are all white. No coloured lights."

"Mysore is indeed a fine place. Why don't you get a job here, Peter?"

"Unfortunately Elizabeth, there are no tea plantations here. These people are all connoisseurs of coffee."

The next morning, again at six, they packed their bags and left for Bangalore. After nearly an hour, they passed Mandya. Peter pointed to the factory on the left and said, "This is the Mysore Sugar Mills. The dam, below which the Brindavan Gardens is located, has a canal that runs to this town Mandya. This has enabled farmers to grow sugarcane in this region. The canal is named after the great engineer-statesman, Sir M. Visvesvaraya. This factory was built to process the sugar canes grown here."

In another twenty minutes they reached the small town of Maddur. Peter said to the driver, "Let us stop near that hotel. We will have breakfast there. It is famous for Maddur vade."

"What's that?" asked Elizabeth curiously.

"Wait and see."

When a plate full of large flat discs appeared, Peter told his wife that it was a deep fried delicacy made out of rice flour, semolina, refined flour or *maida*, chopped onion, curry leaves, coconut gratings and a pinch of asafoetida."You mean the asafoetida we put in *sambar*?"

"Yes. You know what the British call it? Devil's dung. They find the flavour distasteful. Try one Elizabeth. Do you like it?"

"It is not bad, but this *vada*—"

"Maybe it is an acquired taste. They call it *vade* here, and not *vada* as we say."

Afterwards Peter asked the waiter to bring him two bananas from the bunch hanging at the entrance. He gave one to Elizabeth and said, "This is the Nanjangud *Rasa bale*. Special to this area only. Try it?"

"It's really sweet, Peter. What is that name again?"

"Remember we passed the small town of Nanjangud before hitting Mysore yesterday. This banana variety originated there. *Rasa bale* means sweet banana."

"Can I have one more. Take one for the driver too."

By nine thirty in the morning, they reached Bangalore and drove straight to Celina's house. Her husband Dr. Rajan had already left for his clinic. After a cup of coffee Peter went for his meeting, promising to send back the car for Elizabeth.

Celina and Elizabeth went shopping for some Mysore silk saris. The better looking ones were too expensive so she settled for three moderately priced saris, one for Molly, one for her sister and one for herself. But there were women who were buying several really heavy saris without any hesitation.

"Let us go to this popular restaurant where they serve really delicious *masala dosa* for lunch," Celina suggested.

"It is very nice and crispy!" Elizabeth observed, as she took a bite. "Try coffee here. It is also good," Celina told her.

"You mean it is better than tea?"

"Tea? The only good thing about tea is that it supports my sister's family."

"What do you mean?" Elizabeth retorted indignantly.

"I was only teasing you, Elizabeth. But really, coffee here is very good. They make decoction coffee with pure coffee powder and fresh milk."

When Peter returned at night after his official dinner, he said, "I called Molly using the STD facility available in our office."

Elizabeth's eyes lit up, "How is she?"

"She is fine. But Thomachan is not feeling well again. He has some kidney problems. Nothing much to worry, she says. But who knows?"

"Did you talk to Pappachan?"

"He was not there, as usual. He is a gone case. Poor Molly!"

Everybody became silent for some time. Then both the couples moved to their respective bedrooms.

The next morning, the men went to work and the women spent the time cooking and chatting. Celina's daughter, Malini and her husband were coming over for dinner.

Elizabeth enquired, "How is Vijay doing? When is he coming?"

"Oh, he is doing well. He gets a good salary but his company in the Gulf is not giving him leave now. Let us hope they let him come by the end of the year."

Around four o'clock in the evening, Rajan, Celina, Peter and Elizabeth went for a walk in Lal Bagh, Bangalore's famous Botanical garden. "It has many trees that are over a hundred years old and even has a glass house," Rajan told them as they walked towards it.

By five thirty they were tired and in need of refreshment, so Rajan took them to the famous Mavalli Tiffin Room. "This place is known for good South Indian vegetarian food," he explained.

Elizabeth was impressed by its clean interiors, table, and dishes. Rajan continued, "MTR as it is popularly known was started by two brothers who hailed from the Udupi region. When one of the brothers went to Europe he was impressed with the hygiene and orderliness of hotels there. He introduced that concept here. In fact the management encourages patrons to peep into the kitchen. In some way, I think that this restaurant can be considered the world's first fast food joint."

Celina reminded them that a big spread awaited them for dinner so they restricted themselves to only light snacks.

While they were waiting for Malini and her husband to arrive, Elizabeth mentioned the conversation she had had with Malini long ago, how she had described their big house in Bangalore and said that everyone had separate rooms except her poor mother who was forced to sleep in her father's room. Celina smiled and said, "Oh, when she was a child, Malini had many interesting stories like that."

"Tell me."

"One day I cut some mangoes for some guests and gave them fruit picks with two pins to pick the pieces from the plate. I gave some pieces in small plates to the kids also. Vijay went to kitchen and took a fork instead of a fruit pick. I gave a fruit pick to Malini. Just because her brother had a fork, Malini was unhappy with only a small fruit pick. Then you know what she did?"

"What?"

"She threw away the fruit-pick with two prongs saying that she does not want a 'twok', but a 'fourk' just like the one Vijay had!"

Elizabeth had a good laugh and said, "We really miss the kids."

Just then Malini and her husband arrived. Elizabeth embraced her niece and said, "Who is this lovely lady? You have put on some weight, but still look beautiful."

Malini blushed and then said, "How are you aunty? Why don't you come to our house for dinner tomorrow?"

"I would have loved to Molae, but we are leaving in the morning."

Then turning to Malini's husband Elizabeth said, "Why don't you plan a weekend in Ooty? You two would love it."

"That is quite a nice idea, isn't it Malini?"

Chapter 15

George knocked on the door of Lakshmanan, his MD's cabin and went in. "Next week is Onam. Can I take a holiday on Friday, so that I can make a four day trip to Ooty?" he asked without any preamble.

"Why do you want to go to Ooty? Actually I wanted to invite you to my home for Onam *sadya*."

"Thank you Sir, but I have to visit my parents who live there."

"Oh. In that case I'll just hand you an Onam gift from the Company's side before you leave then. Go enjoy your holidays."

"Thank you, Sir."

The next day George went shopping. He knew a place which sold expensive imported items.

On Thursday evening he took the train to Coimbatore for the onward journey to Ooty. He had written to his father about his arrival. Peter had offered to receive him, but George had said no to that. "Daddy, I want to try this Nilgiri Mountain Railway. I am not too sure about its timing and other details. Just tell Mummy that I will be there for lunch on Friday. Tell her to reserve vegetarian food only for Onam day."

Peter had laughed hearing his son's demand.

When the door bell rang at around 1.30 pm, Elizabeth opened the front door.

George had arrived. He dropped the suitcase and bag and embraced his mother warmly.

"George, how are you my son? It's been so long. How was your journey?"

"Very well, Mummy."

Just then Peter came out from his room. After greeting his father, George opened his suitcase and took out the gifts he had brought. “A gorgeous sari for you, the most beautiful woman in the world.”

“Oh George this is too beautiful. I am getting old. You should have given this to Molly.”

“Molly will get one later. And for my dear Daddy a nice watch,” saying so, he opened the small box and took out a Seiko watch.

“Thank you George.”

Elizabeth said, “We were waiting for you. Come, let’s have lunch.”

Peter intervened, “How about a drink first?”

“Yes, why not. Mummy, see Daddy knows your place is a bit cold for a visitor from the tropical coast.”

When Peter left for office, George took a long siesta When he woke up, Elizabeth called him for tea.

Thinking about his choice of beverage, he replied, “Fine, let it be tea. When in Rome do as the Romans do, they say. After all it is our bread and butter.”

“Not like that, Monae. Tea is really great. But don’t be like a Roman when we visit you. We don’t want your pepper extract,” she said with a wink.

She put some cakes and *vada* on a quarter plate and a cup of hot tea in front of him.

“After this, George, have a nice hot bath. By then Daddy will be home.”

When Peter returned, Elizabeth and George joined him on the comfortable sofa in the drawing room. Peter asked, “So how was your adventure?”

“Daddy, it was great. I came to Mettupalayam via Coimbatore by train. There I changed over to the Nilgiri Mountain train. It’s a wonderful journey, taking one back through pages of history, right into the lap of James Watt, the inventor of the steam engine, I’d say. Have you ever taken this train?”

“No George. We should go in it once, Elizabeth.”

“Tell us about this train. Some people want to propose to UNESCO to include in their list of World Heritage Sites.”

“Do you know it’s only about 28 or 29 miles long but the journey to Ooty takes almost five hours. I think in the Moscow Olympics, the winner of the marathon covered a slightly shorter distance in a little over two hours. But why does it take so long?"

"From Mettupalayam which is at 1000 feet above sea level , the train suddenly climbs to over 7000 feet at Ooty. The ascent slows down the train. The return journey takes only about three and a half hours."

Peter bit into another *vada*. "So it is not the gradient alone?"

"Think of over 200 curves, 16 tunnels and 250 bridges. But the gradient also cannot be ignored. I understand that this line has the steepest gradient in Asia!"

Elizabeth was quite amazed and asked, "Will it not slip out of control?"

"A good question, Mummy. They always put the engine at the lower end. That is, during the trip uphill, it is the last compartment. While coming downhill, it is placed in the front. That way they can stabilise the train's movement, it appears."

George picked a *vada* and started eating. He added, "In the steeper areas, I noticed that a toothed central wheel in the engine fits into a toothed track in the middle so that the system functions as a rack and pinion arrangement for better grip and pull."

The couple listened to their son's story in wonder. By that time the sun had set and darkness soon descended. George felt a bit cold and seeing him begin to shiver, Elizabeth went in to get him a full sleeved sweater. But George had already put on a stylish and expensive looking woollen pullover which he had brought with him.

The next day the three of them visited the Botanical Gardens. It was a beautifully maintained garden. They walked through the lawns, adorned with attractive flowers and happy families.

As soon as they entered through the Heritage Gate Building, George felt exhilarated on being close to nature.

Peter who had visited the garden several times earlier explained, "This was a land where vegetables used to be grown. It was in 1847 that the garden was laid in a 55 acre plot."

As they walked across the lush lawns, Peter pointed out the Monkey Puzzle Tree, "It is believed that monkeys cannot climb this tree."

George asked, "And why is that?"

"As you can see, there are spirally arranged stiff leaves with rigid needles at the edges and tip. I guess that's an indication of the challenges that the monkeys trying to climb may face. Look there, that is a fossilized tree trunk believed to be 20 million years old."

When they went past the rose garden, Elizabeth stood fascinated by the flowers. She was about to reach out for one of the blooms when Peter warned her, "Please note that there is a Rs. 100 fine for plucking a flower."

"Oh no," she said withdrawing her hand, "That is too expensive a price for an ordinary flower. Perhaps George may not find it so expensive!"

Peter laughed and said, "So finally your Mummy has made a dig at you! Have you noticed, son, it means that you throw away money needlessly."

George kept quiet. They walked by the Italian garden and entered the glass house. There were plants with flowers laid out in earthen pots.

Peter told Elizabeth, "You should come during the summer festival in the month of May. They conduct a flower show then."

After lunch, George urged his parents to accompany him to the races, which they reluctantly did. Since he declared his intention of placing bets, Peter pointed out the booths to him.

"No Daddy. Those booths are for smaller denominations. I must get to a bookie with whom I can place a larger amount."

At the end of the day George had lost more than he won. Elizabeth remarked, "He narrowly missed it seems. He has no luck!"

"Look Elizabeth, all this infrastructure and club have been built by the money of punters. In the long run everyone except them will lose. But people are stupid and will never realize that. They are waiting to be fleeced, dear."

On their drive back home, Elizabeth said, "Tomorrow George, we are going to the Malayalee Association for Onam celebration and lunch."

"Oh Mummy, even on a Sunday vegetarian food!"

"Onam *sadya* has to be traditional vegetarian. You will like it."

"I guess I will survive one meal."

"There will be young Kerala women performing the traditional *Thiruvathira kali* dance. You'll find many beauties for your eyes to feast on."

"Who is more beautiful than my Mummy?" George said, putting his hands around the neck of his mother who sat in the front seat.

Thomachan was feeling a lot better. He sent word to Vasudevan to see him right away.

"So, what is the problem in the office?" he asked Vasu, as soon as the young man stepped in.

Vasudevan was flabbergasted by the question. In fact it was precisely for this that Vasudevan also wanted to meet him.

"I think our Accountant- cum-Cashier is siphoning off money."

"Well Vasu, that was clear from the words of Mohamedikka. But I want to know the details."

"When he gives money to truck drivers or for any purchases, he enters a larger amount in the register and pockets the difference."

Thomachan and Vasu discussed how much money they might have lost like this until now.

"So what are you planning to do?" Thomachan asked.

"I may have to sack Majeed, but…"

"But what..? Just sack him."

"We have to tread carefully, Appacha."

"I know Vasu what is in your mind. Pappachan is involved, right?"

Vasudevan was taken aback. Thomachan did not stop there, "Please sack the clerk. Make suitable arrangements for a replacement after talking to the Head Clerk. There are times when we have to be bold and direct. Please ask Mohamedikka to see me"

Later when Mohamedikka arrived, Thomachan had a long talk with him, mostly about Pappachan and his regular visits to an old man who used to practice Ayurveda and who was considered an expert in massage. Thomachan did not mind the visits. In his younger days, he himself used to go there for rejuvenation. But he doubted whether his son was telling the truth.

"I want to know where else Pappachan goes. You can take the help of Prabhakaran, my old friend's son. He is a very reliable man. Can you do that?"

The Head Clerk was quite confused and upset. It seemed like a clear case of father against son. He did not say anything. But Thomachan continued unmoved by his expression, "You do it discreetly. This can't continue unchecked. When you are pursuing the truth why should you fear? Even Jesus Christ or Prophet Mohammed will surely stand with us. Go ahead, let us get to the bottom of the matter."

George Peter was a hard working man. The management had already promoted him to the position of Manager. In fact Ramanathan had suggested promoting him to the post of Senior Manager but Lakshmanan had vetoed the suggestion. "Let's wait for a year or so. The present promotion is enough to motivate him for now. If he continues the good work we will promote him to the senior position. That is one way to ensure a continually sustained interest. Don't you agree?"

"There is some sense in that, Lakshmanan."

George rushed to the driving school where he was taking driving lessons straight after he finished work. He had already booked the latest model of the Ambassador car. It was a heavy, unwieldy, old-fashioned car, but was the best available in the market. He told the driving school instructor and owner, "Let us get through it quickly today. I am expecting the car next week."

"Practise another two weeks and then we will schedule the test."

"No date earlier?"

"Well, we could schedule it for next week. But then you need some more driving practice in that case."

"I will pass. Not to worry, I will even take some extra lessons. Don't worry about payment. I will pay you extra, so that you don't lose any additional money."

George had cultivated a friendship with the Circle Inspector of the local Police Station, Vinod Thomas. Since George had a nice house and was a bachelor, the C.I. found it quite convenient to have his drinking sessions there. Being a police officer, he could not be seen drinking in a bar or restaurant. George was not a heavy drinker but he knew that a friendship with the local C.I. could be useful later. Deciding to use his contact now, he rang up the officer. "I would like to have my driving test scheduled for next week, Mr. Thomas. I'm planning to take some extra driving classes this weekend. Can you call the Regional Transport Officer and arrange for the same?"

"Oh, don't worry about extra classes. I will talk to the R.T.O. You can consider yourself passed. You will get your driving licence next week. And we will meet in your house this week-end."

George felt relieved and put the receiver down. But he still wanted to perfect his driving and urged the instructor to take extra classes for him.

The Head Clerk Mohamedikka moved very silently and peeped into Thomachan's room. He found the patriarch taking a nap. Just then Molly came with the syringe to give him his injection. Thomachan was a light sleeper and the sound of Molly entering his room was enough to wake him up. He immediately saw the Head Clerk standing outside.

"Just wait a minute. Let Molly give the injection."

When it was done, he said, "Molae, ask Mohamedikka to come in and close the door."

Thomachan sat up in his chair, as Mohamedikka stood facing him.

"From your tortured look, I can guess that you have the information I was expecting."

Mohamedikka was confused. What was Thomachan expecting, good or bad news?

"Now come on, tell me."

Mohamedikka looked left and right and then peered at the closed door for a moment before saying, "The old man is not practising Ayurveda or massaging any more. He is too old for all that."

"So where is Pappachan going then?" Thomachan asked without any hint of anxiety in his voice.

Mohamedikka stood there not knowing what to say. Then realising that he had nothing to lose, spoke with greater freedom, "Prabhakaran says that if you go a little further there is a small lane. In it there is a tiny cottage, in which lives a woman."

"Is she living alone?"

"Yes, er-no. Most of the time she is alone, her husband is a jawan in the army. He is posted in far away Kashmir."

"Go on."

"Prabhakaran found that Pappachan visits her frequently. He was introduced to her by her distant relative who works on our Estate."

"Does this woman work anywhere?"

"No. Hers is a small land surrounded by coconut trees. She has no children and it appears that she ran away from her house somewhere in the South and settled here with her husband. Theirs was a love marriage. Once a year he comes home from the border where he is posted."

"Tell me openly. Is Pappachan having an affair with her?"

"That is what Prabhakaran said, Muthalali."

"Is he certain?"

"I am afraid so. Prabhakaran has no doubt about it. He even peeped into the house one day."

Thomachan cringed upon hearing this, but composing himself, said, "Then don't tell this to anyone. Tell Prabhakaran also to keep mum. Let me think about it for a day."

Mohamedikka turned slowly, opened the door and left for his work place.

That night Thomachan slept very late. His mind was not at rest. However after midnight he slept deeply until seven in the morning.

So that is it, he reflected sombrely, the minute he woke up. He had been certain that his son had no physical relationship with Molly. But it had surprised him for long, since he knew that

Pappachan had a strong sexual urge. He had read somewhere that extreme inferiority complex and intense feeling of mental inadequacy often played havoc in the sexual lives of men who were basically timid.

No point in inaction now, thought Thomachan. The way out is the way through. If one is gone, let it not contaminate another; that is the way you deal with plantation crops, he began to philosophise his thoughts.

"Something worrying you, Appacha?" Molly asked when she brought him his breakfast that morning.

Thomachan sported a smile with great difficulty and said, "Today I will come to the dining room and have *kanji* with you."

His cheerfulness was infectious. Molly also felt light at heart and asked Kamalam to arrange breakfast for them. Pappachan joined them for breakfast. He made a show of eating and left quickly.

"Molae, can you send word to Vasu that we are coming out there. Probably he is doing something new." Molly nodded and went in to give instructions to the servant.

In an hour, Vasudevan himself came to pick up Thomachan, who had changed into a crisply starched *mundu* and shirt. Then he looked at Molly and said, "What are you simply standing there for? You too come with me Molae. Come quickly, get dressed."

Thomachan sat in the passenger seat, while Vasudevan drove the car. Molly sat behind. She had not seen Thomachan so carefree and jovial for quite some time now. Perhaps he had recovered fully. Going out into the plantation was something she always looked forward to. With her father-in-law in such a relaxed mood, it made the day even more enjoyable.

Meanwhile, in Cochin, Karunakaran Muthalali paced about his room full of tension. He had planned to complete the concreting of a culvert that morning, but the key supervisor had fallen ill at the last minute. Ravindran meanwhile had gone to the Executive Engineer's office to get some bills passed for an earlier work. He also had to give some money to the Executive Engineer as he had been most helpful to their business.

It was a common saying among contractors that in a tight situation, even if it was difficult for God to find a solution, the Executive Engineer would never let go one's hand! But in order to get the smooth support of the official, proper greasing was a must.

While Karunakaran thus contemplated an alternate option for the morning work, Janaki Amma made matters worse by acting all grumpy. Perhaps it was a kind of restlessness caused by her asthma problem. It was at this juncture that Vasudevan entered, with no intimation of his arrival. The sight of their youngest son lifted the couple's mood. It had been some time since Vasu had visited them and Janaki Amma was quite happy to see him. She lifted herself off the bed and exclaimed, "How are you my dear son? Are you getting good food? You are being looked after properly?"

Seeing his wife getting up and hurrying to prepare breakfast for Vasu, Karunakaran teased her, "So all your illness has disappeared now, huh?"

When Vasudevan finished breakfast, his mother raised the subject of marriage, "We want you to get married. I have seen a few girls, but somehow none of them seem to suit your personality."

Karunakaran intervened, "What will you do once Vasu also gets married? Your grandchildren are too young."

"Oh don't be silly. Don't joke while discussing serious matters."

Karunakaran then toned down his sarcasm and added, "Yes, Vasu we want to see you married. Don't you agree?"

"Yes," was all that he replied. It was neither a warm consent nor an outright rejection of the proposal. Perhaps he himself was in doubt whether the time was right to get married. Watching his face, Janaki Amma said, "We really got a fine case, a girl ideal for you. Good looking, educated and from a nice family, but the *jathakam* did not match."

Karunakaran remembered that case with a smile, but put on a serious face. The matter was that the girl's *jathakam,* her horoscope, had warned of the early death of her mother-in-law if she were married to Vasu. Although he had limited faith in astrology, Karunakaran was well aware that marriage should not directly or indirectly be held responsible for someone from the family coming in harm's way. He then asked his son, "What made you come here now?"

"Oh I wanted to enquire about some farm equipments, especially a few high quality water pumps and also a tractor."

"I understand that you have been provided living quarters. Is it convenient for a family?"

"Yes, very much."

Janaki Amma noted that with much satisfaction.

Chapter 16

Thomachan, it seemed had rewound his passing years. He was looking healthier and walking with greater confidence now. One day, he asked Molly to invite her parents to stay for a few days at the estate.

Molly raised an eyebrow unsure whether he really meant it.

But Thomachan had made up his mind, "There's no question of uncertainty. I want your parents Peter and Elizerbeth, both to come and spend some time here. They will enjoy their stay. Call them and connect me to them."

Molly was quite happy. She dialled home, and it was her mother who answered. She passed the phone to Thomachan who invited them very cordially and persuasively before handing over the receiver to Molly.

"Mummy, you must come here. Tell Daddy also that I expect him to be here soon."

"Oh Molly I am sure your father will agree to come. How can he refuse when his darling daughter asks him?" Molly laughed.

Thomachan noticed with great satisfaction the glow which had spread over Molly's face. He said, "Call your younger brother also."

"George, yes, how can I forget him," she said, and immediately dialled his number. She realised that Thomachan was doing all he could to bring her cheer. He was truly like a father to her, she thought.

Next Friday, a little before nine at night, Peter and Elizabeth arrived at the imposing house of the Kollegal family. They found Molly waiting for them at the front door.

After a very effusive welcome, all of them moved inside and made themselves comfortable. Soon after Thomachan walked into the room.

"How was your journey?" he asked them, "It must have been a very long drive?"

"Not so much. The roads are better now."

"Molly, see that they can have a refreshing bath."

"I would like that very much. I am feeling a little nauseous after the trip. I think I'll eat something after freshening up and then head off to bed early."

"Ha, right. I would like to see mother and daughter going to sleep early without a night long tete-a-tete, meeting as they are after so many days," Peter said to nobody in particular.

Thomachan laughed, "Peter, that is what life is all about. Do you want them to be like two hermits, instead? Molly, is the food ready?"

"Yes Appacha. Hot water for bath is ready and in a few minutes dinner will be too."

"Very good, Molly. While your Mummy is having bath, I will give company to Peter although I cannot drink."

Pappachan appeared at the dining table towards the end of the meal. He did not eat much.

After dinner, Peter slept in the guest room while Elizabeth slept with Molly.

When Elizabeth entered the kitchen the next morning she exclaimed, "I can smell *appam* and coconut milk, Molly. Daddy's favourite!"

"Also *puttu* and boiled *nenthran* banana, your favourite, Mummy."

The two dishes, the non-fried *appam,* and the steamed *puttu,* hold a special place in the Malayalee's breakfast plate.

Thomachan took his seat at the head of the table. He did not eat much but participated in the lively conversation during breakfast. Pappachan was present but mostly quiet.

"When is George coming, Molae?" Peter asked, helping himself to one more *appam.*

"I really don't know, Daddy. He said that he had asked for two or three days' leave. I'm expecting him to reach sometime today. God knows how he is coming, if at all he comes!"

Just as they finished their breakfast, Vasudevan arrived. Molly excused herself from the planned field trip citing lunch preparations as the reason. So Vasudevan took Peter and Elizabeth as well as Pappachan for a drive around the plantation.

By the time they returned Molly had arranged lunch in the dining room. They all sat down and were about to start when George walked in, smiling profusely, "Hi, can I also join in the big lunch? You being the mistress of this great house, I have to get your consent first," he said to Molly, who had let out a shriek of joy and jumped up to embrace her little brother,

"*Poda*, since when have I grown so big that you need to take permission to come here and receive my hospitality?"

"Well said Molly. Why don't you visit your sister more often, George?" Thomachan said, smiling at George. Immediately George came to Thomachan and shook his hands with great respect. He then embraced his mother and greeted his father. Then he turned to Pappachan and said, "How are you, Aliya? I have brought a present for you."

So saying he took out a beautiful Citizen watch from his bag, after which he presented an expensive silk saree to Molly. The three older people smiled warmly at the joy and affection displayed by the younger generation. Then George laughingly said, "The rest of the presents can wait. Why don't we start eating, Molly? I am starving and can eat an entire elephant right now."

"Then let us start. I haven't got elephant meat, but almost all others," she said dryly, with a twitch of her nose.

After lunch they again left for the fields where Vasudevan was waiting to show them the estate's various other agricultural operations. The workers were engaged in clearing grass around pepper plants and putting in manure. In the arecanut field workers were removing the old and damaged leaves as well as harvesting the bunches of nuts that were ripe for plucking. There was a lot of activity going on everywhere. Many a time Vasudevan was interrupted by a supervisor for some instructions or advice. Earlier Pappachan had excused himself and slipped away from the group. Thomachan felt embarrassed by his son's behaviour, but not wanting to make an issue out of it, sent the family away with a cheerful wave of his hand.

Peter was curious to see the new Ambassador car which George had recently bought. “I got this, the latest version, what they call Mark IV. It’s not a bad choice. In fact, it seemed reliable when I drove it down here today.”

Peter said with some concern, “But you have just learned to drive. Do you have a driving licence?”

“That I managed to get. I can now drive very well.”

“I find a small scratch on the left side.”

“Oh that? The lorry did not move enough to the left when I was overtaking. It was his fault. Anyway it’s only a small scratch.”

“Always it’s the other man’s fault!” Peter said, half jokingly

Molly and her parents got into George’s car. But he drove well and heeding Molly’s directions entered the rubber garden. Vasudevan received them immediately. George went to him and shook his hand warmly, “Your brothers send their greetings.”

“Yes, I met you during the wedding here. How is the factory running, Mr. Peter?”

“Very well, Sir.”

“Here we don’t do any solvent extraction. What we do are post-harvest operations and primary processing like converting rubber latex into sheets.”

“Oh, I am keen to see that” George told Vasu.

Vasudevan then explained the various aspects involved in processing rubber into sheets, starting from the very beginning, “When Columbus and his men watched the native American Indian kids bouncing balls made of some sort of thread-like gummy matter, they were intrigued. What was later to be called India rubber came from the rubber plants which were later brought here and cultivated by European powers in the tropical colonies under their command. The rest as they say is history.”

George was quite curious, “I have heard about names like Dunlop, Goodyear etc. What have they done?”

“John Boyd Dunlop was a Scottish inventor who developed pneumatic tyres sometime around 1888. He saw his son struggling with his tricycle. So he developed the first practical inflatable tyre for his son’s tricyle. He later patented it and along with a few others started the Company that bears his name. But before him, an American named Charles Goodyear, along with others perfected the process of vulcanization. Rubber is only an elastic gum but it has to be transformed into a thermostable tough elastic material. This was achieved by heating it with sulphur and other additives. Some believe that this important development is an accidental discovery. Goodyear also has a company in his name."

He continued after a pause, "Another name you would have heard is Mackintosh. Also an enterprising Scot, he invented water-proof rain coats and other water-proof materials out of rubberised fabric."

Elizabeth who was listening with much interest added her bit of information, "I have read that the English writer, J.B. Priestley, was the first to use rubber gum for erasing pencil marks. Do you know what they used before? A rough stone like pumice or a bread piece. Perhaps the name 'rubber' came from rubbing."

While the group thus chatted, Peter looked around. Suddenly he asked Vasudevan, "You do not grow tea here?"

"No sir. It is best grown at higher altitudes."

Peter thought about it for a moment, and then said, "Yes, the Chinese do grow tea in the plains, but that is green tea. If you want black tea with aroma, you need elevated grounds like the Assam hills, the Nilgiri Hills near Ooty, the region at the foothills of Western Ghats around Valparai in Madras State and Munnar in Kerala. In fact you get the best aroma at very high elevations as in Darjeeling. You don't grow cardamom either here?"

"No. That too needs higher altitude. But besides altitude, cardamom is also latitude-specific. Other than Kerala and adjoining areas, another place in the world where cardamom grows well is Guatemala in Central America which lies in the same latitude. It is, however, surprising that there is no major cardamom cultivation south of the Equator in the corresponding latitudes. Pepper is also slightly latitude-specific. So you have it growing in Malaysia and also in the corresponding southern latitudes like Indonesia and Brazil."

After a little more touring, they returned to the house. Pappachan did not turn up for dinner which infuriated his father. Thomachan was livid. Probably because of this, dinner time was quiet.

It rained during the night, and the next morning was beautiful. Elizabeth asked George to take Molly and her to the church, "Now that you are here, let Daddy spend a little more time in bed and take it easy."

"You see Mummy, for a working man, Sunday is a day to relax," he replied in a heavy voice.

"But George, your father drives me to church, even though he is mostly an 'outstanding' church goer."

"What do you mean, Mummy?"

"He stands outside the church to chit chat with other 'outstanding' Catholics! I am glad though that he goes to church at least to impress society. Are you also like that, George?"

George pretended not to hear the question.

In some time, the women got ready and George opened the front door of the Ambassador for his mother, while Molly got in at the back.

Later, during breakfast George said, "Daddy, I have taken leave on Monday and Tuesday as well. I am planning to come with you to Ooty. Let Molly also join us and I will drop her back here on Tuesday."

Molly looked at Thomachan, who said, "Yes of course Molly, you must go with them."

"But what about you, Appacha?"

"Don't worry about me. I will spend time with Vasu. I will ask him to join me for dinner."

Peter and family left in two cars to Ooty after lunch. George asked Molly to sit with him in his car. Elizabeth asked in jest, "Molly do you feel safe in his car?"

Unexpectedly Molly became serious, "What is safety for me in this world? I just take everything as it comes."

Elizabeth was taken aback She covered her mouth with her kandkerchief, not knowing what to say. Thomachan pretended to ignore her comment and remained jovial as he bid farewell to the family.

While going on the Ghat section Molly was reminded of her childhood. "Every time I pass through here, I feel like a little girl. What a fantastic view there is!"

George in an effort to cheer her up remarked, "Your estate is beautiful. This Mr. Vasudevan must be good. His brothers are doing a fine job as well."

"I tell you George, the Estate is running only because of Mr. Vasudevan."

Chapter 17

"Let me take this opportunity to congratulate the winners of this year's export awards," the Chief Minister of Kerala announced during a function in Trivandrum to recognise good work in the sector. "I am sure that they will scale greater heights in the coming years and bring glory to our Motherland as well as valuable foreign exchange. *Jai Hind!*"

Lakshmanan and Ramanathan were among the crowd who applauded the speech at its end. They were sitting in the front row, waiting to receive a Certificate of Merit for their promising start in the export business. It was a proud moment for a company that had started only recently. Lakshmanan was adamant that Ramanathan, the brain behind its success, should receive the honour. But his younger brother had refused to do so, passing all credit back to Lakshmanan, the Managing Director. Finally, Karunakaran stepped in with some advice, "I have no doubt that both of you are involved in this success. It is only right that both of you jointly collect the award."

After the function the delegates assembled in the dining hall where tea was served.

"Hi Shyam, how are you?" Ramanathan said as he thumped a man on his back.

The man turned around and his mouth fell open. "Ramanathan. How are you? I am so sorry I haven't visited your company yet. I will do so shortly."

"Ah, that is fine. Lakshmanan let me introduce you to Dr. Shyamaprasad. But you've met him in Mysore, at the Institute. He is the leader of the project team involved in developing the new process for spice oils and oleoresins. He has not come to our place, but his colleagues had once paid us a visit."

Lakshmanan shook hands with Dr. Shyamaprasad who said, "I am thrilled to see you two receive a certificate for your achievement. I hope that very soon your company wins the trophy for the top exporter."

Lakshmanan thanked him and then added, "Ramanathan told me that C.S.I.R. has shifted you here to head a team on plantation products research. How is the work moving?"

"Not bad. These are early days."

"What are you planning in spices?"

"We need to think of other plantation products instead of concentrating on spices. So we are studying coconut, cashew nut, oil palm etc. But spices are still very important and I am working on extracting natural colour from the chilli. I tell you that natural food colour is going to be in great demand in the future."

Ramanathan intervened and said, "In Europe paprika extract is big business. In fact paprika oleoresin can be as big as all the other oleoresins put together. But unfortunately we have no paprika without the innate heat. Sometimes I dream that if only we had the sweet paprika which Spanish people have, we could have made a killing!"

Lakshmanan asked, "I know paprika as an important spice of Europe. But can you kindly explain to me the value of its oleoresin? By the way, Sir, why don't you join us for dinner?"

"Not now, maybe another time. I just had a heavy snack right now. This is not high tea, it is higher tea!"

Lakshmanan was impressed with the scientist's sense of humour. Dr. Shyamaprasad then continued with Lakshmanan's query, "Let me explain your earlier query in simple terms. The chilli, which we produce in large quantities, is rather hot. The hot sensation is caused by a compound called capsaicin as you know. But chilli also has a beautiful colour. This is caused by a class of compounds called carotenoids. Now in European countries, they grow varieties that bear a bright colour but which contain very little hotness. This variety is known as paprika. Paprika has a desirable flavour too. In Hungary and other European countries they produce a lot of paprika that is used as fresh spice and in ground form."

"In Spain particularly, they grow a roundish paprika which is used for extraction. Obviously this variety does not fare well in its fresh form. Because of very, very low level of capsaicin, they get excellent oleoresin with practically no heat. In India we have high coloured chilli but it contains a fair amount of capsaicin. So we cannot produce sweet paprika oleoresin."

"Then why not get the seeds from Spain and grow that kind of paprika here?"

"We have tried it, but it has yielded only limited success."

"So, is there no hope?"

"I didn't say so, that's what my team is working on. We plan to fractionate the capsaicin and carotene colour from our oleoresin. We have high colour varieties like '*Byadgi*' in Karnataka State."

"But can you remove capsaicin?"

"Capsaicin is slightly more polar, that is water loving than carotene colours. So by using a liquid-liquid partitioning system we can do it." There was a lively discussion on the various aspects of separation of two phases in which Ramanathan also took part.

Dr Shyamaprasad saw the puzzled look on Lakshmanan's face and the genial scientist was about to launch into an explanation of the polarity theory. However he was distracted by the appearance of a tall fair woman in an awkwardly worn sari.

"There you are," she said and the scientist smiled and introduced the newcomer, "Meet my wife, Jane. She dropped me here and went to the nursery to select a few rose plants."

Lakshmanan was about to extend his hand when the lady offered a traditional *Namaste* with folded hands.

"We met in the University of Rutgers in America where she was doing Oriental Studies." Dr Shyamaprasad told them. Jane smiled warmly at her husband and asked,

"How did the function go, dear?"

"Oh, it was great." After a moment Shyam added, "She has a passion for roses and is growing all varieties here."

"But only hot spices excite Shyam," she smiled.

"Darling, give me a few minutes to tell them something interesting about paprika as food colour. Just a moment I promise!"

Dr Shyamaprasad turned to the brothers and said, "Where were we? Oh yes, about the use of paprika. Yes, it is used mainly as a food colour. But it has an exotic use. Do you know that in some countries they want the egg yolk to have a reddish tint? To obtain this, oleoresin paprika with high red colour is added to chicken feed. Not to make the feed attractive, but to have the red pigments deposited in their egg yolk. In most countries however, they want yellow yolk. In that case you add an extract of the yellow flower marigold."

Then looking at the bemused expression on Lakshmanan's face he added, "Yes, I know. The good old country chicken was not fed with these to lay eggs with lovely coloured yolk! The pigment, vitamins, minerals were picked up as it wandered about pecking at food that came its way. Today the chicken is a caged machine that is supplied with all the inputs, so that it produces tailor-made eggs!" With a chuckle he looked around for his wife. "I better go and find the lady, or I will be a plucked chicken before you know it," he said with a smile.

"Doctor, this has been a very interesting meeting. We would like to consult you on some of our operational processes. When you have the time, perhaps we can get together."

"Thank you. I will certainly get in touch. Good day."

After seeing them off, Ramanathan said, "Lakshmanan, after listening to the Doctor I feel we can ourselves perfect the process of separation of colour and pungency."

"Don't even mention it, Ramanathan. That would be utterly unprofessional and unethical. How can we take advantage of the good Doctor's openness and all his hard work for our own gain? But somebody will, I have no doubt."

Ramanathan looked embarrassed. "Sorry, I did not think before I made that remark."

Peter drove into his house with Elizabeth by his side. It was dark. Hardly had Elizabeth switched on the porch light, when George drove in with his sister. Peter said, "Tonight, we will have dinner at the Planter's Club. It is too late for Mummy to cook dinner."

Both Molly and George shivered in the Ooty cold. George and Peter put on their blazers and ties and Elizabeth gave Molly a stylishly cut woollen coat that looked smart over her yellow silk sari. She herself had worn a long sleeved sweater and draped a shawl over it.

George drove them to the club. As soon as they entered a hush fell over the room and for a minute everyone stared at Molly. Then a couple of ladies laughed and exclaimed "Oh! It's only Peter and Elizabeth." Elizabeth introduced her children, "This is my daughter Molly. And my son George."

One of the women smiled. "We thought the new film actress had just walked into our humble club room. Some film shooting is taking place in the adjoining regions."

Elizabeth laughed, "Oh no, she is a married woman now! Her family owns the big Kollegal estate in Puthupady, on the way to Calicut."

Peter and George drifted off to the bar. Peter ordered two cold beers.

"Why cold beer in this weather, Dad?"

"You will see George. You will enjoy a cold drink in this weather."

George sipped the beer and true to his father's words, found the beverage tasted better in this temperature.

Watching his son's pleased expression, Peter said, "Cold beer is the favourite of the Germans, Englishmen and other Europeans. Do you know who consumes more ice cream per capita in the world? It's the people of Sweden and other cold countries. And the surprising fact is that hot tropical countries consume a lot of hot tea. If you include the green tea consumed in the Far East and South East Asia also, tea is the second largest consumed liquid after plain water."

"Hi, Peter, stopped playing tennis?" a man called out from behind. Peter turned around to see the man walking towards them wearing tennis shorts and a round neck tee shirt, with a racket in his hand.

"Ah, Mr. Subramanyam, meet my son, George. He is the technical manager in a company in Cochin."

"How do you do, Mr. George? Oh Peter, did you read about the service of the new player John McEnroe? He is the next big one after Borg."

"Yes. But while his smashing with the racket is good, his lashing with his tongue is unbearable!" Peter said and both men laughed. George joined in the laughter.

The next day George took his mother and sister for a tour of Ooty including the Botanical Gardens. After a *masala dosa* and typical South India coffee served in a steel glass, they were satiated.

As she sipped the coffee, Elizabeth said, "You should try the tea instead. It is more invigorating."

Her children shook their heads and laughed recalling the latest passion of their mother.

George then said, "We will go to Doddabetta here in Ooty."

"It's the highest point in South India, Molly. You can see the hills and the plains all around using a mounted telescope, when it is not misty."

During the drive back from the peak Molly said to her mother, "You and Daddy seem to be doing just fine here."

"Yes, but in less than two years Daddy will retire and then we will move to Cochin to be with George Mon."

Molly teased George, "Oh Mummy's little baby!"

Next day after a pleasant breakfast, Molly and George started on their return journey. Molly was very quiet as they negotiated the Ghat section with its hairpin bends. Once they came on to the straight road, Molly asked, "Tell me George. Where do you get so much money from for expensive presents and now this car?"

"Molly, money will come. You can always borrow it from someone."

"What? Mummy and Daddy think you must be getting a handsome salary."

"Nothing like that. I borrow from unofficial banks."

"Don't do that, George," Molly was alarmed and anxious. "Try to live within your means."

"You can say that, with your rich estate behind you."

Molly did not know what to say. She thought how little her brother knew about her life on the Estate. George's statement made her dejected. She maintained her calm for the rest of the journey, trying hard not to let her emotions pour through. As they neared Puthupady George said, "I am sorry Molly!"

Shortly the mood in the car returned to normal. As they neared the estate, George said, "I'll have a simple lunch and then proceed to Cochin. I have to report for duty tomorrow."

Molly went straight to the kitchen when they got home. Kamalam came up to her slowly, saying "Appachan is not feeling very well."

Molly immediately rushed to Thomachan's room, only to find Vasudevan sitting in a chair beside the bed. Thomachan was resting with his eyes closed. Molly sat on the cot and sensing her arrival, he opened his eyes.

"What happened Appacha?"

"Nothing Molae. Just feeling a little tired!"

"We must go to the doctor at the earliest."

"No need. Vasu too suggested the same, but I said no."

After some time, the old man closed his eyes and a few minutes later opened them again.

Pappachan walked in just then, saw his father sleeping and left immediately.

The patriarch's face showed despair, tortured by the indifference of his son more than any illness affecting him. George came in and sat on the edge of the bed where Molly made place for him. Thomachan's face lit up when George stroked his hand affectionately. He said in a low tone, "Molly, why don't you go prepare lunch for George and Vasu. Young people shouldn't be made to waste time over an old man."

Molly moved reluctantly and all of them had a simple lunch while Thomachan slept in his room. After lunch Molly remarked, "I think Appachan will recover soon."

Vasudevan looked into her eyes and said in a low voice,

"Today he sounded very depressed, saying over and over again that he was headed to his end. He even said that the days of visiting the doctor and hospital were over. But he wanted our Head Clerk to meet him."

"What happened?"

"I don't know. He talked for some time with Mohamedikka. And Mohamedikka has arranged for the car to visit Calicut tomorrow morning."

Towards late afternoon, George left for Cochin while Vasudevan walked towards his house.

The very next day, the family car entered the gates of the Kollegal Estate and from it emerged Mr. Kunjali Moosa, a well-established lawyer from Calicut. Behind him stood two people, one Mr. Parthasarathy, the lawyer's clerk holding a briefcase in his hand, and the other, Mohamedikka. Thomachan was in relatively better spirits and was sipping the *kanji* Molly was holding in front of him. As soon as the party entered his room he stopped his breakfast and asked Molly to leave. Thomachan told Mohamedikka to close the door. "How are you Kunjali? It is indeed a long time since we met." Thomachan smiled weakly as he addressed the lawyer.

"Yes, I am fine. What is troubling you?"

"Oh a little problem with the kidney and let us say with most other parts as well."

"I am sure that you will be all right soon."

"No, I don't want to prolong this kind of a life anymore. I had a good life. Why should I be greedy for more?"

Thomachan and Kunjali Moosa were about the same age and had been friends for a very long time. But compared to the fragile looking Thomachan, Kunjali was a robust man, in good health, both physically and mentally. He had been associated with the legal matters of the estate since the time of his early struggling days, when he had helped Thomachan's father sort out a minor legal issue. After getting Mathukutty a favourable verdict, it was natural that he became the legal consultant for all matters of the family.

And in the years that followed, he had established himself as a reliable expert on subjects like property disputes, succession issues and other civil cases.

They spent a long time discussing certain matters, during which Mr. Parthasarathy and Mohamedikka kept silent. Finally the lawyer asked, "Are you sure you are doing the right thing, Thomacha?"

"My dear friend, I have never been surer."

Then the Head clerk and Mr. Parthasarathy left with the Stamp paper to the office, typed out the prepared matter and came back to the room.

After putting the necessary signatures and thumb impressions of Thomachan, Parthasarathy and Mohamedikka who were Witnesses, the old man said in a feeble voice, "I have a feeling that I am bidding farewell to you."

Mohamedikka got up and touched the hands of Thomachan and uttered, "Muthalali, do not say that. You will be with us forever."

Thomachan showed his teeth in a weak attempt to smile again and said softly, "No more Muthalali. Call me Chettan."

"You are like God! You gave me assistance to build my house and also money for my daughter's marriage."

Thomachan simply shook his head. Finally the party left the room. Molly entered immediately and checked his health. He said, "I feel very light at heart now, Molae. Let me sleep for some time."

Molly left quietly. She was surprised that he did not mention anything about the visitors. She had even expected him to call the maid to bring some coffee for the guests, but nothing of that sort happened.

Ramanathan was a confused man. During George Peter's absence, he had done an informal stock check and found some discrepancy in the register carrying details of essential oils. He wanted to talk to Lakshmanan. But his brother's wife had been admitted to the hospital for her delivery. Not knowing what to do, he brushed the matter side, assuring himself that it was just a case of misunderstanding. It would be ridiculous to suspect an important and competent manager of the Company.

Chapter 18

Three days after the lawyer met Thomachan, the patriarch passed away peacefully in his sleep. Molly was the first to notice his departure in the morning. She immediately woke up Pappachan and sent word to Vasudevan to notify all relatives. Vasudevan took charge from there. All the relatives were informed by phone and arrangements were made by family and friends to conduct the funeral the very next day in Thamarassery church.

As per the wish of the deceased, the rituals were performed on a simple scale. All close relatives came. Peter and Elizabeth came from Ooty. George also attended the funeral and stayed at the bungalow for two days with Molly. From Cochin, Karunakaran, Vasudevan's father, came alone as his wife was not very well.

One person who was inconsolable during the funeral ceremony was Molly. She sat through the night for the 'wake' and periodical prayers. When finally the body was taken away, she sat numb in a corner, weeping silently. When asked to go with the body, Molly said softly, "I cannot watch Appachan being taken away from this world!"

Everybody felt the genuineness of her grief. Her mother, Elizabeth, stayed back in the house with her. In a simple but solemn function, Thomachan was buried by the side of his beloved wife Mariam, who had passed away more than forty years earlier.

The following day, Molly regained her composure and took on her duties of mistress of the house. She spoke politely to her aunties and uncles, and warmly thanked George for not only coming, but spending time with her.

Karunakaran stayed with his son, Vasudevan. He used this opportunity to enquire about Vasu's position there. Vasudevan said, "I really enjoy the work here. Nobody interferes with what I do and I can even experiment to my heart's content."

"I am glad to hear that, Vasu. But both your mother and I want you to get married and live like everyone else."

"Well, there is no problem in that."

"You have a good house, but it needs a housewife. Actually Janaki is busy searching for a bride for you. Unfortunately nothing has come through yet. She is also not feeling too well these days. But she is confident of coming up with a fine proposal. You are okay with it, right?"

"Yes, it's fine."

When Mr. Karunakaran visited the house of the Kollegal family, Molly treated him with extreme courtesy and respect. Pappachan as usual, mumbled something impatiently and walked away.

Molly took control of the home and enforced a strict pure vegetarian diet during the forty days of mourning. Pappachan was frustrated. He had little money in his hand and was waiting for the mourning to get over and the Will to be read.

Karunakaran sat beside Janaki Amma who was suffering from an acute asthma attack. He told Ramanathan who was there at that time, "The doctor wants to admit her to the hospital immediately. Just make all arrangements for the same at the earliest, maybe tomorrow itself."

"Yes Acha. I will go to the hospital right now. I have already told Lakshmanan that I will not be coming to the factory for the rest of the week."

The issue concerning the essential oil stock had taken a back seat temporarily. By now Ramanathan had convinced himself that perhaps the fudged accounts were just a figment of his imagination. He was to travel abroad to meet customers in ten day's time, so he wanted to concentrate on that. That evening he telephoned his younger brother in Puthupady, "Vasudevan, how are you?"

"Fine Ramanathan. How is everybody?"

"Amma's asthma is very bad. She is being admitted to the hospital tomorrow."

"Really? I will reach there tomorrow morning itself."

"No, no. Don't come now. Come after a week, and plan your leave so as to stay here for a week. Right now Vanya and I will give Amma company. Next week I need to go to Europe on an urgent business trip. I can't cancel it. All appointments have been fixed."

"Don't worry Ramanathan. I will come next week."

"Thank you Vasu. She will be happy to see you."

"How are Ravindran Chettan and Chechi?"

"He is quite busy. The company received an important contract. If I tell him about your arrival, he will admonish me for disturbing you from your work at the plantation. That is why I am asking you directly."

"Just call me any time you need. Tell Achan not to worry. Let us pray that Amma becomes fine soon."

"She will be. She needs medication and medical care. She wouldn't agree to go to the hospital. But this time upon Achan's and Chettan's insistence, she has reluctantly agreed."

On the forty-first day after Thomachan's death, a special Mass and other religious rituals were conducted. All his sisters and their husbands were present. A simple breakfast had been arranged in the Kollegal house. Molly was busy running around to make the occasion befitting the mourning of the head of the family. Pappachan was present, but showed little interest in being part of the ceremonies. Mr. Kunjali Moosa had earlier announced that the occasion would be used for the reading of Thomachan's Will.

At ten, the lawyer arrived with his assistant and Mohamedikka the Head Clerk. Everyone assembled inside the large hall.

There was total silence but the feeling of anxiety was felt across the room. Molly had arranged for fruit juice to be served to all. The Lawyer had asked for a cup of tea since he had a sore throat he said. Once the tea was sipped a couple of times, Mr. Moosa cleared his throat and started.

"I have pleasure in reading the will of the late Thomachan of Kollegal family of Puthupady village.

"But first let me tell you that my friend and client, the late Thomachan thought about his Will for long before finalising it. When I pointed out certain controversial matters in it, he stuck to his decision making it very, very clear how he wanted the Will to shape out."

Moosa stopped, took a deep breath and continued. "For the sake of easy understanding I am not going to read the Will in its legal style but will give the main gist. I am leaving a copy here for anyone interested to read in detail. He has provided considerable cash payment to Pappachan, as also almost equal amounts to three of his sisters, Chinnamma, Sophy and Thresiamma. Is Mr. Vasudevan here?"

It was Mr. Mohamedikka who answered, "He is out in the field. Do you want him to be called?"

"No. You can tell him later, that an equal amount as given to his sisters, has been provided for him too. There are some lesser amounts kept aside for various employees who have been with him for long. This includes Mr. Mohamedikka."

Then taking another sip, the lawyer said, "The late Thomachan had considerable quantities of liquid cash and gold with him. Nearly half of them have been written off to relatives and employees as just announced."

There was a general surprise among the crowd as to why nothing was provided for Molly who was his favourite. But that was soon put to rest by the Lawyer, who announced, "Now I am coming to the last part. The rest of the wealth including the Estate and the house goes to Mrs. Molly Pappachan Kollegal who is the daughter-in-law of the deceased."

With a flourish, the lawyer closed the file and looked around. There was a moment of silent disbelief followed by a murmur among the crowd.

The three sisters together with their husbands got up from their seats and spoke rapidly amongst themselves. The eldest Chinnamma's husband said aloud, "It is an unusual Will. We are unhappy and may think of contesting it in court, not only for us, but for our poor nephew, Pappachan as well."

The lawyer then stood up to face the audience, most of whom had also stood up by now, "Yes, this is in a way a different style of dividing the wealth. During the preparation of the Will, these matters came up for discussion. One thing I can assure you, it was not at all a case of careless planning. It was well thought out by my friend who was sure about his words when he recounted the distribution pattern of his wealth including this prosperous estate. He asked about any possible loopholes and wanted me to make sure that these are plugged effectively. As per his direction, we have looked into all aspects of the Will. As far as his sisters and employees are concerned I want to say that the document will give you no option to contest its contents. If his son Mr. Pappachan wants to contest it, I admit it can cause some interest, but I doubt that he will have any legal rights. Late Thomachan has asked me to provide protection for Molly from any such legal action. Well ladies and gentlemen, I would like to say that in my firm opinion, this Will is irrevocable and will stand any legal scrutiny."

With this he stood up and left along with his assistant. There was loud discussion and even open display of dissent among the relatives. In the pandemonium, Molly went away to her room and cried silently. She had not aspired for anything, only for peace of mind.

When she woke up from a nap, she went to the kitchen where Kamalam told her that all the relatives had left without having their lunch. Pappachan had eaten something, and then gone off as well. Slowly Molly moved to the dining room and ate her lunch silently.

In the United States a former Hollywood actor, Ronald Reagan was enjoying his success in the 1980 Presidential election. As his Republican admirers recalled it was his brilliant ability to canvas appropriately that turned the tables on the Democrats and now he was showing his capability in administration also. For the Kollegal Estate and the people who lived there, life rolled on as usual. The crops performed excellently which in a way was a tribute to the leadership and expertise of its Manager, Vasudevan. In fact the employees and labourers could not recall a more prosperous season. Molly began to take more interest in the functioning of the estate. But she never interfered in its working.

Pappachan made irregular visits, but mostly he was out. His wanderings evoked gossip and comment from many neighbours and estate workers who believed that he had an illegitimate relationship with a woman from the nearby colony. The prominent people in the locality, who had initially expressed shock at the Will, now began to wonder whether the former patriarch had been indeed right in his judgement.

As soon as Ramanathan reached home from his European tour he asked his wife, "Vanya, how is Amma?"

"She is fully okay. Back to her usual busy life."

Her husband looked at her questioningly. Vanya quickly said with a gentle laugh, "No, it's not a dig made by a daughter-in-law at her mother-in-law. In fact she is my best friend. It's only because we are so friendly with each other that I have spoken like that." Then looking at her husband, she added, "Among other things, she is finalising a girl for Vasu."

They both left for his parents' house. Ramanathan handed over the gifts he had brought for his parents. His eldest brother Ravindran was out of station.

Then after dropping Vanya home, he proceeded to the factory.

"So how was your trip? You have been keeping in touch on the phone and by telex, but I am curious about this curcumin thing," Lakshmanan said as he embraced his brother. He ordered coffee and settled down to hear from Ramanathan.

"It is a good development Lakshmana. Most of them want the yellow pigment in turmeric in pure form. Purity of 95 percent is what they seek."

"But why do they want it? We already have turmeric oleoresin."

"First of all they do not like the aroma of turmeric oil our oleoresin has."

"But how do you remove the aroma? You told me that they are ready to give the process."

"Yes, yes. What we need is to crystallize the pigment from the oleoresin. The pigment is called curcumin, as you know. When you separate curcumin in the form of crystals, all other ingredients like turmeric oil, resinous coloured fraction, etc. get separated. You can filter off the crystals by using a basket centrifuge. And then with a little washing, you get pure crystals, at least 95 percent pure curcumin."

"What do they use this for?"

"For one as natural yellow food colour, without the aroma, but they have found that curcumin has antioxidant properties."

"Oh, so?"

"Yes, adding a small amount of antioxidant can delay oxidation considerably."

"So they want to use this pigment to protect fatty foods?"

"For that there are other antioxidants, even good synthetic ones. But this they want to promote for health reasons. Our body cells are protected by a fat-like tissue. As long as this protective layer, the lipid tissue, is kept intact, cells will be protected from viruses. When the lipid tissue gets damaged by oxidation, cancerous virus can enter the cell. So in a way curcumin is an anti-cancer, antioxidant. Antioxidants also control free radicals in our body system and therefore curcumin can help in controlling cardio-vascular problems."

"So what are we waiting for? Put up the plant soon. What all further help do you need Ramanathan?"

He explained the plan and listed out the items required.

"Then go ahead. Let us build a new plant. Money is not an issue. Spend as much as you need to. "

"Will tomorrow be too late to complete the plant?"

There was loud laughter, hearing which the receptionist knocked on the door and asked, "Some more coffee, Sir?"

She admired the manner in which the brothers worked as a team. There was a high level of understanding of each other's minds and their ability to accept the views of the other was the secret behind their success. Lakshmanan controlled his laughter with some difficulty and said, "Bring some more coffee and some cashew nuts. When I am driving my little brother like a slave, let me at least offer him some refreshments." There was more laughter.

Chapter 19

It was a Wednesday. Molly found a small crowd of workers on the road inside the Estate, not too far away from the house. With Kamalam for company, she walked down the path. Seeing her, the group fell silent. One of the supervisors came up to her and said, almost matter-of-factly, “Pappachan Muthalai has died. It is an accident it appears.”

Another younger man butted in, “I hear it is only an accident and that Saar has been taken to the hospital.”

There were different versions from other members of the group. Molly did not know what to conclude. But any uncertainty she had, was wiped away with the arrival of an ambulance a few minutes later. Two or three people got out of it, one being Vasudevan. Under his direction, four people carried Pappachan’s body inside the house. Vasudevan then approached Molly and said softly, “Madam, I am very sorry to tell you that Pappachan Sir died in an accident.”

It took some time for his words to sink in. One death after another just so quickly was a big shock for Molly. And yet she had a vague feeling that this death did not leave her with a sense of loss. A few minutes she addressed Vasudevan softly, “What actually happened?”

“It is like this Madam. He fell down in the hilly section after stepping on a loose stone and his head hit a rock. He was already dead when we took him to Thamarassery hospital. The doctors there too pronounced him dead on arrival and gave a death certificate.”

Molly went through the motions of the events that followed, as expected of her, the funeral, condolence visits by relatives and friends, business associates, and the Estate labour. Amongst the earliest to arrive were her parents and her brother. She was surprised that during such difficult moments her mind was dwelling on trivial things like Vasudevan addressing her as 'Madam'. Ever since she inherited the Estate Vasudevan was talking to her without using her name. Now that she was the owner and he an employee, however important the position was, a subtle change had occurred in their interactions. It certainly would be going against the social norms if they addressed each other by name.

With the summer setting in, the temperature rose steadily, and the Estate was busy with harvest and post-harvest operations. Molly started going to the Estate once again. Even though she had watched it many times, every step of the operations, be it planting, curing of coffee, harvesting of arecanuts and coconuts fascinated her. Vasudevan took to discussing most matters with Molly. He answered most of her questions about agricultural methods and labour welfare, expenses involved and profits expected frankly and patiently. One day she returned home earlier than usual, but stopped just outside the steps leading to the dining room upon hearing a conversation between two women in the kitchen.

"But how can it be?" one of them was saying. Molly recognised it as Kamalam's voice. The other woman retorted, "Why, you are the only one who says how can it be so."

"But he had a pretty wife here. I am telling you Sudha, don't start some scandal for nothing," Kamalam said.

"Very well then. I won't say any more. You continue to live in your palace cut off from the real world."

But Kamalam's curiosity was aroused. "No, no, Sudha, I was only shocked. Go on tell me."

"He used to frequent this woman which was not a big secret. So as I was saying, this fellow hit Muthalali…"

Just then there was the mild rattle of a window shutter.

"Wait here Sudha. Let me check."

Kamalam walked towards the front of the house and then saw Molly.

"Oh, Kochamma, you are back?" Kamalam said in a loud voice.

Molly knew at once that the loud voice was a signal to the other woman to leave quietly. Molly pretended to have just entered the house and went into her room.

The whole of the next day she found Vasudevan quite busy, always with some group of workers or other. But the day after that, she cornered him and said, "Look Mr. Vasudevan. You have been very kind and considerate to me. You are also running this place very efficiently. So I cannot ask for anything more."

Vasudevan cut in, "It's nothing. You also have been nice to me. Why everyone in your family…"

"Wait, I have not finished. All I want is one more favour from you. I know my husband had not met with an accident as you explained. I know there is a woman involved. Now please, please tell me the truth, in full. Believe me, I can bear it."

"I am sorry. You have gone through too much; I thought it unfair to add more to your burden. Forgive me."

"Please tell me the truth now. I am entitled to it."

"Very well then. I will tell you the whole story. At least it will take a big load off my conscience. Mr. Pappachan had a long-standing affair with a woman staying alone a few kilometres towards the Ghats. Her husband was an army man, posted in Kashmir. He adored her and was waiting for a chance to get a suitable posting where he could take his wife along. He finally got that transfer. Actually the woman had run away from her home for this soldier who belongs to a different caste. Her family did not want her after that. His family was also unhappy with the marriage. But they lived their lives unconcerned about family disapproval. He took a small house nearby and she lived there while he was away. She was lonely and was vulnerable to the guiles of another man, who unfortunately happened to be our Pappachan Sir. A worker in our estate, I understand, helped him get in touch with her at first."

He paused, then said, "Unfortunately the man returned home unexpectedly, excited about the new posting and the hope that they would be together, but what he saw infuriated him. He picked up the small grinding stone and hit Pappachan on his head. It was a lethal blow. One of our supervisors happened to be nearby and he rushed to tell me the news. I went and patched up the matter with the husband. He realised that it could turn into a criminal case and he could be accused of murder. So it was easy for me to make it look like an accident. The police and the doctor were peruaded to accept it as an accidental death."

He stopped, looked around and then added, "I have come clean now on this matter since I know that half the people here suspect his death to be more than just an accident. So there is no point hiding the truth from you. I am sorry dea … er … Madam."

Molly looked vacantly at the distant horizon. Then turning to Vasudevan, she fixed her gaze on him and said, "Thank you. On behalf of the family, I sincerely thank you."

She turned and briskly walked towards her home. She was wearing a simple white saree, the *pallu* of which was fluttering in the breeze flowing in from the hills behind.

What a courageous woman! thought Vasudevan, staring after her for a long time. Yes, what a beautiful, courageous woman!

Chapter 20

The construction of the manufacturing plant for making pure curcumin, the yellow pigment from turmeric rhizome, took much longer than expected. Ramanathan had estimated about three months but it took over six weeks more. He discussed the delay with Lakshmanan, who side stepped the anxiety and replied in an encouraging tone, "Look, it's a lot of work and I feel you have done a fantastic job of it."

"It's nice of you to say so Lakshmanan."

"No, no, it's not just a polite statement. I tell you, you've done a six month job in just, let me see, yes, in four and a half months."

Ramanathan was quite happy hearing his brother's words. Lakshmanan was looking for something on the table, so after a pause he continued, "But I must also mention George Peter's contribution. He was quite willing to take on additional responsibility, outside the purview of his own work."

"Yes, I agree."

"I think we must take note of his knowledge and commitment, shouldn't we Ramanathan?"

"Yes, I think so," Ramanathan replied in a half hearted manner which Lakshmanan did not notice. Ramanathan felt the doubt which had formed inside his heart pulling at him now with greater force. He shoved the thought to the back of his mind, reminding himself that George was in fact doing a fine job at the factory.

Fate seemed to have taken matters into its own hands, though. One day Ramanathan found an opportunity to pry into the suspected misdeeds of his prized worker. One of the newly recruited staff, a smart young man working in the essential oil distillation plant, Vinaykumar, was the catalyst. In a very short time Vinay had proved himself to be a capable worker and when he walked into Ramanathan's office, Ramanathan was more than a little surprised.

"Sir, I have come to ask for a favour," Vinay came straight to the point.

"Favour? What favour, Vinay?"

"I want to continue my studies and apply for M.Sc. With my present qualification, I will be stuck at a lower position forever. With a post-graduate degree, I am confident that I can rise in my career."

Ramanathan saw sense in that. Vinaykumar was a competent technical person with the potential to become a unit head one day. His fears were true as well. Lack of proper qualification could actually be detrimental to his progress.

Ramanathan then cautiously asked, "So, what is it that you want me to do for you?"

"Sir, I want two years' leave."

"You don't want to resign?"

"No Sir. Please understand Sir. I cannot afford to give up this job. I like this company which is very competently led by you in particular, and your brother. When it becomes a big company, I want to be an important member of it."

"Thank you. But how will you manage both job and studies together? Will your family support you?"

"No, Sir, that's why I need your help and blessing. I want a financial loan which you may cut from my salary when I rejoin. An amount of Rs. 50,000 should be enough."

"Fifty thousand! That is a lot of money. Moreover you have put in only a couple of years here," Ramanathan replied, taken aback by the confidence of the young man. He doubted whether he himself would have spoken to a superior in this manner at that age.

"Sir, I won't blame you if you see me as a brash young man. But I tell you, I can help you save that amount in less than six months."

With great difficulty, Ramanathan controlled his temper. The boy had begun to sound arrogant by now, but somehow since he appreciated his work he kept quiet, willing to listen to his proposition.

"Young man, make sure that you are not wasting my time. Say quickly what you want to say."

Vinaykumar took his time to organize his thoughts and in a low voice said, "Sir, I have a feeling that you suspect the honesty of

Mr. George Peter. Excuse me for my impudence, but I have seen you checking the stock, leafing through it and other issue registers. Also do forgive me if I am overstepping the freedom granted to me, but I have a strong suspicion that he is stealing spice oils."

Ramanathan became alert. He tried hard not to show any emotion. In a soft voice he asked, "And what proof do you have?"

"Not clear proof but clear indications. We can get proof if we work together."

Ramanathan immediately felt the potential danger of the conversation. In as low a voice as he could muster, he said, "Mr. Vinaykumar, please come to my home in the evening say by six thirty. I want to talk to you personally. I stay very close, you know my house?"

"Yes Sir, I know. I will be there at the said time."

Much later, Lakshmanan strolled into Ramanathan's room, to show him some of the new enquiries that had come in and the consequent steps to be taken. Lakshmanan watched as Ramanathan cursorily went through the file without saying anything. He asked "Why Ramanathan, you seem a bit preoccupied today?

Ramanathan hesitated a little then shook his head and narrated his suspicion and the conversation he had had with Vinaykumar. After listening to him silently Lakshmanan said, "Ramanathan you are the best person to handle this. Do what you think fit ahead. But tell me why didn't you mention your doubts about George much earlier to me? You know I trust your instincts fully."

"So if the boy leads us to something useful, I will have to grant him his request."

"Of course, why not? This Company has come up from scratch and is going to grow bigger only on the basis of our good business ethics. So we have to keep our word with our staff also."

"Okay then."

"I know I don't have to tell you to be discreet about this matter."

"Of course!"

When Ramanathan reached home, his young wife Vanya served him coffee and *vada*. Quite happy with the way her husband was enjoying the snack she flashed her most charming smile and said, "Let us go shopping as we planned in the morning. I have to buy a present for my friend who's having her house-warming function next week. Besides, I have nothing to wear."

Ramanathan looked at her, surprised by her demand. With some hesitation he added, "But Vanya, a young colleague of mine is coming over and I have…"

"Can't you finish your work in your blessed factory itself and not carry it back home?"

Ramanathan saw that his wife's smile quickly disappeared and her eyes were flashing with anger.

"It isn't like that. It is our factory. It is our bread and butter. Now I have an awkward job which I have to do discreetly. That is why…"

"I have no intention of getting entangled in *your* factory's intrigues. I will go to the temple and pray for sanity in this world."

Ramanathan saw his wife walk out in a huff, but brushed aside the petty quarrel, worried more about how he would handle the situation coming his way. However, a fleeting thought occurred to him that understanding the chemistry of spices was a lot easier than reading the mind of a woman, any day!

At exactly at 6.30 Vinaykumar rang the doorbell. Ramanathan opened the door and directed him to the drawing room. Then he went into the kitchen, prepared a cup of instant coffee for the young man. Vinay stood up, took the coffee and sat on the edge of the sofa. Ramanathan seated himself opposite him and said, "So tell me what you have to say. Wait, first drink your coffee."

"I will sip it in between," he replied, looking around anxiously. He then began talking nervously, "Sir, I am reasonably sure that Mr. George Peter is stealing essential oil."

"But then I should have noticed a serious shortage in stock."

"Partly yes, Sir. If you check the stocks there will be no noticeable shortage."

"Then what is the point, Vinay?"

"Mr. George Peter is an excellent technical man as I am sure you will agree. He has increased the yield of oils in the case of major spices such as cardamom, nutmeg and pepper. All his innovations have worked well, according to me, such as adding an additional chamber to the receiver flask, reducing the temperature of cooling water in the condenser etc."

My God! This chap is good, thought Ramanathan and then asked the youngster to proceed.

"Long back he had explained a point which I recalled only recently. He had said that in the commercial steam distillation process, it was neither economical nor practical to remove all the oil. That would need long hours of steam distillation which would mean lot of wastage of steam. Perhaps extra heating does not do any good to the quality of products either."

"But Vinay, what is the relevance of that here?"

"Sir, let us assume that we have to make an oleoresin containing 30% of volatile oil, something like oleoresin nutmeg 30%. Perhaps, you need add only 25% of oil, the rest 5% may already be present in the solvent extracted resin. Since Mr. George Peter is in overall charge of volatile oils he adds the appropriate quantity of oil, which along with oil contained in the resin will give the right specification for the final oleoresin. But in the register, alongside the column meant to enter the quantity of oil used up for blending, he enters an inflated figure which will correspond to the declared oil content of the oleoresin. When the Quality Control laboratory draws samples and does an analysis they will find the oil content as declared in the register. Since in analysis, effective drastic conditions are employed, the entire volatile oil content, that is both added oil and that present in the solvent extracted resin portion, present in the oleoresin will be shown."

"Yes, I see the point Vinay. Since in England we were not following the two-stage method, these points didn't strike me. So as you said, he makes the oil account seem fine," he took a minute to mentally assess and then continued, "so the smart young man took advantage of that." His voice was almost admiring of the young man's cleverness at noticing these steps as well at George's ingenuity.

Vinaykumar heaved a sigh of relief and said, "Sir, I am happy to note that you understand the situation."

"But how does he take it outside?

"My guess, Sir is that he takes it in his car, not in the boot but inside the car, perhaps in the space in front of the rear seat."

"And how did you arrive at that conclusion Mr. Sherlock Holmes?"

Vinaykumar was tempted to reply, Elementary, Dr. Watson ... but he knew that such banter was the prerogative of the bosses. It would be considered inappropriate and downright risky for an employee seeking a favour. So he said respectfully, "As you know George bought a car some time back. One day we found its windows were covered with dark sun-screen film. He also fitted the car with an air conditioner, perhaps to have an excuse to keep the windows rolled up. This gave him an option to safely keep the twenty litre drum in front of the back seat. Since the windshield cannot be covered with dark film, it would be risky to place the product below the front passenger seat. The watchman at the gate would surely notice it."

Ramanathan was quite astounded by the revelation. Two things were now clear to him. One, George Peter was a clever man. If only he had used his brain positively, he sighed. Second, here was another equally bright person, hopefully an honest worker. Instinctively he felt that the young man in front of him was the right replacement for the egg that had turned bad. He decided to trust his instinct for now, "Look, Vinay I am quite impressed by your reasoning. Let me assure you that the Company will back you to the hilt. Only you have to repay it by serving us well. If you loyally work for us you will be taken care of well, with all perks."

"That I assure you Sir. I will not be stupid like Mr. George."

"But I want you to cooperate with us to trap him."

"I will do that Sir. Tell me how."

"Do you have any suggestions?"

"Sir, Mr. George often leaves the factory by 5.30 p.m. at the latest, usually at five. But on certain days he lingers around till after six. I too generally stay up to six as I need to make arrangements in the plant for the second shift. On such occasions, when he stays beyond six, I am able to watch him from my room. I have found him stop his car in front of the oil storage room, to the side of which his office is located. At that time hardly anyone is around. The next time he lingers beyond six o'clock I may have to follow him. Of course, since by that time in the evening it is getting dark, it's a little hard to see him properly. Further, the view is blocked by the projecting room. I have no clue how to proceed from this point."

Ramanathan thought for some time and then said, "The next time he stops the car in front of the oil storage after 6 pm, immediately phone the gate office using the internal phone. I have a very reliable security guard stationed there. I will instruct him that if he gets a phone call from you he has to stop George Peter and check his car. I will come by then. Just call me at my residence number immediately after you call the gate. You have a phone near your work place. Use it."

"Yes Sir. I can guarantee success, at least ninety percent."

They continued planning and after twenty minutes, Vinaykumar departed, leaving Ramanathan to carry out his husbandly job of pacifying his wife. He hoped that Lord Vishnu to whom she had gone to pray had managed to calm her.

Molly now only had her solitary life for company. Her visits to the Estate had reduced but whenever she ventured there on her own, Vasudevan was present to answer any queries she may have had. But as the sole owner of the establishment, she was exposed to everyone's prying eyes. It made her feel like a gold fish.The only advantage she had over the fish was the home she could call her own, to hide in. Her parents sometimes came and stayed with her for a weekend but otherwise life remained drab and lonely.

One day the priest of the local church called on her. She received him with utmost respect. Father Mankulam appeared too circumspect initially but eventually opened up and was more forthcoming.

"I have come here to ask for a favour in the name of God. We have started a small orphanage and are hoping that the Kollegal family will support us."

"I think this is a good opportunity to do something noble. For the present I will give a token donation. I will have to think a bit for continued support Father, as I don't know how to go about such things."

"That will do. Just think how your family can help in the work of God."

She went inside and wrote a cheque for a thousand rupees from her personal account. With an extremely nervous feeling she handed the cheque to him. Father looked at it casually and then beamed a wide smile. Molly felt relieved. She had not known what was an adequate amount or how much was expected from her. The result of my over-protected life, she sighed.

As he was leaving Father said, "Why don't you visit our orphanage, Mrs. Pappachan?"

Molly liked the idea, "When should I come, Father?"

The priest had not expected such an instant and enthusiastic response from her.

"After four in the evening, maybe? The children would have returned from school by then."

Molly knew that a visit which had a good intent behind it should not be delayed. Like an over eager bridegroom preparing to go to church for his wedding, she got ready much before four, and left for the orphanage.

But there was nobody there to greet her. A few minutes later a nun appeared and timidly explained that her colleague, another nun, had gone to call Father. He arrived panting and gasping in a few minutes and greeted Molly, "The children will come anytime now, won't they Sister?" he directed his question to one of the nuns.

"They usually reach a little after four."

Hardly had she said that, when five children walked in, chattering and laughing. They were all led to a small room where tea had been laid out on the table. Molly's donation and her own visit seemed to have improved the quality of snacks as could be inferred from the look of delight on the faces of those children. "Usually we cannot afford such food. They are given either boiled tapioca or sweet potato. Today we got cup cakes from the bakery. Things can be improved if there is patronage from a rich house."

Molly nodded, satisfied that her contribution had put a smile on the kids faces. For the rest of the evening, she was mostly a listener.

Father spoke a lot while she replied in monosyllables or nodded. But she realised that he was doing his best to present the difficulties they faced in running the orphanage so as to get further support from her.

Fortunately, Molly could also see the bright side of his efforts. She could not help but admire his spirit in pursuing such noble work. She decided that her estate would extend all possible help. But she did not know how to get started. She thought about consulting Vasudevan. Would he find it awkward to advise his employer, she wondered?

It took three days after Vinaykumar's meeting with Mr Ramanathan for matters to roll. Vinaykumar had been on the lookout for hints, but George Peter left early the first two days. On both these days, immediately after five in the evening, George drove his car from the parking shed directly to the gate. On the third day, Vinaykumar had duty till 6 o'clock. He did not notice George going out. In fact his car was safely parked in the shed. A little after six in the evening, Vinaykumar saw George walking towards his car and driving it to the front of his office. He quickly called the gatekeeper on the intercom and told him "Stop that car and inspect its insides."

"Yes Sir, Mr. Vinaykumar, Ramanathan Saar has given me clear instructions. I will be waiting."

Then, rather than waiting for the car to start, Vinaykumar thought it time to call the boss. He dialled his number and the ringing started without any delay, but it stopped abruptly.

"Oh, Damn!" he cursed aloud and dialled again. The call went through but got disconnected immediately. Again he tried, but the same thing happened. Vinaykumar was frantic now. He could hear the car starting. In his panic he tried to remember Mr. Lakshmanan's telephone number. Just then the phone rang. He grabbed it and mumbled, "Hello?"

A tense Ramanathan's voice came across. "Is it Vinay, were you trying to call me?"

"Yes, Sir, I was … but."

"Forget explanations. What is happening?"

"Yes Sir, no time to waste Sir. Come soon to the gate…"

Vinay was puzzled. There was no further response from the other end. He dropped the phone and walked towards the gate. George was arguing with the security guard.

"What are you talking? How can you stop a Manager? Let me go, I have an urgent function to attend."

"Sorry Sir. Ramanathan Saar's instructions!"

George lost his cool completely then. His voice had undertones of panic, although his words and manner were aggressive

"What the hell are you talking about? Open the gate. You know who I am. You will be fired!"

Just then a car arrived from the opposite side and stopped in front of the gate. Ramanathan stepped out. "Please open the door, George," he said. Meekly George came out. Ramanathan opened the rear door and found two 20 litre drums placed under the seats. With the help of Vinay and the watchman, the drums were taken out. Ramanathan opened them and smelled the cap and declared, "Cardamom oil. Check Vinay."

"Yes, Sir, right."

He dialled the Police Station. Ramanathan briefly explained the matter to the Sub-Inspector. The S.I. who was a friend of both Ramanathan and Lakshmanan, understood the gravity of the situation and immediately started for the factory. Ramanathan then called his brother, and told him what had happened.

After all formalities were completed, Ramanathan, George and the Inspector along with a couple of workers left for George Peter's house. Vinaykumar excused himself and went home. Lakshmanan was waiting at George's house for them.

They made a quick search of the premises and recovered five 20 litre drums full of spice oils.

By late evening, after the house was sealed off, the Inspector took George Peter into custody and put him in the lock-up. George was rather defiant. He asked the Inspector to connect him to his friend, Circle Inspector Vinod Thomas who he was confident would bail him out. Vinod Thomas asked the Sub-Inspector, "So what was the offence?"

"Sir, he was caught red handed stealing two drums of factory product in his car, which he was driving himself. That itself is enough proof against him. Now in the presence of other witnesses, we have recovered five more drums, hidden behind a small bush in his residence."

"Can you not arrange to release him?"

The Sub-Inspector who had a reputation for being a straightforward officer was caught off-guard by this response. He replied, "If you can give me a written order, I will do so."

"I'll send it right away."

Although he talked confidently Vinod Thomas was a worried man. The evidence was iron-clad. No doubt George Peter had wined and dined him and even helped him financially. But common sense told him that George Peter's usefulness was over. He had other prospectives for continued hospitality. Why waste my energy to revive a dead horse, he thought to himself, and put his pen down.

He then telephoned the Sub-Inspector after a gap of fifteen minutes and said, "Yes, you are right. The evidence is fool proof. So there is nothing I can do."

The Sub-Inspector was relieved to know that law would take its course. The C.I. requested the S.I. to bring Mr. George Peter to the phone.

"Hello George, how are you?"

"Look Vinod Sir, I am in a tight situation. You had promised that you'd help me in any situation. So get me released now."

"See, things are a little complicated since the accumulated evidence is overwhelming. You will have to remain in custody for the night. Tomorrow I will talk to the Superintendent of Police and ensure that you are freed," he said and put the receiver down.

The deputy of the C.I. on overhearing his superior's words, offered to help, "Sir, do you want me to go to the Police Station there and collect details to bail out Mr. George Peter?"

"Look, we don't know any George Peter."

Chapter 21

During the last week of June 1983, the whole of India celebrated the country's victory in the cricket World Cup held in England. Kapil Dev's team, popularly called 'Kapil's Devils', had won the one-day championship by beating the powerful West Indies team.

But for Molly, 25th June 1983 was one of the worst days in her life. There had been thunder and lightning in the nights and it had been raining cats and dogs in Puthupady for forty-eight hours. A little before noon, she had received a phone call from her father, Peter. His voice was subdued but his breathing was heavy, "Darling Molly, our George seems to be in some trouble."

"Is he sick?"

"Not exactly, he got into some confusion and is now in Police custody. This is regarding the loss of some expensive products. We are trying to sort things out."

"Look Daddy, I have seen much in life, so please do not hide anything from me. Give me the full picture."

Reluctantly, he gave her all details. She bravely held back her emotions and ended the conversation in a steady voice. Then the floodgates opened.

Lakshmanan had called Vasudevan and told him what had happened and asked him to break the news to George's sister tactfully.

Vasudevan started his slow trek towards Molly's residence in the evening. He prepared himself to face her, knowing that she could be hostile to him. Finally when he stood in front of her, he said in a low tone, "Did you hear about your brother?"

"Yes, I came to know everything. Why is it that everything is conspiring to make my life a hell?"

"Take courage, Madam. After all life has a way of providing solutions also."

"Thank you."

"I am leaving for Cochin tomorrow and will return with complete details. Would you like to come to Cochin with me?"

"No. It is nice of you to go there. Daddy has told me not to go there now."

"Madam, you have carried on gracefully so far. Please continue to do the same. Time is a big healer."

"Yes, time is a great healer, but in my case, when one wound heals another appears!"

For Molly the next two days were even more painful. She simply could not come to terms with the latest development in her life. How could my little brother do this to himself and the family, she cried to herself. A bright hard working boy who held a good position in a good progressive company, turns out to be a thief! The manner in which her brother had fallen from grace was too much even for her to bear.

The rain was now playing hide and seek. It arrived with long morning spells, only to quieten down into overcast conditions in the afternoon and then reappear with full force at night. Kamalam prepared some fish curry for her and Molly ate it readily, realising that she had not eaten much in the last two days. From then on she ate it whenever possible, making it her only form of enjoyment.

Vasudevan returned after a couple of days. He called on Molly after freshening up. His arrival was quite a relief for Molly as she was eager to get more details from him. "So how is everything?"

"Quite bad as you know, but things will clear."

"Tell me the truth."

"Your father told me that he has already explained the position to you. George has taken sixty-one drums of various oils from the factory. This includes two which were found in the car. He had disposed fifty four of them. There is an agent in Mattancherry who sells the oils to a dealer in Bombay. George was getting approximately half the price from him."

"What will happen to George now?"

"Achan, that is my father, has requested my brothers to close the case, if possible."

"Is it possible?"

"Well in three or four days, he will get bail, after which your parents will take him back to Ooty."

"So will they come this way?"

"No, I asked Mr. Peter. He says that he will drive via Coimbatore. It looks like your parents do not want to get you involved in any way."

Molly looked hurt, "But then Mr. Vasudevan, will the case against him reopen?"

"Yes and no. They are thinking of getting an out of court settlement, on the insistence of my parents."

"Your parents must be noble people."

"Actually you have to thank Amma. She had a vision it seems, when she went to the temple, asking the family to be sympathetic to a young sinner. Something like forgiving and giving a second chance."

"It is so great of her."

"Yes. Actually my brothers were very adamant that Mr. George pays for his crime. Achan also had an obligation to his late friend, Mr. Sebastian of Calicut; yet he wouldn't have allowed the matter to be closed so easily. You know he is a principled man. Ravindran Chettan also wouldn't hear of anything else. But Amma's is the final word. The family respects her."

"That is indeed fortunate!"

She was itching to ask what Vasudevan himself would have done in a similar situation. Knowing him she knew that he also would have thought like his brothers. Seeing the disturbed look on her face, he said, "I am sorry Madam I have been somewhat blunt. I should have been more diplomatic."

"No, no. You are right in giving me the true picture. So now what happens?"

"Nothing is finalized. Most probably, Mr. George Peter or someone on his behalf will have to pay the actual loss to the Company, which in itself is a generous act."

"Oh, no doubt about that! I am so grateful to your family. I will pray for the welfare of your family, especially for your mother. How can I repay the debt to all of you, Mr. Vasudevan?"

"You don't have to. Incidentally, I must say that you yourself are a noble lady."

Dusk was setting in and abruptly Vasudevan left, mumbling a few words of farewell. Molly stood there for some time lost completely in her thoughts. Later she entered the kitchen where Kamalam was preparing the meal for the night.

After some small talk, Kamalam said, "Why don't you invite Vasudevan Saar for dinner? His cook has gone home and will come only tomorrow morning. Poor Saar has to go out for dinner. In this village there is no proper hotel also. And it will be embarrassing for him to eat with village folks, some of whom will include the estate workers."

Molly woke up from her reverie. She quickly said, "Kamalam go out and call Mr. Vasudevan. He must be on his way out. And for god's sake hurry!"

Kamalam waddled out. After some time she returned and said, "He has already gone out of the gate. Sorry I could not find him."

Molly now berated herself. How could she not think like poor illiterate Kamalam and extend a dinner invitation to Vasudevan? If only the driver was present, she could have asked him to take the car and search for him. But the driver had already left.

After three days, the weather cleared somewhat. Molly was bored being indoors for so long and decided to visit the plantations. She looked at herself and found that her sari was very plain. 'I must change into a better one, in case I meet Vasu.' Then remembering that she was still a widow in mourning, she retained her simple clothing.

On reaching the fields, she went towards the shed where rubber sheets were being made. She was always fascinated by the operations there. Just as she was leaving Vasudevan came in. He stopped and enquired, "How are you Madam?"

"Quite fine Mr.Vasudevan. You have any further news?"

"Yes, I have. Yesterday I talked to Ramanathan. Mr. George Peter is out on bail and is leaving today with his parents."

"Anything about the case? Any settlement?"

"Lakshmanan and Ramanathan have agreed to settle the matter if Mr. George can pay the total loss."

"How much will that be?"

"With the high price this year, tax and other things considered, it will be around ten lakhs."

"Ten lakhs! Oh, my God! None of my relatives are rich enough to afford so much."

"He has a rich sister."

Molly smiled gently and said, "Yes, you are right."

But the rich sister does not know how to go about. Perhaps Mr. Vasudevan will guide me, thought Molly. After some time she said, "Can I go to Ooty?"

"Why not? That is the proper thing to do. Now is the time your parents want you. I will arrange for the driver, a more experienced man, to take you there. One Tamil boy, Arun."

"Thank you."

Vasudevan wanted to ask whether she wanted him to accompany her. But he stopped himself, "Would you like me to send anyone with you? I can send Mr. Abdulla, the Supervisor of the coffee division."

"No, Mr. Vasudevan, I think I will manage. All the same, thank you very much for your concern."

Elizabeth was cooking dinner when she saw a car driving in. She was peering at it only to see who it could be when Molly stepped out from the back seat. She ran outside and embraced her daughter, "Why didn't you call me?"

"Sorry Mummy, it was a snap decision. Mr. Vasudevan made all the arrangements."

By then Elizabeth was silently crying. Molly gave her time to recover.

Changing the mood of the moment, she said, "It was a very difficult drive. With the arrival of the rains, the roads have become very bad. But I had a good driver with me. He helped me reach well before dark."

"Come Molly. What are we doing out here in the cold? Let us go inside."

Elizabeth put some snacks out on the table, and said, "It is cold. Let me make a good cup of tea for you. It will warm you up. I tell you there is nothing like tea."

Molly smiled at her mother's enthusiasm for tea, a beverage she considered nothing short of '*Amrut*', the elixir of the Hindu gods.

Shortly George appeared. Molly greeted him with genuine affection. All the same, conversation was difficult for both of them. Then Peter came in and the entire family talked as one, on every matter except its youngest member's misadventure.

Molly woke up the next morning quite refreshed. After the rainy and overcast weather of Puthupady, it was nice to witness a clear sky with the sun shining bright, even if it was cold.

Peter left for office and Elizabeth went with him. She would pick up chicken, fish and vegetables after dropping him off. Molly met George in the drawing room. She hesitated at first to initiate a conversation and there were some moments of silence between them. Finally she spoke out, telling herself that in her place, Mr. Vasudevan would have done the same.

"Monae, how could you do this?"

She thought she had put forward the question most awkwardly and was expecting George to either reply in a sullen manner or ignore her completely. But in a very soft voice he answered, "Sorry Chechi. I have messed up my life but that apart, I have given hell to Mummy and Daddy. And I should not have given you more grief, after all your sad experiences. It was stupid of me. I can't even ask for pardon."

Molly noted that this was the first time he had called her Chechi. After an interval she opened up further, "Pardon is there without your asking, dear George. But is it okay to ask you why you did this?"

"It is okay. At least it will be some relief to open my heart to you."

Molly could see that her brother's eyes were wet and his lips were pressed tight. After about a minute, which appeared like eternity, he started to speak, "I was living beyond my means. Money was coming from Daddy and then when I got the job I thought that the inflows would stop. But reality was different. There was a money lender and money came even more easily. It was as simple as plucking curry leaves from the kitchen garden. It never occurred to me that one day I would have to return the loan with hefty interest. The seriousness of the matter hit me hard when an enforcer of the loan shark visited me. One day he gave a punch on the upper side of my tummy. It was so painful that tears came to my eyes."

Molly could imagine how he would have cried at the beating received. She had also read somewhere how enforcers hit on body parts that were not visible but gave extreme pain. If there was a visible injury, then the situation had every chance to go out of their control. She listened silently as George continued, "In a way it was my bad luck. I encountered an agent of essential oil who used to sell the oil clandestinely to Bombay. At that time I thought it a god-sent opportunity. To be honest, I started stealing oils from the factory to clear my debt."

"Monae, I hope you don't mind my asking, but did you not ever feel that you are wrong? That crime does not pay."

"Of course I knew Chechi. It was not only wrong but also stupid of me."

"You should have sought the advice of someone who cares for you, George."

"One thing I learned is that when you are prospering, there are people to enjoy your wining and dining, but when you are in need, they are no longer friends. That scoundrel Vinod…"

His sister interrupted, "One thing you should know George, greatness is not in committing no mistake at all. It is in learning from the mistake."

"I hope Chechi, you will guide me in future. In a way I could have got more punishment, but for the grace of Karunakaran Chettan, father of Mr. Lakshmanan and Mr. Ramanathan. No wonder he is a popular and successful man in society!"

Molly's thoughts rushed back to Vasudevan's explanation of how his mother insisted on forgiving the boy. Janaki Amma, she recollected her name.

In the evening George went out for a walk and Molly stayed back with her parents. She raised the subject again, "I was thinking that I'll pay off the amount needed for the out of court settlement, Daddy."

"No way, darling. It was considerate of you to offer though. I have my retirement benefits and other savings."

"But let it be there. Mr. Vasudevan says that I can pay without any trouble."

It was Elizabeth who answered, "Look Molae. In our society the last thing respectable parents want to do is take money from their married daughter. So the matter is settled here."

"But, Mummy, how will you buy a house in Cochin after this to settle down?"

Peter intervened, "There is no special charm in settling in Cochin, now that George is not there."

Since Molly was not very sure herself about how to raise money from the Kollegal Estate, she kept quiet.

Chapter 22

Life in the Estate carried on as usual. The end of the monsoons was near and the weather had cleared as a result. While Molly helped Kamalam in the cooking and enjoyed the variety of food, she had no one to share it with. She ate by herself most of the time wrapped in the shroud of loneliness.

A month or so after her return from her parents' place in Ooty, she had a brainwave. She pondered over it for a day. The more she thought about it, the more she was convinced that it would solve most of her problems. Then somewhat impatiently she dialled her parents' phone number. The phone rang for some time but no one picked it up. 'How could this be, on a Sunday Daddy also should be at home?' An hour later she called again. Again the phone rang and there was no reply.

The next day she rang home once again after breakfast. Her mother answered. Relieved, Molly said, "I called so many times yesterday. Where were you?"

"Oh, we had gone out. What is the matter, dear?"

"I just wanted to suggest that you both move over here. After retirement this will be a nice place to relax. You don't have to worry about building a house and you will be in your home State."

"No Molae now it is not possible. Daddy, George and another colleague of Daddy's who retired last year are joining hands to grow geranium. The friend is also an expert in agriculture."

"Mummy, you want to market geranium flowers?"

"No. The variety that grows well here is good for producing geranium oil. The flowers here are not that good, but the oil is fine according to George. He will steam distil the herbs to produce geranium oil. So we have decided to stay here. Yesterday we all went to see the land. All three of them are very enthusiastic about the project."

"I guess that will be a good option for George."

"Yes, that is the idea. He said that they can add a few more essential oils in the future."

"Oh,Mummy! In that case let me wish the project all success," Molly said, hiding the disappointment in her heart. She was hoping that they would agree to move to Puthupady. All the same, she was happy to see a new ray of hope for her dear brother.

Molly was on her way to Thamarassery where Pappachan's uncle, Mr. Varghese had passed away after a heart attack the previous night. She planned to be with his wife, Thresiamma for some time. Molly knew she would meet Thresiamma's sisters there. In spite of the sad circumstances in which they were meeting, the two ladies did not conceal the hostility they felt towards Molly. However, Pappachan's cousin, John, the son of Paulose and Sophy, and his wife Mercy were extremely warm and cordial towards her. They introduced a young man of around thirty five to her, "This is Pappachan's cousin, Mr. Matthew Kollegal."

"Oh, I am so glad to meet you, especially someone from the Kollegal family. I am Molly, wife of the late Pappachan," she introduced herself.

Matthew was a handsome man with a distinct European look. He spoke with an accent that was definitely not Indian. "I am so happy to meet you. I hear you are managing the family Estate? How nice! My mother is English. And my father as you know is the brother of Uncle Thomas, your father-in-law."

"Where are you working?"

"I am with the Malaysian Palm Oil Board. I was planning to come to the Estate this morning, but then this tragedy suddenly struck."

"I am returning after the funeral. Why don't you join me?"

"That is a great idea."

"You will enjoy seeing our family Estate."

"Dad always used to talk about the place, what is it, Puthupady, right?"

"Yes."

"My father died about ten years ago. Towards the end he was very keen to come back. He married somewhat late. I have two elder sisters settled in Kuala Lumpur. I was married to a Kerala Christian woman and have a three year old daughter. Unfortunately, my wife passed away last year in a car accident."

"I am sorry to hear that."

It was almost dark when Molly left for her home with Mr. Matthew Kollegal. After travelling some distance, Matthew asked, "Do you grow oil palm?"

"I have not heard of it. What is it used for?"

"It is a type of palm which gives fruit."

"Is the fruit like coconut?"

"No, much smaller. Even smaller than betel nut."

"Betel nut, you mean arecanut?"

"Yes. Oil palm gives fatty oil. Like olive it has oil in the fleshy outer portion. The oil has solid fractions. So what we do is to refrigerate and separate out the solid portion. India is importing a lot of this liquid oil from us."

"Yes, I have seen a light yellow coloured oil which my servant bought some time ago. It must be this palm oil?"

"Yes, the oil is rich in carotene and you have to bleach it to get the light yellow shade."

"Is the oil like coconut oil?"

"Not exactly! More like peanut oil."

The conversation was quite interesting partly because Matthew was very clear about what he spoke. Soon the car stopped in front of Molly's house.

Kamalam had prepared *karimeen* curry. Matthew relished the fish curry. "This fish is marvellous. Now I understand Daddy's longing to return home especially during his last days. My Mummy and we, his children, teased him a lot about his fondness for Kerala. He often dreamed about this house and its ways of life. I'm sure he must have been missing food such as this as well."

Molly was quite fascinated to hear about her father-in-law's brother. All along she had the impression that his brothers never planned to return. She said, "Didn't your father have a brother who went to Burma, I think?"

"Yes I have heard about him. Daddy made a lot of enquiries, but couldn't get any solid information. All the reports which he did receive were vague. One even said that his brother was killed in the war."

"So? Would you like to come back?"

"I don't know Molly. Yes and no. My wife would have liked the idea. She loved Malayalam movies and songs."

Molly laughed and then when she noticed him biting into the fish, said, "This fish, Matthew is *karimeen*, known as 'pearl spot' in English. It is a very delicate and tasty fish. But just like the stalk of a rose flower has thorns protecting it, the *karimeen* too has many sharp bones. So be careful while eating it. Use both your hands to pick them out. If you had a third hand, it would have been useful," she said teasingly.

"Hahaaa—Yes, let me make the best of the two I have," replied Matthew, adding, "You know, coconut milk which you make the gravy with is very popular in Malaysia too."

Peter returned from office and sat in the drawing room, sipping the fine tea brewed by Elizabeth. They were waiting for George to return home from the farm where they had planted geranium. He had already placed an order for the distillation still from a firm in Coimbatore that also made small boilers capable of using agricultural waste as fuel.

It was dark when George finally took the bus back home. Rain had made Ooty quite cold. Peter offered him whisky when he came in but he refused it. After a hot bath, he sat down for dinner with them. As he was retiring to his room the telephone rang. It was Molly.

"How are things there Mummy?" she asked cheerfully on hearing Elizabeth's voice.

"Everything's fine, Molea. Daddy is retiring next month. He will join George in our own enterprise which is going well. How are things there?"

"We have a guest, a cousin of Pappachan. He has come from Kuala Lumpur. Nice chap. He is leaving tomorrow."

"I think it is good to have the company of family members. Can Daddy talk to him?"

"Matthew has already retired to his room. I'll call again tomorrow, when he's awake. Convey my love to George and Daddy, bye."

With a happy feeling, Molly moved to her bedroom.

Molly picked up two cups of coffee and went to the portico where Matthew stood admiring the view. The previous night's rain had given the trees a freshly laundered look. In a distant plot he could see pepper plants neatly lined in rows. The rays of the morning sun gave the colourful flowers of the bougainvillea near the bungalow an enchanting look. Far away, the mountain looked as though manicured under the clear azure sky. No abrasive edges of urban life broke the harmony. He turned and smiled at Molly and took one cup from the tray.

"Did you sleep well, Matthew?"

"Yes, Molly. It is very pleasant thanks to the rains. I must also say that you are truly in the lap of nature. The landscape is pristine, the atmosphere tranquil. Quite romantic, infact!"

"Thank you."

He took a deep whiff of the coffee's aroma, let it reach deep into his lungs and then sipped it gently, eyes remaining closed all the time, "I must say that this coffee is superb—just like you!"

Molly thanked him and said, "That is *Arabica* plantation coffee, grown and cured here."

"Oh! You mean you also cure coffee here?"

"Yes, you must meet our estate manager Mr. Vasudevan. He is a wonderful man. But I want to ask you before that … we are making *idiappam*. You like it, don't you?"

"Of course! My wife always made it. The hand pressed wet rice looking like a bundle of threads knit together after steaming."

"Yes. Would you like meat stew or sweetened coconut milk to go along with it?"

"Coconut milk, Molly."

"Eggs, boiled banana?"

"No eggs, only boiled banana. You call it *nenthran* banana, right? When in Puthupady be a Puthupadian!"

Molly laughed and went inside the kitchen.

After a hearty breakfast, the two of them drove to the rubber division. Molly was trying to explain the operations when Matthew interrupted, "Look Molly, rubber is a big commodity in Malaysia. I used to work in a rubber estate myself." She bit her lip, feeling a bit embarrassed.

Just then a jeep arrived with Vasudevan at the wheel. He stepped out of it and said, "Why didn't you call me? I would have come there."

"Oh! There was no need. Please meet Mr. Matthew Kollegal, cousin of Pappachan. He is living in Malaysia."

The two men shook hands and discussed many things. Inevitably the talk veered to oil palm. Molly listened with rapt attention to the two men discuss various aspects of their work. Both are professionals in their approach and thorough in their subjects. She had missed this since her marriage. Suddenly Matthew said, "I think you should go for oil palms here. I will send you all the information on growing it and the prospects for the products as soon as I return."

"That would be wonderful, Mr. Kollegal."

"Another thing we have implemented successfully there is drip irrigation. Do you have it in India?"

"There is no commercial firm which installs such systems, as far as I know. I know the advantage, you can save water. But I would like to show you an indigenous system of drip irrigation."

They all went in the jeep to a nearby garden where young pepper vines were growing. Vasudevan explained, "What we have done is, we have half buried a mud pot with a narrow mouth. At its base we have made a small hole, through which we have inserted a thin cotton wick. We fill the pot with water, and after that allow it to drip drop-wise. So instead of watering every day, we need to fill the pot only once in four or five days. The top is covered with a piece of broken tile to reduce evaporation loss. Now of course there is plenty of rain but in summer it is useful."

tomorrow, either morning or evening. I need you to come with me to Calicut for the same."

"What is the matter, Madam?"

"Oh! Nothing. Kindly make all arrangements and inform me. We will go according to his convenience."

"Right, Madam."

Mr. Mohamedikka later informed Molly that the lawyer had given an appointment for the next day at three in the afternoon.

As per plan, after lunch the following day Molly left for Calicut. Mohamedikka sat in front next to the driver. She found a lot of changes especially in the size of buildings enroute Calicut. Ever since her marriage she had rarely gone beyond Thamarassery. As they approached the town centre, more big buildings popped up. She was told later that the one at the centre of the city was the Civil Lines where the State Government offices were located.

Arriving at the lawyer's office, Molly was received very warmly by Mr. Kunjali Moosa.

"How are you Molae?"

"I am fine, uncle."

She felt that it was better to frankly present her ideas to the old man before he began advising her in return. So she said, "Uncle, I have to talk to you alone."

He asked his stenographer who was in the room and Mohamedikka to leave. Then he closed the door and invited Molly to join him on the comfortable sofa in one corner of the room. Before beginning, he asked whether she would like to have some refreshment. But Molly was too excited to even think of refreshments at this stage.

"Uncle, I have given a lot of thought to what I have to say before deciding to come to you. Kindly listen carefully and look at the proposal from my point of view. I don't want to say that I am perfect, but kindly cooperate with me to carry out my wishes."

"My dear Molly, nobody admires you more for your sense of discretion than me. You have gone through the vicissitudes of life very maturely and carried out your duties sensibly. My dear friend Thomachan had spoken a lot about you. So please present the matter boldly."

Then they had a long conversation. The lawyer asked for clarification on several occasions. But eventually he said, "Are you sure that you are doing the right thing?"

"I have no doubt about it. I am doing the right thing, uncle."

"But remember Molly, the Kollegal family has over two generations transformed the Estate into a very prosperous one. Have you thought enough about its heritage?"

"Yes uncle. In fact there are a lot of families that depend on it, both directly and indirectly. For their sake at least, it has to become even more powerful and rich. Its continuance is of utmost importance to me as well. That is why I have chosen this path."

The old lawyer closed his eyes and thought for a few minutes before saying, "Management matters are important but there are also matters like history and culture of the place. Have you thought about all these? What I would advise is that you return and think about this for a day. If you still think that you want to go for it, then I will support you."

"I have given enough thought to the matter and seek no change of plans. Now, uncle, can I ask you something?"

"Please go ahead."

Molly assumed a serious face for a few minutes and then said gently but emphatically, "Do I have the power to enforce this change? Will all this be legally correct?"

"Yes my dear. You have been vested with all power and rights over the Estate as per the Will prepared by Thomachan and me. It will be one hundred percent legally binding."

"Then I most humbly request you to make the changes as I wish."

Mr. Moosa rose and put his arm around Molly affectionately, "Dear Molae, I am now convinced that you have given full thought to the changes. I know you are strong willed. I knew Thomachan and his father Mathukutty Chettan, and I can say that they displayed a special strength of character. You have their same spirit."

Molly was silently crying now. The old lawyer gave her a few minutes to collect herself, and then said pleasantly, "Come my little strong willed woman. Let us first have a good cup of coffee."

By then Molly had washed her face in the wash basin in the room, wiped her tears and was once again the gentle beauty that she was. She smiled at the lawyer who called out for coffee, after which he asked his clerk to prepare the papers.

About half-an-hour later the clerk brought some papers for her to sign. The old lawyer then said, "I cannot but admire you, my little angel. I have to register this in the court. I will send you a notarized copy for you to act by tomorrow evening."

"Thank you, uncle."

"You take a few days to spend time with your parents."

It was getting dark when she and Mohamedikka started their journey back to the estate.

After a good sleep, Molly felt quite relaxed and light hearted the next morning. Kamalam actually noticed the change, because after listening to her usual complaints about pain here and stiffness there, Molly laughed and said, "Well, if you are not too well, I shall grate the coconut myself."

"You mean Kochamma that you will grate the coconut?"

"Why, will the coconuts refuse to be grated by me?"

"Not exactly," Kamalam replied with a smile.

"Then watch."

Molly finished grating the coconut and gave it to Kamalam to squeeze out its milk. In the meantime Molly picked the full fish, cleaned it and cut into pieces.

Towards late afternoon, as she sat on the porch finishing her coffee, Kamalam came and said, "Kochamma, Mohammedikka Saar and another person are waiting to see you."

She went outside. They handed her a big cover and left. Molly carefully opened the cover, and studied the sheets of paper inside. They had several signatures including hers on them, with big round seals in some places. When she tried to read it, she found that it was in the usual legal language with words like 'whereas' and 'hereinwith' repeated many times. But the matter was completed as desired by her.

That night Molly could not sleep peacefully as her mind was filled with anxiety. With much tossing and turning, hours passed by, and it was only just before dawn that she managed to enter deep sleep. She woke up only after Kamalam brought coffee to her room at seven o'clock.

She picked up the Malayalam newspaper which featured a review of the Los Angeles Olympics. Rather than praising the brilliant sprint effort of Carl Lewis, the reviewer had focussed on his disappointment at the local sprint queen, P.T. Usha missing a medal in the 400 metres hurdles by a whisker.

Kamalam complained about general weakness in her body again. After breakfast Molly told her, "Kamalam, you take this cover to Vasudevan Sir. Are you okay with that?"

"Yes, Kochamma, I will do that." Going to Mr. Vasudevan with an important looking envelope would enhance her prestige in the eyes of other women in the estate. All her illness vanished when entrusted with the errand. She came back with a bag of mangoes in one hand.

"Kochamma, there are one or two mangoes in this lot which are ripe. I will cut them for you."

"If you are not feeling well, you may leave for your parents' house after lunch and take rest. Take the mangoes also with you. I need to take a short nap after lunch."

She had a longer than short nap and woke up only by four in the evening. Not wanting to waste more time, she took a bath and applied a pink *bindi* on her forehead. It was the first time that she had worn a *bindi* after Pappachan's death. She also carefully applied eye-liner around her eyes and kept her hair loose as it needed to dry further. She wore a white cotton saree with pink design. She rarely used lip-stick, and avoided it today as well, as her full lips were naturally pink.

After a cup of coffee, she looked out of the window of her bedroom. Suddenly she found a spider's web in her line of sight, under the window sill. Her attention was drawn to an insect that was caught in the web. Poor thing, it was struggling to wriggle out of the trap! Would it free itself, she wondered.

It was a pleasant evening of a clear day. She was so engrossed in the sight of the spider and the insect that she was startled when the front door bell suddenly rang. Instinctively she stole a glance in the big mirror. She could not help but feel pleased with the image that was reflected in it. She adjusted her sari and stepped out into the portico. Vasudevan was standing there. He surveyed her and with a faint smile said in a low voice, "Molly, it is indeed generous of you to pass on the ownership of this huge estate solely to me. I have always dreamt of possessing a place like this, where I can try out my ideas and make it a realisation of my dreams. Needless to say, I accept the gift."

At least the irritating word 'madam' had ceased to be used now, thought Molly. She had a vague fear the previous night that he would reject the offer. Now she felt relieved. But all the same did his voice reflect enough gratitude, she wondered. She had mentally rehearsed several times her response to the expected conversation, but right now she was hopelessly tongue-tied.

However she was confident that under his benevolent leadership this place and the people working there would attain heavenly prosperity.

Vasudevan had alway admired the good looks of Molly, but right now he looked totally lost at the angelic beauty of the woman in front of him. He picked up courage but lowering his eyes and in an almost murmuring tone put across what had been in his mind for long now, "My dear Molly, there is one more thing I am aspiring to possess, and that is you! Will you be my wife?"

The bluntness of his remark stunned her. She was dumbfounded. All her pent up love towards Vasu gushed forth and erupted like a lighted cracker. Like the petals of a sunflower drawn towards the first rays of sunlight, she moved towards him slowly until her head rested on the chest of the only man that mattered in her life. Instinctively, Vasudevan placed his swarthy hand around her, protectively.

After a few moments he lifted her tear-streaked face towards him and planted a kiss on her lips. They remained like that for a few moments, soaking in the new found bliss, like a graceful pepper vine twining around a majestic coconut tree. She then smiled gently and looked over his powerful shoulders to see the coconut fronds fluttering in the evening breeze. A couple of pigeons were flying across the horizon towards their favourite ledge nearby where they had built a simple nest. Behind him towards the east, the mountains looked enchanting as the setting sun over her shoulders threw an orange ray which on striking the blue sky over the hills breathed out a poem of ethereal glow, with a hue that looked distinctly rosy!

-- :: o :: --